TO DIE NO MORE

MILES NELSON

WORKING STIFF PRESS
www.MilesNelsonAuthor.com

WORKING STIFF PRESS
www.MilesNelsonAuthor.com

❀ Created with Vellum

To those family members who have gone before - I'm sorry that you didn't get to see this, but I'm thrilled to be able to do it in your honor.

Any American city of a certain size has at least one area that's been beaten down over time, for one reason or another. As companies and their employees move out and away from the downtown area, they leave empty streets cutting through blocks of huge old brick buildings full of empty space. Once bustling streets then see less and less traffic. If someone is spotted on the sidewalk, there's a good chance that they're either engaged in some shady activity, or maybe just lost in the wrong part of town. San Diego is no exception.

After driving past a dozen dark and dirty buildings, I turned onto 18th Street, and the GPS in my rental car announced that the target address was a few blocks ahead. As arranged with the people I was meeting, I made a right onto the next cross street and parked behind an unmarked gray van. As I exited my car, I noted that there was a second unmarked van halfway up the block on the other side, with two San Diego police cruisers behind it, all with lights off. I guessed that they would be the backup team standing by and ready to come running.

After a light knock on the van's side door, I was ushered inside to join the four men already there. I didn't have their names memorized, but I had seen the faces a few hours earlier in a DEA conference room in a better part of town. I knew that the two DEA agents were dressed in the dark blue tactical gear, while the two guys from San Diego SWAT were in black, like me. Fortunately, all four of them had a little name tag stitched onto their shirt above the left breast pocket. We all nodded our hellos.

One of the DEA guys spoke first. His name tag read 'Claxon'.

"Good to see you again Boudreau. We're just about ready. The last call they made, the guy named Bishop, was almost six hours ago, but we figure they must both still be inside. We set up cameras early this morning to watch the front and back of the building, and there hasn't been any traffic in or out. We were just settling on the best way in when you pulled up. We all onboard with that back way on the second floor?" His eyes tossed the question to the other three men, who all gave a verbal assent. Claxon turned his attention back to me. Producing a hand-drawn diagram, he said, "The target building is 126 18th, almost three blocks down on the right. Most of the inside was leased by a dressmaker, so we're expecting large empty spaces, probably with a variety of work tables spread around, with offices and whatever else around the perimeter. We didn't have time to get the actual floorplans, so we may have to adjust when we see inside the place. We have the keys for the building just before it on the same side, which is also empty. The two buildings have the same owner, and there's a connecting walkway on the second floor at the rear. Made it easier for the cleaning crew to get back and forth or something like that. Anyway, if we go through the first building and find that walkway in the back, we should have just a regular door to get through to 126. We're equipped to pick most locks, but we also have breaching charges if we need them." He looked around at the group again. One of the city SWAT guys spoke up.

"We don't have any reason to believe that the two of them are expecting company, except that it makes sense for them to be on edge and on guard. If they're watching, we hope they're watching the street out front, or the old employee entrance at street level in the back."

"Right, thanks Dave," Claxon said. "After the fireworks last night, if they have any sense at all, they'll be on their toes. Now, I have operational command. I hope we're all clear on that. Our orders are to do whatever we can to grab these guys in one piece. We need them to tell us where all their friends took off to. It's them that started shooting the other night. DEA lost two good men, with three more shot up. And your group lost one or two also, correct, Boudreau?"

"Yeah, that's right," I said. "One killed, one injured. That's why my boss made sure I was here to assist."

"And who are you exactly," the second SWAT guy asked, looking at me. "I mean, no disrespect. Is it true that you're Homeland? Some special unit? I was ordered not to ask you any questions, but, you know, I don't always follow orders."

"That's okay," I said. "No sweat. I don't always follow

orders myself. You're right—Homeland Security is close enough. I got your back, don't worry about that."

"We all lost friends the other night," Claxon said, "but we want these two alive. Boudreau, the four of us have worked together before. I want you to hang back and provide backup and support only. Got it?"

I nodded, and the other three nodded with me.

After a few minutes of looking over the hand-drawn diagram, and doing a weapons and comm check, the five of us left the van. It was almost midnight, and there was no traffic as we made our approach. We walked slowly down 18th Street, in single file and hugging the faces of the buildings.

Just twenty-six hours before, almost to the minute, the DEA-led raid on a meeting of some big meth dealer and his gang had erupted into a massive shootout. People had been killed and wounded on both sides. Two members of our small, secret team—one of them my best friend Tommy, and another guy—had been along for the ride in response to a high-level request for extra firepower. The initial impression in the aftermath was that someone on the inside must have tipped off the gang at the last minute. Aside from the two guys they left dead on the dock, most of them had been able to slip away into the night, but a patrol unit had been lucky to spot two men tearing off by themselves. With some hasty after-action investigation, it was determined that they had probably been stationed a few blocks away from the meet, as lookouts or drivers, and had not been present for the actual raid.

The quick thinking patrol unit had managed to track them most of the way here before losing them. In a stroke of luck, officers found two homeless men on the street who had seen the car in question enter the garage of our target building.

As I brought up the rear of the five-man stealth team, I felt my anger coming to a boil, and commanded myself to stay level and cool.

Sure, I'll hang back. I'll be your backup. I thought to myself. *If it's gonna help me get my hands on the guy who gunned Tommy down. And Stillman. You better believe I am going to come for you, wherever you are.*

Claxon, in the lead, motioned for us to stop as he came up to the main entrance door of the building just before the target. After a moment of fiddling with keys, we were inside, leaving the door unlocked for any officers that needed to get in behind us. Our flashlights illuminated what looked like the wide-open space of a long-forgotten factory floor. We could see orphaned electrical cables laying here and there, along with the odd chair or small table. Bits of packing material and an assortment of discarded soda cans and coffee cups dotted the floor. Whatever machinery or other equipment that had once filled the space with the clanking and whirring sounds of industry was long gone. Offices and various other utility or service rooms, mostly with large windows facing out to the floor, lined most of two sides of the interior. The ceiling was high above, at twenty feet or more. A wide walkway went around the perimeter at the second level and gave access to more offices and small rooms directly above the ones on the ground floor. The effect was not unlike looking up from the ground at the second level of an old-fashioned indoor shopping arcade.

"A guy back at the station told me that these were sister buildings," one of the city SWAT officers said. "So, depending on how much the one next door's been altered over the years, it could look a lot like this inside."

"Let's hope," Claxon said. "That would be a good break."

As we traversed the expanse of floor, we approached a hallway that appeared to lead back to where the rear door to the alley must be. Above that, stairs on both right and left led up to a sort of balcony overlooking the factory floor. After taking the stairs up to that level, we followed an upper hallway back to a door at the rear. There, at the back of what appeared to be a small supply room, was a steel door with a square, wire-reinforced window set up high. Pulling on a pair of night-vision goggles, Claxon looked through the window for a full minute before pulling them off and turning back to the rest of us.

"Can't see much, even with these," he said, "but it looks like what we expected. A walkway, almost like an enclosed porch, leading off to the left. I'm guessing if it goes that way maybe thirty feet or so, there should be another door like this one. Hopefully they haven't walled it off or welded it shut. Let's find out."

One of the SWAT guys lifted the wooden security bar off the door and set it aside. Claxon used his keys to unlock and open the door before pulling the goggles on again for a quick look up the hallway.

"Okay great," he said, after his brief look. "There's an outside window up closer to the other door that's letting in a little moonlight. Looks like it's just past the door, so we won't have to worry about shadows if anyone happens to be looking out. Let's go."

With me again bringing up the rear, we started down the narrow corridor, testing steps carefully at first to learn how creaky the floor might be. A minute later, Claxon was at the door, and I could see that he was examining it closely. He stepped away to whisper to the rest of us.

"It's the same door, but the window is blacked out. We can't see in but they can't see out."

He gestured to the SWAT guys, who went to the door quickly but quietly. The one named Dave pulled out what I recognized as a listening device. He put small earbuds into his ears, and then held what looked like a suction cup against the door. There was just enough light in the narrow hallway for me to see that he closed his eyes while he listened intently. He moved the plastic cup around the door several times, listening for twenty or thirty seconds from each location. After a while, he shook his head to tell us that he had heard nothing, stowing the listening equipment into a cargo pocket.

His SWAT partner took his turn at the door. After examining the lock, he chose a few items from a small kit, and set to work. After a minute, he made a "get ready" gesture to the rest of us.

I was the only member of our group to be armed with just a pistol, which was a customized Para-Ordnance .45 auto. In addition to their own side arms of choice, the SWAT and DEA men were all carrying short-barreled M4 assault rifles, with either twenty or thirty round magazines. I had declined the offer of a loan of one of the same, preferring to stick with one of my favorite automatics. I knew that with it, I could shoot rings around whatever most people could do with any kind of gun at short range.

When the SWAT guy gestured to us, we all checked and raised our weapons, clicking our mental switches over to the next higher level of combat readiness. He pulled the door open just enough to disengage the latch, then open further to allow his partner to take a quick look inside before whispering to us.

"Looks the same as next door. Small room just inside, then a corridor towards the front. I'll take the lead." He looked at Claxon, who gave him a thumbs-up sign, then opened the door again and stepped inside. His SWAT partner followed, with the two DEA men on their heels. I came in last, taking a moment to close the door against a thick piece of cardboard to make sure it didn't latch. I turned back to the room just as the last of the other four guys left to move up the corridor.

As I started across the room to follow them, the roar of a violent explosion filled the rear of the building. The shockwave blasted down the corridor and into the utility room, filling the small space with smoke and dust and knocking me to the floor.

Grenade? I wondered. *Or some kind of booby-trap? They must have been expecting us.*

Having been in combat situations before, I came to my senses quickly, grateful that I had decided to wear special shooter's ear plugs that protect my ears from loud blasts while still allowing me to hear normal conversation. Gambling that there wouldn't be any further explosions, I pulled the plugs out and shoved them into a pocket.

Hearing the moans of an injured man somewhere out in the corridor, I shook myself off, re-checked my pistol, and left the room. As I moved up the hallway, stepping on chunks of wood and mangled wall board, I could see that, like the building next door, it opened up ahead at a kind of landing where the stairs on either side came together. The huge open factory space would be beyond and below. There were no lights on in the short hallway itself, but enough light spilled in from the ceiling fixtures in the big room that I could see a body twisted against the wall near the end of the hall. I knelt down to feel for a pulse, finding no trace of one. There was just enough light for me to see the man's name tag—it was Claxon. I heard more moans and realized there was another body—this one moving a little—just outside the end of the hallway on the wide landing. The thought occurred to me that whoever had thrown, or set off, that bomb might be thinking they had killed all of us. If I was quiet enough, I might maintain some element of surprise.

I moved as silently as possible over to the injured man, seeing that his eyes were open but he was torn up and bleeding from a dozen terrible wounds. His left arm was gone, with the shredded cloth of his uniform shirt hanging from the shoulder. The part of his shirt that would have had his name tag sewn to it was gone. I'd seen plenty of combat injuries in my day, and it didn't look to me like there was enough of his shoulder left to put a tourniquet on. The blood puddle under him was growing rapidly.

"Please," he said, with remarkable clarity, considering his condition. "My arm. Get my arm." He pointed to an object on the floor and I realized that it was most of a severed arm, still inside its shirtsleeve.

"Sure buddy," I said. "Hang in there." I reached across and grabbed the arm by the wrist, pulling it over to him.

He hugged it to his chest like it was a long lost favorite puppy. In the dim light, I suddenly realized that he was wearing what was left of his black uniform, while the arm he was holding so tightly was wearing a blue sleeve.

"Hang on man," I said. "Doctors can do anything these days." *Shit, this is not going well.*

Just then, someone started shooting, and as bullets ripped up through the floor near me, I realized that someone must be just below, blasting away with a high velocity weapon. I shoved myself clear back against the wall in time to see the one-armed SWAT man get hit from below a half-dozen times, finally laying still. The shooting suddenly stopped and I heard what sounded like someone running across the floor below.

I jumped up and went to the railing to look out at the open expanse of the factory floor, seeing a man moving quickly away towards the front of the building. Taking careful aim with my pistol, I put one bullet into the man's upper back, and he stumbled, still standing. I fired again and he dropped to his knees, but then managed to twist around back towards me, attempting to raise his rifle. My third shot caught him in the upper chest, causing him finally to drop the rifle and fall back. I was amazed that a hand still tried to reach back for his weapon. I took careful aim again and put the fourth bullet through the top of his head.

That was one tough fucker.

Still at the landing rail, I made a quick scan of the area, not seeing anyone else. I took a minute to check the carnage around me. Claxon was dead in the hallway, the SWAT guy with the arm was now gone also. A few careful steps down the mangled stairs to the left I found the other DEA officer, clearly dead from numerous blast injuries, and also clearly the former owner of the arm I had given to the guy on the landing. I looked around for the missing second SWAT man, finding him at the bottom of the staircase. Based on the impossible position he was in down there, I figured he had to be dead, but knew I needed to check him. Before starting down the stairs, I picked up one of the discarded M4s and slung it over my shoulder, also taking a pair of spare magazines from one of the dead men and shoving them into a cargo pocket.

I paused at the bottom of the flight of stairs to check the SWAT guy. It wasn't hard to see that he must have been blown down with great force, breaking his neck and probably killing him instantly. I checked for a pulse, found none, and lifted him to help him lay flat. As I did so, a pack of cigarettes fell out of his breast pocket, followed by something shiny. I picked the thing up, seeing that it was a lighter. I guessed it to be sterling silver, and saw that it was engraved with "To The Best Dad Ever – Love Lizzie". I had to take several deep breaths as a wave of emotion washed over me—sadness to anger, then to rage, and then back to sadness—all in seconds. I closed my eyes for a ten-count to gather myself as the feelings dissipated. Having the fine lighter in my hand reminded me that the disposable one I usually carried for general utility had recently run out of gas. I flicked the flint wheel and it lit up on the first try. Just as I stood up, dropping the lighter in my hip pocket, a fast series of gun shots rang out from somewhere above and behind me. The bullets missed me, and I heard and felt them slamming into the stairs and wall next to me.

Someone was blasting away sloppily. I realized that the shooter must be on the long side walkway above me, and probably had to lean way out to fire down in my direction.

A few quick steps brought me under the upper walkway, and just outside the first of the small rooms that stretched all the way along to the front end of the building. I paused to listen for a moment before moving forward quickly, but as quietly as possible. Thirty or forty feet along, I stopped and froze when I heard what sounded like a step on the wood floor above. The ceiling I looked up at was the underside of the wooden flooring above. I guessed that the planking that made up the floor was probably oak, and was at least an inch thick, supported by vertically situated pine boards. I holstered my pistol, knowing that it wasn't the right weapon to shoot through heavy oak boards. The compact M4 assault rifle, on the other hand, should do nicely. With the rifle pointed up and ready, I listened carefully. Breathing softly, I pictured someone just above me doing the same—holding their breath and nervously frozen in place.

After what seemed like forever but was probably less than ninety seconds, whoever was up above either took a step or shifted their weight in place, causing the tiniest of oaken creaks to ring out above me and to my left. I shifted my focus to what I thought was the right spot, braced the M4 on my shoulder, and fired.

In just under four seconds, the M4 spat out all of its thirty rounds, and the hard-jacketed, super-sonic bullets tore through the wood easily. There were screams and a crash as someone fell to the walkway above. Gun smoke and the metallic sounds of the ejected brass hitting the floor filled the air around me as wood chips rained down like old dry snow. Then came the shuffle of someone up there dragging himself across the floor. I slapped a fresh magazine into the rifle, adjusted my aim, and made another ten holes in the ceiling. The shuffling stopped as more wood chips fell. Blood started to drip through several of the many new holes above, and I stepped clear to avoid it.

I went quickly back to the staircase at the rear of the building, up past the bodies of the DEA and SWAT guys, and then across to the wide walkway that served the upper level of offices and other rooms. The guy was in the middle of the walkway outside one of the small offices to the side. The office was dimly lit, and I guessed that he must have been hiding in there before popping out to the railing to shoot at me. There was no need for me to look for a pulse to see that he was as dead as it gets. His body had been shredded by at least half of the high-powered slugs from the M4. Jagged splinters of oak reached up from twenty or more holes that had been punched through from below all around him.

Well shit, So much for bringing either of them in alive.

A lot had happened in what really was only a few minutes, and I suddenly realized that I had never called in for the backup team. Certainly, none of the other four guys would have been able to do it. I set down the rifle and reached for my comm unit, stepping away from the bloody mess on the floor and into the adjacent office.

Just as I was about to press the transmit button, I heard something behind me, and turned towards the sound in time to feel the rush of air as a figure launched out from behind the office door and swung some kind of stick at me. In an instinctive blocking move, I was able to raise my right arm enough to deflect the blow. I yelled out as the pain flashed through my upper arm and shoulder. I knew right away that I wasn't seriously hurt, but I could also tell that it was going to take some time to recover. As the guy drew back to hit me a second time, I kicked out with my right foot, hitting him firmly on his upper thigh. That gave him his own dose of pain, and he stumbled backwards and into some debris on the floor, which I saw was a paint tray with a hardened roller stuck in it. It was then that I realized the floor of the room was littered with tools and other painting-related junk. As I stepped back to get more space between us, my foot kicked a gallon-size can, causing some liquid to splash out. The smell of turpentine filled the room.

He was big, at least a few inches taller than me and maybe forty more pounds. He had long dark hair hanging loose, and a mangy beard. He looked scared and angry, which I knew made him dangerous, but he didn't look like any kind of trained professional. I decided that the stick he was holding was probably one of those extender poles meant to let a painter reach high up with a roller. He yelled out as he drew it up again to swing at me and took a step forward. I went to draw my pistol, finding that my right arm wasn't yet up to speed. I got the gun clear of the holster, but my grip wasn't good enough and it clattered to the floor and slid out the door towards the dead guy on the walkway. I dropped to a squat just in time for the pole to swing over my head, missing me closely enough that I felt it touch my hair. I put out a hand to the floor to brace myself as I kicked out at the guy a second time, this time catching him in the groin. He screamed and dropped to his knees, knocking over a paint can, and spilling lumpy white paint out in a large splash in my direction. As I tried to rise up from my squat, my right foot slipped on the paint puddle and I went straight down, slamming my back into the floor and briefly stunning myself.

What a shitstorm. Why didn't I think to check for anyone else?

It must have been only a few seconds before I was able to get into a sitting position. I looked up in time to see him coming at me again with the pole raised high and with rage in his eyes. I bumped into the can of liquid again, and a quick glance told me that it was about half full. Grabbing the container by the rim, I hurled it at the guy as he came at me, a paintbrush smacking him in the face as the liquid went all over his head and chest. He screamed out and stopped in his tracks, dropping the pole and rubbing at his eyes. My nostrils again filled with the smell of turpentine.

With one eye open, the yelling man lurched towards me in a zombie-like motion, flailing away at the air. Standing now, I backed away to avoid him. Both my pistol and the borrowed rifle were somewhere out there on the floor, but at this point the guy was blocking my path to them. I looked around the room for a weapon, seeing that the pole he had used was now at his feet. Something on the floor caught my eye—a flash of blue and yellow—and I realized that it was a can of WD-40 household lubricant. I scooped it up, glad that it didn't feel empty. I stepped to the side to avoid the guy as he came close and tried to swing at me. I dug into my hip pocket to grab the silver cigarette lighter, flicking it open and spinning the wheel. With my other hand, I brought up the can of WD-40 and pressed the dispenser button. As the spray crossed the lighter's flame, it ignited instantly, becoming a compact flamethrower. The guy was barely more than an arm's length from me as the two-foot torch hit him in the face and torso. His turpentine-soaked shirt and hair caught fire, and within seconds he was in flames from the waist up. He screamed horribly, turning and running out the door to the walkway, where he stood at the railing, desperately trying to pat out the flames.

I ran out after him, grabbed my pistol from the floor, and did him the favor of shooting him. It was the sixth fat .45 slug that sent him over the rail, with a final scream and a whoosh of flame. I walked over to look down at him where he lay, a smoldering, bloody mess.

Retrieving my comm unit, I pushed the button and spoke into it.

"Boudreau here. Come on in. Four officers down, believed dead. Three hostiles down, also dead."

"Roger, we're only a minute out," came the reply. "Did you say THREE hostiles?"

"Yes, three. There must have been one already here inside the building. I think that's it, but come prepared to check. Oh, and somebody bring a fire extinguisher."

And maybe some marshmallows.

I pulled out my cell phone and punched the button to get my boss on the line. The Colonel answered right away and I filled him in as concisely as I could.

"How are you doing?" he asked. "What shape are you in?"

"Oh, you know, I've been blown up, beaten up, and shot at. I'm covered in bruises and white paint, but it's nothing that a hot bath and a few drinks won't fix."

"Good, well, take care of yourself," he said, "I need you in one piece. There could be more to this. And Dean, wanted you to know that Tommy's surgery went well tonight. He's going to be okay."

Whew, that was a relief to hear, I thought to myself. *Tommy's going to be okay.* We finished our conversation and I ended the call. I walked down the stairs and over to the dead SWAT guy, dropping his silver lighter back into a breast pocket.

"Thanks for the loan buddy, much appreciated."

I heard doors opening and people yelling, radios squawked loudly.

The cavalry had arrived.

2

About twenty-four hours before I set a man on fire in San Diego—just after two-thirty in the morning—my phone started buzzing away on the bedside table, yanking me out of a deep sleep. I snatched the thing up, pressed the button to answer, and said a quick, "Hang on." I got out of bed, shaking my head to help wake up, and looked over at Jenny, who briefly opened her eyes. She spoke a few sleepy words and adjusted herself and her pillow, but otherwise didn't appear to be much disturbed. Grateful for that, I went out into the living room.

I looked at the phone screen. Sophia—at three in the morning—interesting.

"Hey, Sophia, what's up?"

"Dean," she said, "I'm sorry to wake you up, but I knew you'd want to know right away. Tommy's in the hospital. He's alive but hurt pretty bad. Shot at least once. I don't know much more than that."

Dammit, I thought to myself, *I should have gone with him.*

My throat tightened. "The thing in San Diego, then, right? Wasn't Stillman with him?"

"He was, yes," Sophia said. "And he's hurt too. I don't know how bad, but I think it was him that got Tommy out. Several other agents got shot up also, some kind of ambush. I got fragments from the DEA comm guy. He only had a few seconds to talk, so I really don't know much."

"Shit, okay," I said, "so Tommy's hit bad, and you don't know any prognosis, right? Where is he? They?"

"A navy hospital in San Diego is all I know," she said. "Look, I'm sorry I don't know much, but I wanted you to have the heads up. Call The Colonel if you want, but probably he'll be calling you anyway."

"You're right," I said. "I'll give it till the morning and call him if he doesn't call me first. Thanks for letting me know. I'll call you tomorrow when I know more."

We said our goodbyes and I ended the call. As I set down the phone I felt a rush of emotion come over me and dabbed at my eyes before steadying myself. I knew Tommy would be getting the best care possible, and I would know more soon.

I stood and looked out the floor-to-ceiling windows at the city of St. Louis laid out in front of me, a gridded carpet of night-lit streets and dark buildings spreading eastward to the edge of the Mississippi River. The massive yet graceful shape of the Gateway Arch stood bathed in light at the riverbank, ruling and defining the night view of the city. Through and behind the great arch, on the east side of the river, the darker expanse of Indiana reached out into the night and the distance.

Too wide-awake at that point to try to go back to

sleep, I started the coffee pot brewing and turned one of the counter stools around to face the wall of windows. My thoughts drifted as I gazed again out into the summer night. Up to the left and north of the big arch, I could see lights from several of the bridges that crossed the river over to Indiana. Though I couldn't see it from where I stood, the old Chain of Rocks Bridge was farther upriver, just below I-270. Decommissioned now for decades, it had served for years as part of the original Route 66—the main east-west highway crossing from Indiana into Missouri north of the city. You could still use the bridge to walk across the river, but it was long closed to vehicular traffic. *One day*, I thought, *maybe I can get Jenny to follow the whole length of the old Mother Road with me.*

A series of beeps from the coffee maker brought me back from my road trip and I fixed myself a strong cup. It wasn't yet three-thirty.

I didn't know much about the San Diego job, but I did know that neither The Colonel nor Tommy had thought it would be a big deal. The DEA had asked for a little help from our small group because a few of us had worked in the area in the past and knew the local geography—sort of like a "ride-along."

One of the local DEA people had become unavailable suddenly, and they had not been able to fill the vacancy in time for the op. The Colonel had consulted with Tommy before volunteering him, and Tommy had brought Stillman along, knowing that he had lived in the area for several years and knew it well. Stillman was a solid guy. They all were, Damien and Kevin too—a good team. My thoughts naturally ran to my old friend Tommy, but I also hoped Stillman was going to be okay.

In general, when any of our small group worked with some agency in this sort of capacity, it was expected that we would give advice, train, or otherwise assist as needed, but also would endeavor to stay out of the real action. Clearly, albeit without any solid information to go on yet, something had gone seriously wrong. A trap, an ambush, a double-cross perhaps? Maybe it was just a good old fuck-up that had started the lead flying.

The thought of my best old friend lying in a hospital somewhere—with bullets in him—was twisting me up inside. I knew getting hurt or killed was always a possibility when we went out on a job, but that didn't stop me from getting pissed off. I made myself take more deep breaths to tamp down my anger.

Don't overreact, I thought to myself. *Keep cool and wait for more information. There will be plenty of time to overreact once I have more information.*

I had just poured a second cup when my phone rang again. The screen ID'd the caller as The Colonel—my boss. I answered with my name.

"Dean," said The Colonel, "you already talked to Sofia, correct?"

"Yes, but her info was thin. What happened, and how are Tommy and Stillman?"

"Looks like Tommy's going to be okay, but Stillman didn't make it. I understand he had a lot of internal bleeding that they didn't catch in time. Went into cardiac arrest and they couldn't save him. He was a good guy. They're still assessing Tommy. Looks like he took a bullet in the shoulder, so let's hope it didn't hit any vital organs. The DEA team lost two also, with three more in the hospital. Several dead bad guys too."

"Shit," I said. "Stillman. Dammit, Colonel, what happened? Wasn't it just a raid on some drug gang? I thought we were just there to help with the lay of the land."

"That was the idea, though we did have a suspicion that the gang was into more than just drugs. Looks like we were right on that point. Must have been a tip-off somewhere, and our guys walked into an ambush. Or at least a very prepared reception."

"That's just so crazy though," I said. "It doesn't make sense. I mean, could they really think they could get away with this? How many are they?"

"The DEA was expecting twelve or thirteen total, including their inside guy. They left two dead behind last night, and neither of them was him. So now it looks like ten, give or take, including the mole. Here's the thing though—the local cops think they tracked two of them to some old building in the factory district. They're working on plans to snatch them later today. I think I can get them to wait for you if we can get you out there as soon as possible.

There was silence on the line for a minute and I sipped my coffee. This was a real shitstorm. Tommy shot up, Stillman and a bunch of feds dead or shot up. The day was not off to a good start. The Colonel broke the brief silence.

"Look, Dean, get your toothbrush packed up and I'll

have Sophia book you on the earliest flight she can find. I'll send you what I can about who to link up with when you get out there, and whatever we know about Tommy. I'll pave the way for you so nobody's asking too many questions. You've probably got a few hours if you want to grab some more sleep."

We ended the call, and again I sat looking out into the night. I felt something against my leg, and then Jenny's cat, Hazelwood, jumped up and began maneuvering around my lap in search of a comfortable perch. Knowing that Jenny's alarm would be going off in less than three hours, I decided to camp out on the couch rather than disturb her sleep any more than I already had. I figured I'd try to do some dozing myself; she would wake me up as soon as she was up and around.

I picked up Hazelwood and took us both to the couch, settling down amongst the pillows. Thoughts of violent revenge against unknown, faceless people swirled around my head until I managed to push them aside with a relaxing combination of meditation, deep breaths, and the purring of a large cat.

I awoke to the smell of toasting bread and fresh coffee. Jenny brought a cup to me and sat down in one of the side chairs with her own. I sat up, ran fingers through my hair, stretched a bit, and sipped the strong brew.

"You got a call," she said. "Almost three, wasn't it? What's going on?"

She was accustomed to my getting calls at all hours. My

job frequently had me going places and doing things that I couldn't talk about. But she had met Tommy a few times, and knew we were close.

"Tommy and another guy on my team were along for the ride last night on some kind of DEA raid and it looks like the whole thing blew up. Some kind of ambush maybe —I really don't know yet. Tommy's hurt, but I'm told he's going to be okay. The other guy, Stillman…he didn't make it. I've known him for less than a year, but I liked him. He was a good man."

Jenny quickly came over to sit beside me, putting her arms around me from the side and resting her head on my shoulder. Her light brown, shoulder-length hair was still wet from the shower and smelled faintly of some tropical flower.

"Dean, that's so terrible, I'm sorry to hear that, but I'm really glad to hear that Tommy's okay at least. What happened to him? Was he shot? Haven't you guys been shot enough already?"

Despite everything else, I had to laugh at that. She was familiar with all my scars, inside and out.

"Yeah, I guess we have at that. Let me tell you, you get shot once, that's already enough. It's my plan to not have that happen anymore, just so you know. And yes, I'm told he got shot, but that it isn't life-threatening. Must have been some kind of graze or flesh wound."

"Good," she said. "I mean, it's not good, but glad to hear it sounds like he's going to be okay. I guess this means you'll be traveling somewhere, right? To see him? Tommy?"

"Yes, to San Diego, though I don't know exactly where

yet. I need to get it together this morning and get to the airport. I'll let you know details later."

Her phone rang from somewhere in the kitchen and she jumped up to find it. "I need to get this. Today is the first day for the new franchise."

I took my coffee off towards the shower.

When I emerged from the bedroom twenty minutes later, shaved, clean, and mostly dressed, Jenny was just checking her bag and looked ready to go out the door.

"So, the new franchise," I said, walking towards her, "that's fantastic. How many is that now—seven?"

"Close, this is our eighth. This will make us the third biggest cleaning crew in St. Louis."

"Fantastic, congratulations," I said. "You and your sister have worked hard. Today St. Louis, tomorrow the world."

"Paula and I have worked hard, yes, but we've also had a mysterious silent partner who has been very generous." And she gave me one of those kisses that, for me, set her apart from any other woman I'd ever kissed. She gave me a quick hug.

"You can have more of that when you get home. I guess call me later if you can and let me know what's going on. Tell Tommy I'm thinking about him and I'll expect him out here for one of our summer barbecues. Gotta go meet Paula at the office."

With that, and with her bag over her shoulder, she scooped up her keys and phone and went out the door.

3

A long flight is a great occasion to think.

In order to get one of the earliest flights out to California, I was flying into Los Angeles. I had a first-class ticket, and was thrilled to find that the seat beside mine was empty. Once on the ground, it was my plan to rent a fast car for the hundred-mile drive down "The Five" to San Diego. Traffic permitting, I hoped to reach Tommy's hospital by late afternoon for a quick visit. After that, I needed to get to the local DEA office for a rendezvous with the agents who were planning to round up the two fugitive gang members later in the evening.

I was aching for a chance to find the people who had gunned down my friends and dish out a massive dose of lead poisoning.

It was just over a year since we'd wrapped up the BEQ business. Old friends of ours had paid Tommy and me an obscene sum of money to crush a corporate embezzling ring led by a pair of executives from multinational corporation BEQ—Benson, Ellis, & Quentin. Because Tommy and I, along with that whole family, had our own personal reasons to hate the corporate crooks, and to blame them for indirectly causing the deaths of several people we cared about, we had ended up taking care of them in a very final way. That job had been a bit of a bloodbath, but fortunately it hadn't been our blood. Including the stolen funds we'd been able to recover, we had each walked away with something north of four-million dollars.

Tommy had been approaching retirement at the time, after a long career in the navy and Special Operations, with the last ten years attached to the CIA. A few months after the end of the BEQ mess, he had been relaxing on the beach outside his small house on St. Croix when a man claiming to be from the State Department had come to talk. Tommy could spot someone from the CIA a mile away and hadn't been fooled by the guy's cover, but had listened to his offer. Unnamed higher-ups wanted him to help form a small and super-secret unit.

"I'm really surprised you're even thinking about it," I said, when he had called to discuss the idea. "Don't tell me you're already bored with the rum and the palm trees?"

"No, I'm not," he said. "I love it down here, but I get restless. You know what I mean, right? I miss the action. They're offering a ton of money and lots of freedom too—that doesn't hurt."

We talked for a while longer and he told me what he knew about the proposed team and its mission. We talked about what the command structure would look like and how he thought it might operate.

I had used some of my blood money to buy my own beach house on one of the quiet Bahama Out Islands. I had enjoyed many hours there, sitting by the warm, calm water with a good book and a cold Kalik beer. I had earned that beauty and relaxation, but I often missed the action myself. Once you've experienced the excitement of a gunfight, and the thrill of surviving it, little else could compare. A week had gone by before Tommy had called me again.

"Well, what do you think?" he said. "You wanna do this thing with me? For the good of the country and all that?"

"I figured you were going to ask me that," I said. "You said the money's pretty good?"

"Better than Blackstone and the other contractors."

"And will there be lots of travel, explosive violence, and excessive drinking?"

"I'm pretty sure about all of those things, yes," Tommy had said. "Maybe even exciting women, but it seems like you're already covered for that. Just leaves more for me."

He didn't have to turn it up much higher than that. I called him back ten minutes later and told him I was in. After me, he had recruited two others—Bink Stillman and Kevin Briggs. Stillman had worked with him in Naval Special Operations long after I had gotten out twenty years ago. Briggs had been with the Army Delta Force. Tommy had found them both working for the same security firm as bodyguards to the rich and famous.

The last operations person to join us was Damien Stevens, a twenty-something veteran of the army's elite 75th Ranger Regiment, who had done two tours in the

Middle East. I had met him in Rhode Island when I was just starting to get involved with the BEQ thing. He had not been part of that action, but I, and then later Tommy, had been impressed with him. Recruiting him had been delegated to me and I had gone to find him on Block Island, a favorite getaway off the coast of Rhode Island. Circumstances had found him suddenly single, bored, and liking the idea of making some serious money. He made no secret of the fact that he was also looking forward to working with Tommy and me. Damien was a fast yes.

The sixth team member was Sophia. She had worked with Tommy and me—for a substantial financial consideration—on the BEQ job. It was her prolific technical skills that allowed us to fleece the fleecers before they met with their unfortunate accidents.

Sophia was a master hacker, and performed those duties for the team as needed, but was also our main and central communications point. She set up email dropboxes, handled ID issues when we were not able to travel as ourselves, helped with all computers, and generally served as a sort of high-tech "eye in the sky" for our operations. With the access given her by The Colonel and those above him, she could tap into just about any database in the United States, and presumably most of those not in the United States.

The mission of our small team was not one of law enforcement. Our friends in Langley, Virginia, along with the old Soviet KGB, and probably countless authors of spy fiction, would have called us a "wet affairs" department. "Wet," as in blood. Though it didn't happen as frequently as you might gather from watching movies, the government certainly did need to do away with people now and then. The FBI is strictly a law-enforcement body, and the CIA is prohibited by law from operating within US borders. The CIA does plenty of things that they're prohibited by law from doing, but then they also have to worry about Congress breathing down their necks.

So, we got called in on those occasions when one agency or other wanted a bit of dirty work done. There might be a federal witness who had worn out his welcome and was making noises about revealing some misbehavior on the part of law enforcement. There could be some militant group that hadn't yet committed a crime, but authorities were not comfortable with the idea that they wait until that crime was committed—better to just nip it in the bud.

There are occasions when the CIA or one of the other intelligence agencies learn of a crime in progress, or soon to be in progress, where the agency itself was not free to act on the information they have. Or, in some cases, the actions they were permitted to take wouldn't stop the crime nor result in convictions.

And then there are occasions like last night's DEA raid in San Diego. In that case, with my current limited understanding, two of our team went along just to help out with logistics and maybe serve as an extra gun, but only in a backup capacity.

The leader of our small team was Colonel Cameron Bixby, who we called "Colonel Bixby" or more often, simply "The Colonel." We knew that he reported to a small top-secret group of highly placed veterans of the intelligence community that he referred to as 'The Council', on the rare occasions when he referred to them at all. He told us that The Council had been given special authorities by the president, and was not overseen by Congress. They had been deliberately insulated from the standard bureaucratic command structure, while still enjoying a huge budget. Our paychecks came from the Treasury Department, while our Government IDs and gun licenses were from Homeland Security. In any case, the checks were good and The Colonel obviously had a lot of juice.

Colonel Bixby had retired from the Marine Corps after a long and distinguished career that had included plenty of combat action. Tommy probably knew more about him than any of the rest of us, and that wasn't much. The important thing is that he had earned our respect and we knew he would look out for the team members on all occasions.

When our team was formed, we all spent a week together at a secure complex in the foothills of the Sierra Nevada Mountains east of Sacramento, California. We did lots of eating, drinking, bullshitting, hiking, shooting, and generally getting comfortable with one another. Each day we would spend some time going over hypothetical situations meant to represent the sort of missions for which our team had been formed. Those sessions would be handled like a proper briefing, with time for questions and answers.

"This team is not about arresting bad guys or taking prisoners," The Colonel had said on more than one occasion. "There are enough other agencies that do that shit. This team is about eliminating problems. We are here to do some of the dirty work that those agencies either aren't allowed to do, are afraid to do, or don't have the balls to do. We will be a blunt instrument—that is, a finely-tuned, razor-sharp blunt instrument. I don't want anyone here under any illusions. We will be executioners.

"Having said all that, there may very well be times when we are needed to assist some agency or other with arresting or capturing bad guys, but that is not our port-folio and I will try to keep that to a minimum.

"While we are out here this week," he had said, "I want all of you to think about our mission and make your own decision about your involvement. Most of us have already done some killing, and some of us have been shot or blown up once or twice. There is no shame if anyone wants out, but make that decision this week."

Nobody had wanted out.

Other than The Colonel, Tommy and I were the oldest team members, being both in our mid-fifties. That made us pretty ancient for most commando-type operations, but it was considered part of the overall plan for the team that we might be able to blend in more than the younger guys in some situations. If the target was in a wary mood for example, the lines on my face and the gray hair at my temples could make me appear less threatening. In fact, like many active-duty Special Operations people, we were encouraged to have non-military haircuts and any kind of facial hair we pleased.

When not out on missions, we spent lots of time train-ing. We practiced old skills and learned new ones. We had access to whatever weapons and technology we wanted. We were a small, tight group, and were very well paid. Our budget appeared to be quite large for such a small team, though was probably more like a tiny rounding error in terms of the overall intelligence community.

It was a good job, as long as you didn't mind traveling on short notice and killing people. I knew that for me and Tommy that was not much of a problem. We accepted the basic premise that our targets were people who really needed killing. Terrorists and murderers probably, and threats to national security at the very least. I had been sent out on eight missions since the team had come online, and I had seen more than my share of blood and gun smoke.

A big fat pile of money wasn't the only good thing that came out of the BEQ job for me. I met my girlfriend Jenny Mason when we had been thrown together by chance while both crossing the country by car. She was being harassed and bullied by a guy she'd known for less than a day. We had felt a natural connection during our first brief meeting, and I had been in a position to rescue her from the overzealous suitor. It had been an exciting side trip that had all played out in a matter of hours, and as we drove away together afterwards, she had been under the impression that I had successfully scared the guy away. Understanding that she hadn't really known him, I had never seen any point in telling her that I had watched him get blown up and incinerated in a high-speed crash that I might have helped to bring about. After all, the highway could be a dangerous place.

After our eighteen hours together, Jenny had continued on to St. Louis to help her sister build up a business while I had continued down the highway on my mission of justice and revenge. Something had sparked between us though, and when I had crossed the Mississippi almost two months later to find her, she welcomed me into her arms and her life.

I bought us a large condominium in a new high-rise at the western edge of the city. It was the fanciest place that either of us had ever lived. I liked it, and enjoyed being able to share the small luxury with her. When I had taken the new job, I had explained to her that I had gotten the position by virtue of my past service with the navy and the Special Operations Command, along with my relationship with Tommy. She knew that it was a very unusual team, with some kind of law enforcement function. She knew that we frequently worked with and assisted other better-known agencies. She accepted that I couldn't discuss most of what I did except in the vaguest terms. She knew I went out on raids, arrests, or other dangerous jobs, and she worried some, but hadn't yet made a thing about it. She was, after all, extremely busy growing the office cleaning business that she shared with her sister.

I sold my house in the Philadelphia suburbs and bought a small apartment in the Rittenhouse Square area of that city. Sometimes, after a job, I stayed there for some private "decompression time," and to get my fix of a big East Coast city. Jenny had joined me there on several occasions when her schedule allowed, and we enjoyed the city together. Between the places in St. Louis and Philadelphia, along with the Bahamas beach house, we had plenty of room to spread out.

"Excuse me, Mr. Boudreau," the flight attendant said, gently pulling me back to the present. "We'll be starting our final approach into the Los Angeles area soon. Would you like some coffee?"

She stayed and chatted with me for ten minutes or so. I said vague things about working in the security field. She must have been ten years younger than me, friendly and charming, and radiating a warmth that could have thawed a hole in a frozen lake. I sensed that her sunny conversation carried an invitation, but I wasn't in a time or place to try to run with the idea. I was thinking again about Tommy in the hospital, and what I'd like to do to whoever had put him there.

A little over an hour later, after retrieving my special checked bag, I was driving down the 405 Freeway in a Ford Mustang convertible. The junction with I-5 at Irvine lay ahead. From there, San Diego was a straight shot.

4

I was amazed at how good he looked. At least, that is, in terms of how good anyone can possibly look while lying in a hospital bed with lots of tubes and wires and who knows what else sticking out all over the place—little glowing screens and beeping things attached.

"What took you so long?" Tommy said. "Shit, next time you get shot, I'm gonna take my time." His voice was low but clear, and he looked mostly like himself.

The drive south after my flight had been uneventful, and the car's GPS had brought me right to the hospital. I had no trouble finding Tommy's room, but the nurse had told me in no uncertain terms not to bother him for long. She filled me in on the surgery they were planning to get the bullet out later in the day. They wanted his blood pressure to stabilize, but otherwise he was doing well.

I pulled a chair up close to the side of the bed.

"I'll try to be faster next time," I said. "Hey, the nurse is going to kick my ass if I stay very long, but, man, it's good to see you. You scared me, you rat bastard. Don't do that again."

"I'll try not to," he said. "Scared me too, even after all these years. I'm really pissed about Stillman. I'm telling you, he was great. If it hadn't been for him, I don't think I would've made it out of there. I really thought he was going to be okay."

"He was a good guy," I said. "Really good. We'll all miss him, but I'm sure you both did what you could. If I know you at all, T, you're blaming yourself for this, but don't. This is dangerous stuff we signed up for. Anyway, we might get a chance for some payback. I'll be meeting with The Colonel soon and we'll see what's what. You need to take it easy and get better."

"Shit, yeah, man, I know," he said. "I'll be out for a while. Guess I was lucky, you know, considering. Lots of fun rehab coming up."

"You'll get through it just fine," I said. "Hey, I don't want to wear you out, but can you take a few minutes and just tell me what happened with this raid? Summarize it for me?"

Tommy nodded and started talking. I leaned in as he went through a rough outline of the whole thing. A warehouse along the waterfront, an exchange of drugs for cash witnessed by the feds, then suddenly sirens, cars and men moving in, and everything blows up into gunfire coming and going every which way. Men dying, others escaping in cars and a speedboat. It all sounded to me like an episode of *Miami Vice*, but I knew that was how these things could really go.

Tommy went on for almost fifteen minutes before he

reached the end of the story, and I could see that he needed a rest. As if on cue, the nurse poked her head in and gave me a look that ordered me to wrap up. I stood up and started to get ready to go.

"San Diego PD tracked two of them to a building in the old factory district," I said. "We're hoping if we can grab them, that they'll lead us to all the others who took off. I'm headed to the DEA office now to get up to speed on that. They're planning the op for late tonight."

"Dean," Tommy said, "remember what I told you about that one guy—the leader—Puckett. It was him that started blazing away. He's really good. One of the feds told me about him. A serious gun guy. If you run into him, you put him down from as far away as you can, you got me? I know how you are, but don't fuck around with that guy. No fair fights. Somebody had to have tipped them. That must have been it. Watch your back."

"Okay, boss," I said. "I hear you. I'll be fine. You just lie there and worry about healing up. When you're ready, we'll celebrate something."

"We'll go places and eat stuff," he said. "Drink stuff too." He laughed and waved me towards the door. "Be careful and lemme know what happens. Now get outta here."

With that, I was off to meet up with a group of DEA and SWAT officers to plan the evening's festivities. I had hopes that it would be a simple matter of picking up these two punks, who might then lead us to this gun nut character that Tommy had warned me about, and then finally, a taste of payback...

5

By the time someone finally came into the old factory building on 18th Street with a fire extinguisher, the whole place smelled like a Texas barbecue gone terribly wrong. The man I had set ablaze was nothing more than a smoking lump on the floor. After an army of police had completely searched the building, a smaller army of paramedics came in to check everyone for signs of life. The dead were carried away in a parade of ambulances, with no need of sirens. I was interviewed by a DEA agent who seemed to be in command, and then again by a San Diego detective while he rode with me to get myself checked out at a nearby hospital. It was halfway to dawn by the time I made it to my hotel, with the hot bath and triple bourbon I'd been dreaming of.

I slept late into the morning, only dragging myself out of bed hours after the sun had started streaming through the gap in the room's heavy curtains. A long hot shower and a room service breakfast washed down with lots of strong coffee brought me gradually back to life. I was sore in spots where I hadn't known I had spots. My right upper arm was painted in a riot of black, purple, and blue, but aside from some stiffness, everything was in working order.

Knowing that Tommy had just gone through surgery the night before, and that he would probably be sleeping most of the day, I decided to spare him a visit from me. Instead, I enlisted the aid of the hotel concierge to send him a "get well plant". I included a note telling him that things had gone well since I'd seen him and that I would try to visit tomorrow. I figured that when I saw him I could be more honest and explain how things had actually not gone so well.

I made a call to Jenny back in St. Louis, passing on vague updates to her, and she was very glad to hear that Tommy was in decent shape. I kept the part about the late-night fight and shootout to myself, not wanting to alarm her unnecessarily, and hoping that my bruises would be healed up by the next time we were together. Knowing that she was busy with work, we kept the call brief. I told her I would let her know about my travels and schedule when I knew more.

I had an email from The Colonel telling me that one of the other team members, Damien Stevens, would be arriving in the area tonight to rendezvous with me. The Colonel wanted us both to meet him for lunch the next day. After sending my response, I was closing my laptop when my phone rang. The caller ID showed me that it was Damien himself, and I answered immediately.

"Hey, Big D," I said, "I just heard you were on your way. Good to hear from you. Are you already in San Diego?"

"Not there yet, but I'm in transit and I have a reservation at your hotel. I should make it there by about seven. How 'bout dinner?"

"Dinner about seven sounds great," I said. "Give me a ring when you get in and we'll meet up. The hotel restaurant looks nice."

With the business of communications taken care of and a plan in place for dinner with Damien, I had the middle of the day free. I walked across the road from the hotel and spent an hour exploring a lively neighborhood of shops, restaurants, and tourist-oriented activities, forgoing the wax museum and the mini-train tour. The Southern California sun was blazing away, and I was happy to stumble upon a lovely garden café where I enjoyed a cool glass of sauvignon blanc and a light lunch. After that, as the call of the hotel pool grew louder in my ears, I bought a pair of swim shorts in one of the shops, and claimed a poolside lounge chair for the rest of the afternoon. It was a quiet day at the pool, and I luxuriated in a lazy routine of cooling dips, drying off in the sun, and sipping rum punches from the tiki bar in between.

I topped off the afternoon at the pool with a visit to the hotel spa, where I was able to get a Swedish-style massage. The muscular and capable masseuse honored my request to take it easy on my right arm, but showed the rest of my body little mercy. By the time I had showered and dressed back in my room, I felt relaxed and refreshed, and almost completely free of the horrible events of the night before. Damien called me just before seven, having already checked in, and we agreed to meet.

We found each other in the hotel bar, and right away

asked to be seated for dinner. It was a quiet Tuesday night, and we were taken to a table in a sparsely-populated area outside on the patio. The temperature was in the nineties, but there were a few well-placed fans that complemented the light breeze coming in from across Mission Bay. The hotel property as a whole was beautifully landscaped, with numerous fountains and koi ponds tucked in between the palm trees. Bougainvillea and Hibiscus plants lined the pathways. I made a mental note to add the place to the growing list of destinations that I might like to come back to with Jenny one day.

We ordered dinner and Damien picked out a bottle of wine to start with. I remembered that we had first met over an impromptu wine tasting. It seemed to me like a long time ago, but really hadn't quite been a year and a half. He had been cleaning up behind the bar when I'd wandered into a restaurant looking for a meal near closing time. We had sampled a number of wines, chatted away, and had both enjoyed the brief connection. He must have remembered enough about that night to know that I would appreciate the 2014 Lodi Zinfandel he ordered, and it was delicious.

I told him about my visit to the hospital the day before, and my interpretation of Tommy's condition and state of mind. I also told him all about the debacle on 18th Street the night before, including the bombing and the use of the can of WD-40.

"We didn't get them alive, obviously, and I'll take some blame for that, but when those guys were blown up, I just wasn't thinking much of reading anyone their rights. Anyway, from what I understand they recovered a laptop and some phones. With luck The Colonel and his friends will be able to figure out where the rest of them took off to."

"WD-40, very creative," Damien said. "Not sure I would've come up with that one."

"Probably just because you weren't enough of a delinquent when you were a kid," I said. "You should see what you can do with a can of Lysol or Aqua Net some time. Better yet—don't."

"Somehow, I think I'll just take your word on that," Damien said. He was quiet for a minute and we both sipped our wine. "I worked with Stillman a few times. He was a good dude. There was that thing in Cheyenne with just the two of us, and then with Briggs on the New York job. He was very professional—a real ace. But very private too. He had walls around him at all times—I don't mean he was mean or rude, just that he had barriers."

"That's how a lot of people handle this kind of work," I said. "I don't think there's anything wrong with it. It's a survival thing. Walls. Calluses. Whatever you want to call it."

"Yeah, I know you're right," he said. "There's nothing wrong with it at all. Anyway, I'll miss him being one of us. He sure had your back in a fight. I hope I get to kick some ass in his honor."

"I have a feeling you'll get your wish," I said. "I'll be surprised if we don't get a stamp-out mission after all this shit. We'll know more after lunch with The Colonel tomorrow. I hope—we'd better."

"Yeah, I agree," he said. "There's one thing—when I first talked to him, you know, when he called to tell me to meet you here, he said something about the Salton Sea. It seemed like he let it slip, and then decided to wait till he got us together. Funny, because we had a bad connection for a minute and all I heard was something like 'out by the Salton Sea,' but then he moved on and I had the feeling that I should wait for tomorrow."

"That's interesting," I said. "Now I really can't wait for that lunch. The Salton Sea is some big lake way east of here, right? Just north of Mexico?"

"Yeah, that's right," Damien said. "My parents took me there once on a road trip when I was a kid, and then later, when I lived in Rancho Mirage for most of a year, I read up on it and drove down there a few times. It's really a crazy place. A crazy thing, actually. It was just desert, pretty much, the Imperial Valley. In the early 1900s, '06 or '07, I think, some irrigation channels coming off the Colorado River overflowed, and water flooded the valley for more than a year before they fixed it. Ended up with a lake maybe fifty miles long."

The waitress stopped by to tell us our dinner would be out soon. I poured out some more wine. While we had been talking, a trio had started playing on a small stage below us near the pool. The night was still hot, and a thoughtful staffer had set up a large fan to point right at the stage. The singer, a young woman—maybe thirty—had long, straight, blond hair, and as she sang, the big fan blew right towards her, causing her hair to blow freely back from her face as though she was singing into the wind. I found it mesmerizing, and after watching for a moment, I realized the effect made me think of a mermaid, her untamed hair flowing back and forth in the waves.

"Quite a picture, isn't it?" Damien said. "Beautiful hair. I might ask to buy her a drink after dinner."

"Why not?" I said. "I think you should. Don't forget to make up a good story about what you do for a living." We both laughed and continued to enjoy the old jazz classics until dinner arrived. Damien ordered a second bottle of wine and we ate without speaking for a while, enjoying the music.

"So back to the Salton Sea..." I said. "The people out in the desert must have been thrilled to have a new lake, right?"

"Some of them, sure," he said. "The place had its heyday, mostly in the forties and fifties. A few small towns popped up, marinas, fancy resorts. They tried to make it a big vacation destination. The problem was that there wasn't any constant inflow and outflow of fresh water, and over the decades, runoff from farms and other surrounding land made it more and more polluted. With the constant evaporation, the shoreline has receded and the water's gotten too salty for most fish. Far as I know at this point, it's mostly surrounded by ghost towns with a few diehards hanging around for who knows why."

"Well, if you heard what you think you heard from The Colonel, maybe we'll get to see it."

We ate the rest of our dinner at a leisurely pace, and afterwards moved to a table closer to the singer with the wind-blown hair, where we sipped a fine Armagnac brandy. After a few more tunes, I started to feel how dead-tired I was.

"Well, I'm beat," I said. "Don't stay up too late, sonny."

"I won't, pops," Damien said. "And hey, it's good to be

working with you again. I mean it. Looking forward to knowing more tomorrow."

We made a plan to meet for a run in the morning, and I started off along the palm-lined pathway to the main building. Ten minutes later, I had the air conditioning cranked way up, the curtains drawn tightly, and was under the covers drifting off in search of some much-needed sleep.

6

We found The Colonel in the restaurant at the agreed-upon time. The three of us sat down at a table in a corner away from any other diners. He was our height—within an inch of six feet—and very fit looking. If his sixty or sixty-five years had given him a few extra pounds around the middle, it didn't show. His dark brown hair was generously flecked with gray, spreading out from the temples. He was neatly dressed in his standard uniform of a light charcoal two-button suit, with polished shoes and a light blue silk tie in a perfect Windsor knot.

In contrast, both Damien and I were casually but neatly dressed in khakis, with a polo shirt for Damien and a blue oxford button-down for me. Though we were dressed-down relative to our boss, our belts still matched our shoes and everything was neatly pressed. We could have easily fit in with the thousands of business travelers who crossed the country every day for project planning meetings and other corporate events.

The Colonel had his old leather briefcase with him but hadn't yet taken anything out of it. We ordered our lunch and made small talk until after the server had brought our beverages.

"First of all," he said, "I know we're all tough guys here, but I want you to know how sorry I am about Stillman, and of course Tommy. We're all veterans, and we all signed up for this, but that doesn't make it easy to lose somebody. Stillman was a good man, and he'll be hard to replace. Now with Tommy on his back for a while, you guys and Briggs are going to be busy."

"May I assume," I said, "that you're planning to hire a replacement for Stillman?"

"Absolutely," The Colonel said, "and probably a sixth also, but I'm going to put Tommy in charge of that as soon as he's ready. It'll be good light duty for him to work on for a while, rather than running around getting into firefights and blowing things up.

"I know that Tommy told you what he knew about the raid, Dean, but let me take a few minutes to summarize for Damien's benefit, so we're all on the same page. After that, I'll tell you about what I've learned since."

He then spent about twenty minutes going over all aspects of the DEA raid against a criminal group led by the man Tommy had told me about—Clarence Puckett. We already knew a lot of it, but he fleshed it out for us and filled in some blanks. While the raid was a DEA action, the whole Puckett operation was also being closely watched by the Bureau of Alcohol, Tobacco, and Firearms. The BATF strongly suspected Puckett of being involved in an illegal cross-border gun-running operation. The Colonel didn't have a lot of specifics on that part of Puckett's business, but he gave us what he could.

Apparently the DEA officer who had approved the raid on Puckett had his hands full fending off calls for his resignation, while at the same time the folks in the offices above his were miles apart on what to do next. A quietly powerful figure had reached from the shadows outside Washington to contact The Colonel.

"So, as you well know," The Colonel said, "the operation that Dean took part in the other night didn't work out quite the way we would've liked, but the DEA and San Diego PD were able to put together some info that got passed up the chain very quickly. We now believe that this Puckett character and his gang—nine left now, after the last two nights—regrouped and beat it out into the desert. Latest info is that they're shacked up in some old resort hotel somewhere by the Salton Sea. Something like seventy miles from here. We know this because the DEA still has a man inside. He has some kind of transmitter and he's been able to send a few short messages. They don't think he's blown. We certainly hope not."

"Was he with them the other night?" Damien asked. "I'm just wondering if he tried to show himself or get out at the time."

"I asked the same question," The Colonel said. "What I got from the commander is that he—their inside man— was somewhere in the background and didn't realize what was going down until it was too late. Then he decided to stay low and keep passing on information. Everything I hear on him is that he's solid."

"So, we have Puckett and his gang of nine," I said, "ten

total, holed up out by the Salton Sea. One of the nine is undercover DEA, and as far as we know he's still okay."

"Right, that's pretty much it," The Colonel said. He reached into his briefcase and withdrew two large envelopes, handing one across to each of us. His look around the room first was almost imperceptible, but I knew it had happened. I looked around as well and saw no other diners or staff within earshot.

"This is a clean-up mission. You are to go out there to this Salton Sea place and take the necessary steps to make sure Puckett and his people do not cause any further trouble for anyone. Your secondary mission is to get the DEA's undercover agent out of there safely. Get him out if you can, but don't compromise the primary mission to do it. Obviously that last bit does not leave this table. Aside from yourselves and this agent, nobody else should be in a position to leave that place. Is that clear?"

"Clear," I said. Damien echoed the same a second later.

"In your envelopes, you'll find a summary of most of what we've discussed, along with information on the DEA man, and also on the hotel out there and some material on the area. A friend of ours has been nice enough to loan us an apartment in Palm Springs that the two of you can use as your base of operations for this." He passed a set of keys across the table. "You'll find the address in with the other materials. Use Sophia as your main contact. She put together the information packages you have, so she's familiar with the overall. After this meeting, I'll be heading up to the base at Twenty-Nine Palms to check in with some old friends. I imagine I'll be there for a few days at least."

"Time frame?" I asked.

"It's Wednesday afternoon," The Colonel said. "This needs to be completed before dawn on Friday, so you have about thirty-six hours. I know that isn't a lot of time, but it looks like you probably have a straightforward assault—you know, plus getting the guy out. Get your shopping list to Sophia by early tomorrow morning and I'll get you whatever you need. You'll find some of your standard items waiting for you in Palm Springs."

He stood up and we stood with him. He spoke with a tone that sounded very serious, even for him.

"Good luck. Come out of this safe. We can't lose anyone else right now, and I don't like funerals. Let Sophia know anything you need."

With a final look to each of us, he turned and walked out.

7

B y a little after seven that evening we had made it up to Palm Springs and were settled into the apartment, which appeared to have begun its architectural life as a pair of adjoining motel rooms. The style and décor were classic 1960s Mid-Century Modern. It looked to me that the property must have originally offered about twenty ground-level rooms that now were half as many condominium apartments surrounding a central courtyard with a large pool and patio.

On our way out of the San Diego area, we had stopped at the airport to get Damien a heavy-duty Jeep Wrangler that we thought would be a good vehicle for the following night's activities. We had also stopped at the hospital for a quick visit with Tommy, who again appeared to be in good spirits, if quite tired. He had already gotten a call from The Colonel, who had updated him on the mission at hand.

In the apartment, we had found a large case with a note indicating that it had been delivered on The Colonel's behalf. Inside was body armor, an assortment of combat webbing, utility vests, and several other goodies that might come in handy. There was also a supply of spare ammunition for each of our pistols, and a note reminding us to get our shopping list to Sophia by eight the next morning so that further equipment and supplies could be delivered to us on time. We decided to start formulating a plan over dinner, and set out walking the few blocks up Palm Canyon Drive in search of a restaurant. Ten minutes later, we were seated at an Italian place, chosen not just for the extensive menu, but also because there were only a very few other customers. Once again, I let Damien order the wine.

We had brought a small map of the Salton Sea and the surrounding area, along with a hand-drawn representation of the hotel where Puckett's gang was shacked up.

"So, we need to do this thing," I said, "and get out of there by dawn on Friday. We have tomorrow to prepare. I'm thinking we want to be down in that area at midnight tomorrow, with the operation to start within two hours after that."

"That sounds about right," Damien said. "Get there at midnight, then we have about six hours before sunrise." He pointed to parts of the drawing. "I've been thinking about this. There's a highway on either bank of the lake, both going roughly north and south. They're just state highways, really just local roads. But look, on the western side —Route 86—you can see how around the middle of the lake it's a good several miles away from the shoreline, see? Puckett's place is about midway down the lake, and sits right on the beach. To get to it, you would have to turn off the highway and go three or four miles down a long access road, like a long driveway, really. If I were them, I'd feel pretty safe as long as nothing was coming up that road from the highway."

"I agree," I said. "I don't like the idea of us driving up that road for so long. Even with lights off, they could see us without too much trouble. We could go in on foot, but that's a long walk."

"Here's what I was thinking," Damien said, pointing to the drawing again. His finger was on the large open space to the east of the hotel—the lake. "Let's take Route 111 down the other side of the lake. On the east side, the highway is much closer to the shore. We park at one of the old recreation areas there and go straight across over the water."

"Hmmm, I like it," I said. "That idea could work. They'll probably be on the lookout for some kind of police raid, like cars and helicopters. Can't imagine they'll be expecting a small commando mission from the water. Problem though ... we have tomorrow and that's it. That doesn't give us much time to come up with a boat, not to mention the right kind of boat."

"I don't see that being much of a problem," Damien said with a laugh. "The Colonel might need to flex some muscle, but between San Diego being the home of the Seals, along with half the Pacific Fleet, and the world's biggest Marine base at Twenty-Nine Palms, we should be able to get what we need."

"Yeah," I said, "we should, but there isn't much time to spare. After we eat, let's put together that list and get it to Sophia right away. We should try to get as much sleep as we can tonight too, because I don't see us getting any at all tomorrow night."

Dinner arrived. We ate at a leisurely pace, savoring the semi-dry Italian red Damien had ordered. The wine choice was beyond reproach, and the slight fruitiness was an excellent counterpoint to my tortellini Bolognese. I tried not to look over at Damien's plate, which held some sort of seafood riot in red sauce, complete with legs, claws, and antennae sticking out every which way. Neither of us were in the habit of ordering rich desserts after dinner, but knowing that the next night was going to be all power bars, bottled water, and flying lead, we yielded to temptation and enjoyed large squares of freshly made tiramisu, along with glasses of a well-oaked Napa Cabernet.

"I like traveling with you," Damien said. "Even with the dirty shit we do, you always seem to fit in some luxury. It's not like the movies, you know, when the detectives on stakeout are always eating cold sandwiches and donuts. This is better."

"Oh, I think it's very important," I said. "Critical even. When you're going out to get shot at—or shot even—you need to take the time for a good meal. A fine wine—cigar if that's your thing. I don't want to be lying somewhere dying and thinking 'Shit—that was a crappy hotdog and a Mountain Dew.' Even when you're not with me, Big D, make sure you treat yourself well. Get the room with the hot tub if you can."

"As always, your logic is undeniable," he said. "I'm going to take your advice from now on. Though, I'll admit, I do occasionally have a hankering for a hotdog and a Mountain Dew."

We settled the check, leaving an exorbitant tip for the waitress, and started on the short walk back to the apartment.

We spent two hours going over everything in the information packets The Colonel had given us, and kicking around ideas. We committed the photo of the DEA agent—guy named Pete McAdam—to memory, along with his code word, which, for reasons unknown to us, was "Roseland."

By one-thirty in the morning we felt we had a solid plan for the next night, and I emailed our equipment list to Sophia up in Seattle. I knew her to be something of a nocturnal person. I wasn't surprised that she immediately acknowledged the message.

We poured ourselves one stiff bourbon on the rocks and took our glasses outside into the steamy night. We sat beside the pool, alternating between easy silence and non-mission chat until our drinks ran dry, and then went off to bed.

8

A fter sleeping later than usual, and taking a short run through town together, the next day was spent quietly, and mostly indoors.

There were several calls back and forth with Sophia, after which we were comfortable with our plan for equipment delivery later that night. Our special package would be coming to us courtesy of the U.S. Marines at Twenty-Nine Palms.

I disassembled and cleaned my pistol carefully. I then spent an hour practicing my draw, until I was confident it was as fast and smooth as it ever had been. I noticed Damien watching from across the room.

"You should be in professional competition. Your hand is just a blur when you do that. How did you ever get so good?"

I laughed, feeling a little embarrassed.

"That damn thing called 'long, hard work,'" I said. "When I was a kid I had a BB gun that was a replica of a Colt Peacemaker. Had a real leather holster to go with it—

the full cowboy rig, like I was the town marshal or whatever. I practiced with that a lot until the gun finally fell
apart. When I was old enough, I got one of the real ones
and spent a lot of time shooting cans as fast as I could. I
guess there's a part of me that always wanted to be a
gunfighter. I used to think that I was born a hundred years
too late, but look at us now—both of us—gunfighters after
all. I don't put much stock in destiny. I think we make our
own. But … I don't know, maybe it's real and maybe that
was my destiny. Listen to me—getting full of shit as I get
older."

"Nah, no way, not you," he said. "But it's a good story—
really pretty cool. I like to think I'm pretty good myself,
but I'm not anywhere near your level. Now I think if we
run into Doc Holiday or Johnny Ringo, I'll step aside and
let you handle it."

By late afternoon, some pool time in the blazing sun had
me relaxed enough that I was able to get in an hour nap.
After a walk into town and a simple dinner with Damien,
we were ready to start loading up the Jeep.

It was shortly after eleven when we set off in search of
the mysterious Salton Sea.

9

As we drove south along the east coast of the Salton Sea on State Highway 111, I told myself that Damien had given it to me straight. This had to be one of the weirdest places in the country—even for California. The vast, empty, moonscape to the left, along with the shining surface of the huge inland lake to our right, made for a scene that would have been at home in any number of apocalypse films. The sky was more than half cloudy, which was unusual for the desert, but at that time, for us, a welcome happenstance. It was just after midnight, and cool for this part of the world in August, a comfortable ninety-five degrees.

After passing the bullet-riddled sign for some abandoned restaurant, we started watching on the right for the turnoff to the lake. Less than a mile later, Damien took the exit and steered the Jeep down a dirt road towards the lakeshore. Within a few hundred yards, the path opened up to a large, level clearing that I knew had once been a nicely-groomed parking lot for this long-forgotten swimming beach. Damien had warned me to expect the smell of the dead and rotting fish that frequently washed up along the shore, due to the great salinity of the water, and the rancid smell filled our nostrils as we pulled up and got out of the jeep.

I checked my watch, noting that our delivery should be arriving shortly. While Damien started to unload and check gear, I got up onto the hood of the Jeep and scanned the sky to the east with binoculars. I soon spotted the blue light of the special Marine helicopter. The old parking area was more than large enough for a landing pad, so I set the landing marker light in the middle and switched it on. It started to flash its own blue light, emitting a signal for the chopper to home in on. Within a few minutes, the darkest and quietest helicopter I had ever seen was on the ground and a trio of Marines was completing final assembly steps on a fifteen-foot inflatable Zodiac speedboat. Damien and I spoke briefly with the commanding officer, a Marine captain from the huge base at Twenty-Nine Palms, about a hundred miles away to the north.

As the crewmen finished up with the Zodiac, one of them called us over and gave a quick tour of the important controls and features. After that, another crewman produced a large canvas duffle bag from the chopper and opened it. The Marine captain stepped up to go over the contents, which appeared to include all the goodies on the list we had given to Sophia. We walked briefly around the perimeter, agreeing on a spot where we could leave the equipment for later pick-up, and thanked the captain and his crew. Within minutes, the big chopper was fading back into the night sky and away from the lake.

With a last check of the area, we pushed off from the beach and started the small outboard. Soon, as we moved out away from the shore, the combination of the fresher air over the water and the light breeze created by our movement provided a degree of relief from the rotting fish smell that was thick in the air. Damien was driving the boat straight out, consulting a small screen on his wrist.

"Alright, I'm picking up the transponder. Looks like it's straight across for about fifteen miles, almost due west. When we get closer, we should be able to see that old boat on the beach to the north. That's our landmark."

"Sounds good," I said. "Let's go electric, what, about two miles out?"

"Aye-aye, Captain Dean, two miles out it is. That should do it. We should be on the beach in about fifty minutes."

The main outboard was a special one, and very quiet indeed, but because the design of the small boat was based on a need for stealthy approach in life-and-death situations, it was also equipped with a small electric motor, along with a set of oars.

Our target was a run-down and long-closed former resort hotel that sat on a small point of land jutting out from the western shore of the lake, about ten miles south of the decrepit settlement of Salton Sea Beach. Due to the nature of the high-salinity, steadily-shrinking lake, with its constant fish kills and algae blooms, almost everything in the area was abandoned and rotting away. I conceded that the old resort waiting for us across the water was probably an ideal location for a criminal lair.

The few short transmissions that had come through from the DEA man on the inside—McAdam—along with whatever intelligence The Colonel had been able to gather from other sources, painted a picture of a heavily-armed gang hunkered down and waiting for a chance to make a break for the Mexican border, about fifty miles to the south. The last transmission sent to McAdam was an order for him to get out and get down as soon as the shooting started. We were on radio silence at this point, so we could only hope he had gotten that order and would comply. We knew he was a trained agent, at least as far as standard law-enforcement went, but we didn't have good on-site communication with him, and in any case we needed to just have him out of the way in order for us to do our jobs. Damien and I both had a small device on our wrist, the size and shape of a watch, which was supposed to vibrate whenever it was within about thirty feet of McAdam's transmitter. Between that and the established code word, we hoped to avoid mistakenly shooting him.

Clarence Puckett himself had an interesting history. He grew up wealthy, heir to one of Arizona's largest construction companies, which happened to be the owner of record for the old lakeside hotel as well as the old brick factory building on 18th Street in San Diego. Somehow, a falling out with his family, along with his own problems with drugs and several arrests, had led him to go rogue and build up his drug empire. An interesting part of his biography was that for years—before the drugs took over I guessed—he had been a well-known competitive pistol shooter on the national circuit. A very serious gun guy. While researching him the other night, I had found a video of him at some fast-draw competition.

In front of a crowd of witnesses, and with cameras

rolling, he dropped a rubber ball from belly height, drew his pistol, fired three shots which broke three china plates mounted on posts several feet apart, re-holstered the pistol, and then caught the ball in his right shooting hand as it bounced back up from the floor.

Some incredible stuff, to be sure, that few people anywhere could pull off. I was hoping the drugs had slowed him down. *Better to shoot him in the back, or better still, from far away*, I thought to myself.

But then I would never know if I could take him. Can I pass up a chance to find out?

It was Puckett who had put my oldest and best friend Tommy in the hospital, and another friend, Stillman, onto a cold slab in the morgue. Puckett and his lightning fast gun.

I am coming for you, Clarence. I hope you felt the sun on your face today, and took the time to look at something beautiful, because I will be with you soon.

I felt the boat slow down suddenly and realized that Damien was preparing to switch over to the electric motor. I was pleased to note that the increasing cloud cover was dimming and softening the moonlight above. The air held the potential of rain. I could see the lights from the old hotel ahead in the distance. The place had been built in the sixties and was in the style of one of the great old national park lodges, though with only twenty-four guestrooms. Plans filed with the county, along with some old brochures that someone had been able to rustle up, indicated a large and multi-story central lobby, with guestrooms wrapping around three sides on the second and third levels. The restaurant, bar, offices, and various utility or storage rooms ringed much of the perimeter of the first floor. There was also a full basement. One of the garbled messages received from McAdam had indicated that the people inside were mostly hanging out in and around the central lobby.

A wooden deck wrapped around most of the main level of the building. We expected that sentries would probably be posted out there. We were hoping they would be focused mostly on the front of the building and the long driveway that led out to the main road.

As we approached the shore, Damien steered towards the decaying hull of a beached sailboat that sat a few hundred yards away from the old hotel. He drove the Zodiac up onto the beach beside it, where we wouldn't be seen by anyone looking this way from the hotel, got into our Kevlar vests, and loaded up with other equipment and supplies. There was a Heckler and Koch MP5SD submachine gun for each of us, fully suppressed, with laser sights, and plenty of spare magazines. Damien had a standard military-issue Beretta in a combat shoulder holster, and I had the .45 auto strapped to my right hip. Knowing that I might soon be going up against a world class shooter and fast-draw expert, I took a moment to adjust my gun belt so the holster hung lower on my right hip than it usually did, the butt of my pistol now positioned at the ideal height for the fastest possible draw.

I've put in some practice time myself, Clarence.

Using a pair of light-amplifying binoculars, Damien peeked out from the shelter of the old sailboat down the beach at the hotel. After several minutes of careful surveillance, he said, "I see two men outside on the deck.

They appear to be watching the front, just like we hoped. It looks like they each have some kind of rifle, but not ready. They're going through the motions—doesn't look to me like they're expecting trouble. I don't see anyone watching the lakeside or this end."

"Good," I said. "If they really aren't expecting anything, then hopefully that also means McAdam is still safe." I pulled a plastic-wrapped bundle out of the Zodiac and started to unpack it. "I'm going to go a hundred yards farther up and rig this. Keep watch and give me a ping if you think anyone's looking this way. Two pings from me means I'm on my way back." He nodded at that and turned back to his binoculars. I set off up the beach with the package, counting off a hundred paces with no signal from Damien.

While cramming for the mission, I had learned that it was very common for people to light off fireworks in the remote and mostly empty settlements scattered around the lake. That was illegal for most people in California, but driving past the north end of the lake earlier we had seen fireworks in the sky several times. What I had brought with us was what a fireworks store would call a "36-shot cake." When set off, it would launch individual shells high into the air, which would then explode into showers of multi-colored sparks. After setting the thing up on a level stretch of ground and activating the remote igniter, I keyed my transmitter twice to tell Damien that I was headed back.

Once again beside the old sailboat, we squatted close and held a whispered conversation.

"Alright," I said, "we need to end up with nine dead bad

guys, and hopefully this McAdam guy still alive. If you find him, try to get him out and down and signal me. Same goes for me. If we can just get him out of the way, then we know we're free to take out everyone else we see."

"Got it," Damien said. "I'll try to get him out the front as fast as I can. I've been watching, and I still don't think they're expecting trouble. Two on the deck, mostly looking out front towards the road. A third guy came out to talk for a minute but then went back in."

"Let's move on down there and get close," I said. "We'll take down those two guys and get them off the deck and out of sight. Then we'll set off the light show and deal with whoever comes outside to look. After that, I think the shit will be hitting the fan and we'll take it from there. You okay with all that?"

"All fine," Damien said. "When we get up there, let's get up on the deck at the rear. That'll help us get behind the sentries and get them over the rail. If we're lucky, more of them will run out and we can do it again. Only, let's keep close enough to our targets to give these gizmos a chance to go off if it's McAdam." He gestured to his wrist to indicate the special receiver.

After a final weapons check and a look through the binoculars, we set off down the beach towards the hotel. We kept close to the sparse line of low bushes that bordered the beach, ready to duck down and lie still if needed, and stopped every hundred feet or so to look through the binocs. After checking that the two sentries were still around on the front side of the building, we made a sprint for the last stretch, flattening against the slatted fencing that closed off the space under the deck. A person would have had to lean well out over the rail and look straight down to see us. We could hear the men slowly pacing the deck around front, and faint sounds of music coming from inside. Through hand signals, Damien and I agreed that the group still did not appear to be on high alert.

Moving as quietly as possible, we made our way around to the rear of the building, where there was a stairway up from the narrow beach. I picked up a small dried branch. Two minutes later, we were up on the deck and tight up against the wall, several feet from one of the dark windows, listening carefully. A bar of light from a door on the north end of the building reached across the deck towards the railing. I tossed the branch over the railing and off into the brush.

It caused a small but discernible noise that could easily have been made by some animal moving about. Almost immediately we heard the two men come around from the front, where they leaned against the rail to look out at the rough landscape. One of them was shining a flashlight down, but neither of them seemed alarmed.

Damien and I stepped just far enough out from the rear corner to line up the laser sights of our MP5s on the backs of their heads and fired. Our first shots certainly killed the two men, and our second and third shots helped them tumble over the railing to the dirt and sand below, rifles still slung across their backs. The built-in suppressors did their job beautifully; the loudest noise was that of the two bodies hitting the ground below. We ducked back to the rear wall and listened carefully for any reaction from inside. We heard nothing.

Two down now and seven to go, plus McAdam.

I dug in my pocket and pressed the button on the remote switch, setting off my little fireworks display. Within twenty seconds, the first aerial shell shot three hundred feet into the air and exploded with a bang and a bright red shower of sparks. The second one was bright blue, and then more and more spaced a few seconds apart. We heard sounds from inside and then someone burst through the door out onto the deck to our left, soon joined by two more men. They all had pistols at the ready.

"Oh, it's just more fireworks," one said.

"Yeah, I see that," another said, "but why so close? There's nothing up that way."

"Where the fuck is Deckard? And Jimmy?" said another.

We heard someone crack the door and yell back into the building. "Just fireworks, boss, but we're looking for Deckard and Jimmy."

Ah, so Puckett was still inside. Good to know. Damien and I exchanged a look and I gestured to my wrist and shook my head. No friendly vibration yet. We moved the selector switches on our MP5s to burst mode. It seemed like a good time to start blasting.

We stepped out around the corner again, moving six feet apart and dropping to one knee. I put a three-shot burst into the torso of the guy on the left, and then another, while Damien did the same for the guy on the far right. They both crumpled to the deck like the skeletons had been yanked out of them by some giant hand. The unfortunate third man in the middle got it from each of us at the same time as we both swung our aim inward. His heavy frame took in a spray of a dozen bullets within two or three seconds. He managed to fire his pistol into the wooden decking several times as the hail of high-velocity punches sent him flying backwards over the railing to join his two friends below.

After a quick self-check, we signaled to each other that we were both uninjured. As we moved carefully and quickly towards the side door, we heard a series of yells from inside the building. Several wild shots from within shattered the glass panes.

"The game is on," I said. "McAdam's code word is 'Roseland.'"

"Right, Roseland," Damien said. "I'll try to go for him if I can. Puckett is all yours."

Silently, Damien ran around the corner of the deck towards the front door. I ducked and waited as multiple shots came through the door by me and more through an adjacent window. As soon as the firing stopped, I yanked the door open and tossed an M84 stun grenade into a hall-way. I ducked down again and held my ears tightly as the blast went off, then opened the door and ran in, keeping low, the MP5 pointing the way. I found myself in what looked to be about a twenty-foot hallway that opened up into some larger open space dead ahead. The grenade had not made it all the way into the big room before going off. I hoped the explosion would still have had some effect on any occupants. McAdam would just have to deal with it.

A few more steps brought me to the end of the hallway. Several pistol shots echoed somewhere in the open space off to the right. Then I heard a loud crash that I guessed was probably Damien kicking open the front door. More shots rang out. I reached the corner and looked out in time to see two men about ten feet apart pointing handguns at a third armed man near the door that Damien had just come through. Some sort of a stand-off was playing out. Lingering smoke from the stun grenade made it hard to see everything, but the guy by himself looked like he was probably McAdam.

Suddenly that whole part of the room erupted into a smoking storm of gunfire. Several figures dropped from view. I heard yelling. I thought I heard someone yell the code word, and maybe someone else too, but I wasn't sure. I figured McAdam was either safe or dead at that point, but in any case, he was over there somewhere. Trusting that Damien would sort it out, I turned my attention to scanning the rest of the room ahead.

I caught a flash of movement as a man jumped from behind a large sofa and started to run towards the long wall at the far end of the lobby. I realized what he was going for when I looked past him and saw an AR-15 style rifle leaning against the wall. I flicked the MP5's selector switch to full-auto and ran straight towards him to close the distance between us. He was within a few paces of his goal when I dropped to one knee, put the laser in the middle of his back, and spat out the last twenty rounds in the magazine in just over two seconds, turning the running guy into a bloody ragdoll. The wall behind him looked like something Jackson Pollack might have done if the only paint he had was red.

As I slapped a fresh mag into the MP5, I saw more movement over towards my left, at the rear of the big space, and realized that another man had jumped up and was running towards the corner of the room. *That's got to be him*, I thought. *Puckett.* I took off after him, rounding a corner and seeing a man running towards a door at the end of the hallway. I saw him reach the door and then struggle with it, apparently surprised to find it locked.

"Puckett!" I yelled. He looked back quickly but continued to fumble with the door.

I flicked the selector switch to single shot and sent a fast dozen bullets into the woodwork around him. That made him stop and raise his hands. He turned around slowly to face me as bits of wood and plaster drifted down around him to fall at his feet. I saw that it was indeed him, tall and slim, but solidly built. My first impression, seeing him now in the flesh, was one of neatness and order. His thick blond hair had been cut recently, and he had a neatly-trimmed beard that went more towards red. He was wearing well-fitted blue jeans, with clean work boots and a Western-style chambray shirt. Somehow the shirt was still firmly tucked in despite all the commotion and the brief chase. Like me, he wore a leather gun belt slanted across his hips so that the holster hung low on the right side for a fast draw. From where I stood, the pistol in the holster looked like some model of German automatic, probably a Sig Sauer or an H & K. I walked in closer, stopping at about twenty-five feet. His face was impassive. He appeared to know the drill and was awaiting either a bullet or instructions.

"You killed my friend the other night," I said. "Nobody gets to do that to my friends."

He nodded in understanding, but otherwise gave no answer.

"I saw a few of your old videos," I said. "You were really good. Really good. Have you kept up with it?"

"I've been mostly busy with other things," he said, "but I have my good days." I thought he smiled a bit.

What was it my father had said to me that one time? Something about, what is the privilege of the dead? Ah, yes—that was it—"to die no more." But that had only been a dream. *Man, I may regret this, but I'd really like to know. I think I can take him.*

Still with his hands above his head, he gave a slight start as I switched the MP5 to my left hand and into a one-handed hold. I held up my right hand to him, palm out, in a "wait" gesture. He watched carefully as I slowly lowered the MP5 to set it gently onto a small side table that stood against the wall. I thought I saw the shadow of a smile as I squared up to face him straight on, my feet just slightly more than shoulder width apart. I lifted my left hand briefly, gesturing to him with a downward wave. He thought for a moment before nodding in understanding and slowly lowering his hands. He took two steps out from the wall.

And there we were. Puckett smiled, but look perplexed. "Why?"

"Fair question," I said. "And I'm not sure I know the answer. Maybe it's because you're so bad. Or, maybe, just maybe, it's because you're so good."

He appeared to think about that and smiled again. I saw several things in his face at that moment. I saw humor, confidence, and the satisfaction of achievement. I did not see hate, anger, or fear. I realized he knew he had me. He knew it.

And then, heralded by a thunderclap, the desert sky opened up and it started to rain. Deep inside the decrepit hotel, we both instinctively looked up and around as though we could see through the old walls as the drops started to hit the tin roof high above. Our eyes came back again to rest on one another.

In a barely perceptible flash of motion, he went for it. His right hand moved with a speed and a grace that could only have come from a combination of natural ability and hundreds of hours of dedicated practice spread across years. In a fraction of a second I knew that the drugs hadn't slowed him down one bit.

Damn, he was good.

10

Puckett drew his pistol within a span of time somewhere between the blink of an eye and the beat of a hummingbird's wing.

There was probably only a handful of people on the planet who were as fast as him.

His gun hand was halfway through its upward travel when my first shot plowed into his chest.

Any single fat slug from my .45, optimally placed, would have printed out a first-class ticket to oblivion, but I gave him two more, and then a fourth, because I like even numbers. He bounced against the wall and then tumbled to the floor, where he lay on his back. His pistol clattered down beside him. I walked over to stand above him, figuring he had a few seconds at most, if he wasn't dead already. His left hand was moving in some indecipherable gesture over his mangled chest, and he was trying to speak. I leaned over to listen.

"…ossible…" He shook his head slowly, back and forth, mouth open.

"What's that, Clarence?" I leaned in closer to hear him.

"That…that was…impossible," he said.

"Well, then your day hasn't been a total loss," I said. "You got to see something impossible."

He managed a slight laugh and gave a weak nod.

"This is for Stillman," I said, and shot him in his right thigh. His leg kicked a few times but nothing new showed on his face.

"And this is for Tommy." I put a bullet through the center of his forehead. His head bounced once off the floor and then, with a last exhalation, he was still. His eyes looked off into a future that he would never know.

I keyed the radio as I turned and walked away. "All done here. You still alive?"

"All good here," came Damien's response. "Right outside the front door with McAdam. Where's Puckett?"

"He's somewhere in the past tense," I said. "I'm on my way out."

Damien and McAdam were a little banged up. McAdam had managed to take out two of the gang members himself, but had paid the price in the form of a bullet graze to his upper arm. It didn't appear to be too bad and Damien had patched it up as well as he could. McAdam was handling it well. Damien had taken two pistol shots to the chest himself; his body armor had done its job and stopped the bullets, but he would have sore muscles for a while, and possibly a few cracked ribs to boot.

"What about all the others?" McAdam said. "There were nine guys. I saw two go down before we got out here."

Damien and I exchanged a quick look. This guy would have to be trusted to some extent and would certainly be debriefed extensively by higher-ups.

"All dead, Pete," I said. "Unfortunately, they were all shot while resisting arrest."

McAdam thought to himself for a minute before speaking. "Okay, okay. Yeah, that's a shame that they wouldn't come quietly."

"Yeah, a damn shame," I said. "Really sad. Alright, let's get it together." I looked at McAdam. "You take it easy for a few minutes and we'll get you outta here. This place will be crawling with your guys soon. They'll clean up and take credit for everything, but we need for you to come with us for now."

McAdam nodded and made no protest.

"We need pictures of all nine stiffs," I said to Damien, "and be sure to verify their status." Damien would know I was telling him to make sure everyone was dead as doornails. "You get the five guys outside; I'll do the four inside. Oh—did you signal Sophia?"

"Yes I did," he said. "I told her the mission was complete and that we had McAdam. She will pass it on to The Colonel. I told her we'll report again from the other side of the lake."

Fifteen minutes later, the three of us were back at the crumbling old sailboat, half-soaked from a light rain. Forty minutes after that, we pulled the Zodiac out of the water on the other side of the lake. We packed up what gear we needed to return to the Marines and stashed it, along with the boat, in the agreed-upon location.

As Damien drove us away in the Jeep, I sent the signal to our Marine contact, telling them to come back and pick up their stuff.

It would be dawn in not much more than an hour. I was wet, sandy, and fighting the wave of exhaustion that follows the ride down from a massive and prolonged adrenaline high.

Once again, I found myself looking forward to some air conditioning, a long hot bath, and an ice-cold glass of bourbon whiskey. Not necessarily in that order.

11

Gavin Bartlett was having the kind of day that couldn't end soon enough to suit him, but as the CEO of a company that employed twelve-hundred people in five states and four time zones, his workdays never really did end. He looked at his watch, as if doing so might make the remains of the day fly by faster, but found no help there. The profit margin for the company's most popular fencing products was being beaten up by the rising price of steel and the associated tariffs. A bungled renovation of the cement works at one of the two Texas manufacturing plants had production there bottle-necked at forty percent capacity. And the required minimum wage was going up all over the damn place.

Can I get a fucking break please? He thought to himself.

Bartlett figured he had about eighteen months before he'd have to tell his department heads to start slashing and reorganizing big-time. The company's cash-flow problems were upsetting to him on a gut level, because the leadership of Consolidated Barrier Corporation had been entrusted to him by his father and uncle, shortly before they had both passed away within the same year. It was their long years of hard work and smart decisions that had established CBC as one of the largest providers of fencing and wall solutions in the country. He knew the list of once-great companies that had been run into the ground by the second or third generation of family leaders was a long one, and he didn't want his name to get anywhere near it.

Bartlett turned his office chair around to face the wall and thought about the potential big break that had been teasing him for months. He wasn't very political himself, but as a business person he made a point to know what was going on in that arena, and he was aware that there was a fiery national debate going on about the need—or lack of a need—to build some kind of huge wall along the border with Mexico. His personal view that the whole idea was a silly and unnecessary waste of public funds was something that he wrapped up tightly and shoved down deep inside himself. His managers and employees, almost without exception, were chomping at the bit to get a piece of any wall action, and if contracts for such a wall were ever actually awarded, CBC would certainly be in the running. In fact, it was Bartlett's powerful politician father-in-law who had told him that he thought he would be able to influence the bidding process to heavily favor CBC. After all, he would say, he wanted his daughter and grandchildren to be well taken care of. A contract to build even a portion of this "great southern wall" could mean hundreds of millions of dollars—even more possibly—for CBC. An influx of cash like that could free him once and for all from the specter of crashing his father's company.

And so it was, that two months earlier he had begun work on a scheme to influence the outcome of the heated national debate.

With a nudge—no, a shove—from his wife's powerful father, the game was on. Bartlett had gotten a call from the senator one afternoon.

"I have some friends," the senator had said, "who share my disagreement with the way this country has been headed. They have agreed to finance our efforts to effect some change. A man named Sykes will be contacting you at your office. Please meet with him and extend him every courtesy. He has the skills and the experience that we will need to get this done."

Bartlett had met with Sykes and had been impressed with the power of his personality, though at the same time put off by what seemed like coarse violence simmering within him. The strength of Bartlett's personal convictions, however, could not stand up to the crushing weight of his company's problems. Sykes' proposal, if it ever came to fruition, would literally cost lives. Was the survival of the family company worth that?

In the end, after several sweaty days and tormented nights, the answer was "yes." He would work with Sykes and follow his instructions. If the whole scheme came together, Consolidated Barrier Corporation would be solidly in the black, and Bartlett and his family would live happily ever after. If in the process his ambitious father-in-law came closer to his political objectives, well, he was in no position to argue with that.

He had used his accounting expertise to set up a sham

real estate development corporation whose headquarters' address was an empty storefront between a dry cleaner and a dollar store in a strip mall outside of Dallas. He had provided the shell company information to his father-in-law, who presumably had passed it on to the mysterious benefactors, because two million dollars had appeared in the fake company's bank account overnight. The fake corporation had then put in several fake CBC fencing orders that were promptly paid for in real money. That money was then used to pay the very generous salaries for CBC's new "special consultant"— one Bernard Sykes, and his assistant, James West.

Bartlett didn't know where the money came from—and didn't want to know. He would help them do their ugly work and he hoped they would then go away, quietly and permanently. After that, having secured the solvency of his company and provided for the long-term comfort of his family, maybe he'd have enough time left to try to earn back his soul.

It was during the second long meeting between Bartlett, Sykes, and West, that they had worked to refine the idea that Sykes had first put forth. Sykes and West, who, Bartlett learned, went way back together, had first met while they were both serving with the DEA in El Paso. After several years of reasonably good law enforcement work for each of them, they had yielded to the temptation of making big money, and had gotten involved in a group that smuggled opioids across the border. They soon found out they had been ensnared in a sting operation designed to ferret out a particular double-agent they didn't even know. Having come quite late to the party, they were able

to avoid prison time by agreeing to resign, accept proba-
tion, and go away quietly.

Sykes had told Bartlett about how both he and West
had spent time flirting with different white supremacist
groups, and how, in particular, they had both spent time
with The New Confederates. Neither of them were card-
carrying members, but they were both on friendly terms
with the brothers who led the group—Darren and Bobby
Booth. It was through occasional contacts with the brothers, along with some more deliberate communications
with other acquaintances still in the group, that they had
learned of the recent falling out between Darren and
Bobby.

"Bobby's fed up, you see?" Sykes had said. "He feels like
he's been second in command for too long, and they aren't
doing enough to further their cause of making sure the
white Christians are always on top. Darren won't listen to
him anymore. Getting soft, he says."

"Do you think we can use Bobby, then?" Bartlett had
asked.

"That's where I'm headed," Sykes had said. "I got in
touch with Bobby, just like, you know, old times' sake sort
of thing. I took West and we met up with him in a bar. We
didn't have to go too far into a bottle of Jack Black before
he started opening up about his brother. 'Gutless,' he called
him. Then he started telling us about an idea he had to
stage some big attack that would get blamed on someone
else and start a big government crackdown. He went on
about blacks, Muslims, just about all immigrants—fill in a
minority—you name it. He didn't seem to make much
distinction. He thought if there was some big explosion,

like in a city park or something like that, and some little white cheerleaders got killed, then they'd finally get their wall built and get all immigration locked down. He said that after the attack, all the new anti-minority and anti-immigrant laws that would surely follow would be a 'righteous steamroller.'"

"Sounds like he's certifiable," Bartlett had said. "Did you get the sense that he was just ranting, or do you think he's really up for doing something?"

"I think he's hot for the idea," Sykes had said, and then had gone on to tell the story of how Bobby Booth had already started working on his rough plan. He had a cousin out in California by the name of Clarence Puckett. Puckett would be able to get his hands on some serious explosives and might actually know what to do with them. He had contacted Puckett, who had approved of the plan in general terms, and had suggested that Booth contact a friend of his in the Philippines. As Sykes told the story, Booth had been trying to get hold of this guy, Nikola Petrov, but hadn't yet gotten a response. He had called his cousin again in frustration.

"And here's where the plot thickens," Sykes had said. "When Bobby Booth called Puckett again, the guy answered from some hideout in the desert, out by the Salton Sea. Told Bobby about a big DEA raid that had gone down and busted up his whole crew. He told Booth that he was trying to get out of the country and that he wouldn't be taking any more calls for a while. Told him to keep trying Petrov in Manila."

"That's quite a story," Bartlett had said. "So what happens now?"

"I told Booth to keep trying this Petrov character. I told him that if that didn't work I might have some other ideas we could try. I also told him that I would be contacting a friend of mine from my DEA days to see if I could find out anything about this raid on his cousin Clarence. I'll call as soon as I have anything."

In his office outside Louisville, Bartlett was still gazing at the wall, but had managed to tamp down his slight panic. If everything fell into place in the near future, he and his Consolidated Barrier Corporation would be flying high with lucrative wall-building contracts, Bobby Booth would get his knee-jerk attack on non-whites and immigrants, Sykes and West would walk away with a pocket full of cash for services rendered, and Bartlett's politician father-in-law and his wealthy silent partners would ride the breaking wave of anti-immigrant hysteria to a new term in office and even more power than they already had.

Bartlett's phone rang, snapping him quickly back into his workday. He answered, recognizing Sykes' number.

"Just wanted to let you know that what Bobby Booth told me about his cousin getting raided by the DEA is apparently true. It happened just the other night in San Diego. My contact tells me there was lots of shooting. People were killed on both sides. A real clusterfuck, sounds like. And the next night, three more of his people were taken out by local SWAT. So it seems that this guy Puckett is too hot right now and won't be able to assist us after all. I've already called Booth and reminded him to keep trying the Manila contact for at least a few more days. He'll let me know how that goes. For the moment, let's hope that works out and that we'll be able to move forward."

A DEA raid. Bartlett didn't like the sound of that one bit.

"This DEA raid, do you think there's a possibility there could be any connection to this thing we're working on? Maybe we should bail out…"

"I really don't think so, Mr. Bartlett," Sykes said. "I don't like coincidences any more than you do, but it seems like one on the surface. Booth told me that this guy's main business was drugs, hence my old employer, the DEA. It looks like a coincidence that happens to be bad timing for us. In any case, my friend on the inside is going to do a little more digging for me. I'll let you know if I get anything from him."

Bartlett ended the call with Sykes and went back to looking through his office wall and into a pleasant daydream, finding a degree of comfort in an imagined image of a twenty-foot high pile of money snaking along the U.S. side of the Rio Grande.

The drive back up to Palm Springs from the eastern shore of the Salton Sea took just over an hour, factoring in a stop in the town of Palm Desert, where we handed McAdam over to a pair of men in dark suits who flashed the right IDs and knew the right password. Dawn was breaking as we neared the end of our drive, and the weather guy on the radio promised a hundred-percent chance of heat.

Back at the apartment, we did a quick unload of the Jeep, then a quicker wash-up. Despite our exhaustion, we wasted little time in pouring the stiff drink we'd both been dreaming of. I raised my glass in a toast.

"Here's to truth, justice, and the American way, or some shit like that."

"Whew," Damien said, laughing, "yeah, something like that anyway. You didn't tell me you fell and hit your head inside that place." We both laughed and drank heartily.

"Here's to a successful mission and rescue," I said. "We made a good team, didn't we? I hope we get to do it again."

As it had been for me many times in the past, the good Kentucky whiskey was a potent elixir, hitting my throat with a gentle wave of fire. It couldn't have been ten minutes before the glass was empty and I felt myself becoming part of the retro Mid-Century sofa. I looked over at Damien on the other sofa and saw that he was already sound asleep. Like a vampire running from the first rays of the morning sun, I dashed off to my room and dove under the covers.

I awoke to the sound of someone moving around a few rooms away, and spent a groggy minute thinking about where I was and why. By the time I had it all figured out, I was smelling coffee, and came out of my bedroom to find Damien having a cup in the kitchen. I fixed one for myself and we went out to the patio.

"Went through my emails already," he said. "The Colonel says I'm free for a few days as long as you don't need me for anything. If you think you don't, I guess I'll head back out to Rhode Island to check in with some people. Just call when you need me and I'll be there."

"That's fine. Go ahead with that. I'm not aware of any reason to keep you here for now. You may as well grab some R & R while you can. If something's cooking, I'll let you know."

My own email from The Colonel asked me to meet him tomorrow morning in the town of Twenty-Nine Palms, which was about an hour away on the north edge of Joshua Tree National Park. It was in an area commonly called "the high desert." He had been staying at the Marine base up that way.

We got it together and hit the highway at the same time, both headed back towards San Diego. Damien was bound for the airport and a flight out to the East Coast, and I was on my way to the hospital to see Tommy again.

"You are punished. I am so pissed at you. I told you that guy was a serious gunslinger. I told you to put him down from far away. Why did you not listen? Do you have a death wish?"

I knew right away I shouldn't have told him about Puckett. Tommy and I were the same age, but in some ways I still thought of him as a sort of older brother, and I never wanted to experience his disapproval.

"Come on, T," I said, "I'm no dope. I was pretty sure I could take him. There aren't many people faster than me. A few, I know, but he wasn't one of them. I mean, in this day and age, how likely is it that we get to do something like that? Showdown the bad guy? When will I ever have a chance like that again? Let me answer that for you ... never."

Propped up in bed, arms folded across his chest, he was glaring at me. I saw he really needed a shave.

"You can't do that shit in real life. This is not a fucking movie."

"Okay, okay," I said. "I shouldn't have done it. But I did and I'm here and he's dead and you're bitchy. The mission was a success by any measure. Can we move on please? When do you think you'll get out of here?"

He scowled at me for a half a minute before shaking his head and finally speaking.

"Another two days maybe is what they're telling me, as long as my vitals are all okay. I'll be able to go home, but I'll have to take it easy for a few weeks at least."

"The Colonel told me that he plans to ask you to find two more guys. That'll need to be done pretty soon."

"Yeah," he said, "he told me that too. That'll be pretty urgent. I don't know how easy it's gonna be to find people nuts enough to do this stuff. But I have a few ideas already. There're a lot of good guys out there. We'll get it done."

"Did Julie and Gayle come down to see you?"

His face lit up at the mention of his two daughters.

"Yeah, they were here yesterday, or maybe it was the day before. I was groggy as hell but it was great to see them. I told them I'd be back in Seattle as soon as I could. They think I'm with Homeland Security now, which I guess I am. Fighting the good fight and all that, you know."

"I know, same for me," I said, "with Jenny. She worries all the time but mostly keeps it to herself. We can't do this shit forever you know. It can't always be our fight. Hey—before I forget, you might want to update the next of kin in your file. Sophia told me it was still your ex. Maybe you want Julie and Gayle. Anyway, that's your business. Just mentioning."

"Oh yeah, you're right," he said. "I'll take care of that. Should be the girls, just like you say. I guess The Colonel must have you busy as a one-legged man in an ass-kicking contest. Where you off to next?"

"I've gotta get up to Twenty-Nine Palms. He's visiting old friends up at the Marine base and he wants to meet with me. I'll tell ya, I'm just about ready to find out what's what with all of this."

"Let me know what you can," he said as I stood up to go. "And Dean, I hope you got that out of your system. No more quick-draws, okay?"

"Yes, boss, got it," I said. "That'll hold me for quite a while. Heal up and I'll be in touch."

I did my best out-of-practice salute and he answered with a grin and a wave of dismissal.

Traffic was light for my drive up to Twenty-Nine Palms. The Mustang purred along happily. I passed Palm Springs, along with several other desert towns, curved around the western edge of the Joshua Tree National Park, and finally headed due east for the last thirty miles. The small but sprawling town was mostly clustered along an east-west stretch of Route 62, just to the north of the park. I knew the enormous Marine base was outside the town to the north, its thousand square miles stretching up and out into the high desert. The base, along with the Marines who lived there, was an integral part of the economy and life of the town that shared its name.

After passing through the center of town, I turned up the lane to the historic inn where I had stayed once in the past, and in short order was checked into my room. My appointment with The Colonel was for ten o'clock the next morning, so I had the evening free. After a long walk around to explore the property, a dip in the pool, and a simple but fine dinner in the inn's restaurant, I called it an early night and was asleep before ten.

It was already over a hundred degrees when I shut the door of my room the next morning and started down the path leading to the main building and restaurant. My walk took me past several small adobe structures housing more guestrooms, all named for desert wildflowers.

I was slightly startled when a large roadrunner ran out from between two of the buildings, passing just in front of me to run off into the expanse of Mojave Desert that bordered the property. I half expected him to yell out "beep-beep," but he just ran by silently. I stood for a moment and watched the tall, slim bird run off into the desert until he became a small spot, finally vanishing like a ghost into the shimmering heat. I turned back to the path and found my way to the lodge.

Inside, I found the main dining room to be comfortably air-conditioned and only about a third full. A long table was set up with a generous breakfast buffet. As I looked around, a staffer pointed me to a small side room that appeared to be meant to accommodate a private party of six or eight people. The Colonel was already there, sipping coffee and sorting through a small stack of files. He stood and we shook hands. We went back out to the buffet table together and loaded up plates before sitting down. He poured a cup of coffee for me and refreshed his own.

"I thought it would be good to get together for a few

minutes while we're both still out this way," he said. "I talked to Tommy yesterday, but it's been a few days since I've seen him in the flesh. How's he doing?"

"I stopped in on him yesterday before I drove up here," I said. "He was pretty groggy, and I only saw him for a few minutes, but he seemed as good as can be. Nurse told me he was right on schedule. He thinks he should be able to bust out within a few days. He didn't say it, but I think he's still pissed at himself for Stillman."

"Understandable feelings, of course," he said, "but that certainly wasn't his fault. Well, he'll have to work through that himself. We all do. He'll be okay before long. Good job by you and Stevens the other night," he said. "You got Agent McAdam safely out of there and wrapped the rest of it up nicely. Good work. The DEA got some good intel out of it too."

"That's good to hear," I said. "We were lucky there were no major snags. Colonel, my understanding is that the DEA first got onto Puckett for his meth dealing, but when we met with you the other day you told us that there was some intelligence that he was also some kind of gun runner. I'm thinking that must be why he started shooting in San Diego. What do you think?"

"I think you're right. It's hard to say. Meth dealing is serious business, but would you gun down federal agents for that? No doubt some would. But adding in the chance of going down for smuggling small arms into the country really ups the ante, don't you think? Could have pushed him to slap leather.

"In fact, that brings me to part of the reason I asked you here. Aside from all the lovely vistas of Joshua Trees and tumbleweeds, that is. Forget about Puckett's drug dealing for now. That isn't our concern, and anyway he's dead. We, along with the other agencies, are more concerned with the arms smuggling at this point. It looks like he had a line on basic infantry small arms—rifles, mostly—but explosives too. Maybe grenades and plastics. We're still going through intel and cross-checking everything. The concern is that he may have been in bed with some home-grown terrorist or anarchist group. I don't know enough to be very specific right now, but everyone's looking at that angle. Whether we're talking about neo-Nazis, white supremacists, the good old KKK—not sure yet. As you know, with today's political climate, all these nuts have been coming out of the woodwork."

"Right, yeah," I said. "I'm aware of that being a big thing in the past few years."

"Good," he said, "because I think that is probably where all this is headed. CIA, DIA, FBI, and ATF are all in on it at the moment, and it looks like we might get a slice of the pie too pretty soon."

He shuffled some papers around and opened a new folder. "How is Damien doing?"

"Solid," I said. "He was all professional on the Puckett job. Great reactions, doesn't freeze up, very cool when he should be. I wouldn't hesitate at all to work with him again."

"Good to hear," The Colonel said. "That matches up with what Tommy has said in the past. I hope we can find a few more as good."

The Colonel poured more coffee for each of us. We took a moment to doctor up our cups and take a few sips.

"Do we think Puckett's arms racket is done with now?" I asked. "With his recent demise?"

"The ATF and FBI seem to think so, yes," The Colonel said. "It wasn't a big operation anyway, but they think it's done for at this point. So, to your question a minute ago, the thinking is that this arms business that Puckett was into was probably the reason for the heavy response the other night. They were into something bigger than anyone thought."

"Hmmm, yes," I said. "That makes sense—and it's scary. So now I wonder, if Puckett's candy store is all boarded up, whoever he may have been talking to, are they kaput now, or are they looking for another source?"

"Good question." The Colonel nodded and sipped at his coffee. "And I don't have a good answer for you right now, but I'll let you know when I do. I hope that'll be within a day or two. If we get involved, and with Tommy out for a while, I'll probably need you to ride point.

"I want you to hang around Southern California for a while until I know more. Go see Tommy again if you want. I'll be in Portland tomorrow for Stillman's funeral. I hate that shit, but it comes with the territory."

We spent another thirty minutes drinking coffee and talking about other department business before The Colonel took off for a meeting back at the Marine base. I went out to stroll around the grounds and enjoy the novelty of the extreme heat. I saw a small scorpion and a variety of lizards, but the roadrunner was nowhere to be found.

13

Two days after my breakfast meeting with The Colonel in Twenty-Nine Palms, I got an email from Sophia, asking me to be available for an online conference that evening. She would be sending me, Damien, and our other team member, Kevin Briggs, a link to a secure video chat. The Colonel wanted to meet with us all together.

That evening, at the specified time, I started up the secure meeting software and used Sophia's link to log in. Damien, Briggs, and Colonel Bixby were already there, along with Sophia. We said hellos and chatted casually for a few minutes while Sophia made some adjustments to the sound. Everyone's face was displayed in a small square, and there was an area where other pictures or documents could be displayed if desired. The Colonel started the meeting.

"Evening guys, thanks for being here on time. I asked Sophia to set up this call so all of you can get this at the same time. Sophia – please stay on, I want you to get all this too. First of all, Tommy continues to do well, and his daughter Julie is escorting him home today. Probably there by now in fact. He won't be operational for a while, but will be doing desk work for us as needed, as long as he takes it easy.

"The Council and I, together with the other agencies, have been sifting through the information recovered after the DEA raid last Sunday, along with the operation in downtown San Diego on Monday, and then the one out at the Salton Sea. A lot has happened quickly, but we are starting to make sense of it. We believe that we've uncovered the early stages of a domestic terrorism plot.

"So then, some background is in order. We all know there are lots of white supremacist groups all over the country. It's been mostly on the FBI to watch as many as they can, and that organization has recently been very interested in one group that calls itself 'The New Confederates'. They're based in Alabama and we think they have about a thousand members. The FBI has several informants that bring in information from time to time about the group's plans and activities. They get together at rallies and picket this or that politician, occasionally get an interview on some small town TV show, maybe write in to a newspaper. The group hasn't yet done anything to make them look like any serious threat, though it is headed up by some really nasty characters. The leader is a man named Darren Booth. He was kicked out of the army for spreading racist propaganda. His long-time girlfriend—lady named 'Lana'—did six years for armed robbery. A cop and a bank customer were killed in that robbery, but she got off light by taking a deal. Not pleasant characters, all in all.

"Now, here's where it gets even more interesting. About six months ago, one of the sources that the FBI has on the inside reported in that there was a lot of disagreement at the top. The man they consider to be the second-in-command of the NC is apparently fed up with the mostly passive nature of the group, and has started to make a lot of noise about how they should be much more militant. He, along with some twenty or so loyal followers, has broken off to form his own group. The man leading this splinter group is none other than Darren Booth's younger brother, Bobby Booth, also an army veteran."

"Man," Damien said, with a laugh, "this shit is pissing me off. These guys are giving the army a bad name."

"You said it," Briggs said. "They need a big punch in the face at a minimum. Colonel, do you know if the younger brother had an honorable discharge?"

"Yes," he said, "Bobby Booth did, but cool your jets, guys, there's a lot more. Okay, so, moving on. Unfortunately, the FBI wasn't aware of what was going on in Bobby's group because his true believers didn't include any of the informants from the NC. Not until a recent breakthrough that is. Someone approached the Alabama State Police and started talking up a storm. The State Police immediately brought in the FBI. The story is that this person was alarmed when they learned that Bobby Booth and his inner circle were seriously thinking about some big attack right here in the U.S. The guy overheard Bobby and a few of the others talking about building some kind of bomb—a dirty bomb maybe—and setting it off in a majority-white city. He believed the basic idea was that they wanted to kill as many as a few hundred people—white Americans, mind you—such that it pointed towards Islamic extremists as the culprits. Somehow, the FBI was able to convince him to stay in the group and try to pass on more information.

"Of course, as you all know, that exact scenario is one that the intelligence community has been worried about for years. Their end goal would likely be that Congress and the president would rush to close the borders and crack down on all immigration. They would also hope to start a new tidal wave of fear and hate aimed at blacks, Muslims, Latinos—you know, everyone that these nutjobs are always ranting about.

"Now, we know that if a group of racists from Alabama ever managed to pull something like this off, the FBI, CIA, and everyone else probably wouldn't really be fooled for more than a minute as far as who did it, but that wouldn't matter. All it would take is a few news reports, a few interviews on TV, a few politicians jumping up and down screaming, and the country would be freaking out. It all sounds absurd at first glance, but if you think about it, it's not too much of a stretch to see that, in the world we live in today, it could possibly work.

"So, to recap: we have two racist brothers, Darren Booth and Bobby Booth. Darren heads up a mostly run-of-the-mill white supremacist group, and Bobby gets pissed because they aren't militant enough. Bobby breaks off and starts working on this crazy dirty bomb plot. Only thing is, some of us have to take it very seriously. Deadly serious. That brings me to this past week, when Dean and Damien met up with one Clarence Puckett, meth dealer, gun nut, and dabbler in illegal arms. Digging into Puckett's past, we can see that he grew up in a small Alabama town called Union Springs. Anyone like to guess who else grew up in Union Springs, Alabama?"

It was Briggs who spoke first, but I could tell from the small portraits on my screen that everyone knew the answer.

"Gotta be the Booth brothers," he said. "Darren and Bobby. Puckett must've known them."

"You got it," The Colonel said, "Clarence Puckett was Darren and Bobby's cousin. So if you're Bobby Booth, and you've gone off the deep end and want to get your hands on bomb materials, you'd probably call the first gun guy you can think of—your cousin."

"Then like I asked you the other day," I said, "with Puckett out of the picture, is Bobby Booth dropping his whole idea, or trying to find another contact?"

"Good question," The Colonel said, "and we think the answer is that he's actively trying to find some other source. Just yesterday we had some help on that end from our friends at CIA. They've picked up both emails and cell phone calls in the last few days between Bobby Booth and a Ukrainian citizen by the name of Nikola Petrov. They already have a fat file on Petrov, and they consider it possible that he could have obtained some amount of radioactive material and could be trying to peddle it to Booth. Petrov is currently in Manila, where he is under heavy CIA surveillance. They think he's cooling it there while he negotiates with Booth."

"Do they think this Petrov guy actually has these materials with him?" Briggs asked. "Or somewhere nearby?"

"Not sure yet," The Colonel said. "Our friends are working on that as we speak. We have to assume the worst case, which is that there is something and he has it, or ready access to it. Regardless, CIA is not planning to let him leave the Philippines, one way or the other. They have the resources to take care of him there whenever they want to, and the local secret police would probably be thrilled to help out. They're watching and listening to see what they can get from him about this Bobby Booth link before they do anything with him."

"Do we have eyes and ears on Booth?" Damien asked. "And the brother—Darren?"

"The FBI will be monitoring everything from any cell phones or land lines related to them. We hope we can also get bits and pieces from the human contacts. The informant inside Bobby's group could help us to keep tabs on his frame of mind. Who knows, if CIA squashes his second attempt to get bomb materials, he may just go nuts and run into a crowd with a machine gun. But let's not let that happen."

"Do we know where all these people get their operating money from?" I asked.

"We do have some information on that," The Colonel said, "and you'd be surprised. They get a lot of donations from outsiders—people who like what they're doing but don't want to publicly support them—people who hate the same people they hate but won't say it out loud. After the secret warrants came through, the FBI found quite a bit on that. Darren Booth has had several famous donors. You know that conservative radio host—Gus Lindburgh? He donates regularly. The FBI has pictures of a Lindburgh staffer handing over a bag of cash to one of Booth's men earlier this year. Which, by the way, is not currently illegal. And you've probably heard of Sam Hargity, you know the guy with the show on FIX news? He's a generous donor to The New Confederates. There are lots of others, but remember, that's interesting, and maybe even despicable, but not our business or concern.

"For right now, let's assume this team will be called upon to execute some form of strike against one or both of the Booth brothers' groups. We will watch for word from our friends on this Petrov character in Manila, and will react to that information as appropriate. That about covers what I know now. This situation is very fluid, so everybody keep your phones charged and be ready to move. I'd be very surprised if something doesn't happen in the next week or two. Okay, I'll be calling each of you within the next hour. Any questions before that?"

Nobody spoke up.

My call came in less than ten minutes.

"I've just spoken with Briggs," The Colonel said, "and asked him to get to Manila right away. He'll hook up with CIA out there as our man on location. Tommy will be home sometime today and will be resting up. I know you two are close, so feel free to visit whenever you have time. We can use him for light duty, but until he's firing on all eight you'll be second in command. That means, depending on what this mission turns out to be, you will have operational command in the field. I'll make sure the rest of the team, including Tommy, knows that. Okay so far?"

"Got it, Colonel," I said. "No problem at all. Do you really think this is all going to come to something as fast as you say?"

"I'm afraid that I do, yes," he said. "I don't know if I've ever seen dirty water boil so fast as it's been doing this week. The higher-ups are rubbing their necks from the whiplash. So yes, things are happening fast. I know that isn't ideal, but our role will be limited, as usual, and we will have all the help or tools we need—I'll see to that."

"All right, then," I said, "I'll get up to Seattle tomorrow and check in with Tommy. I think Damien's back east. Can we get him up there too?"

"That's what I was going to suggest," he said. "With Briggs on the way to Manila, I want you and Damien out there where you can hash things out with Tommy to help. Sophia will assist as usual. She can be a central repository for equipment needs, travel, research—you know what she can do."

"Anything else for now, Colonel?"

"That's it for now. Keep your ears open and your powder dry. Something's going to be happening soon."

14

I arrived in Seattle the next day and made a quick stop to see Tommy, who was settling in at his home with help from his daughter, Julie. I promised to be back in the morning and went off to check into a favorite downtown hotel where I'd stayed several times in the past. I strolled around the area within a few blocks of the hotel, visiting the historic Pike Place Market and then doing some window shopping. I found a small, family-run Italian place for dinner before heading back to the hotel.

The hotel bar had a fine bottle of calvados brandy, and the way that the warm liquor carried the scent and taste of the fresh apples it was made with was mesmerizing. Sipping it slowly, my thoughts ran to fond memories of a trip to the Normandy region of France I'd taken many years ago. I remembered that two-week trip as being filled with long walks in the sun, invariably followed by a leisurely lunch at a tiny table at a shady sidewalk café. I took a second glass up to my room, where I returned a few emails and enjoyed a twenty-minute call with a sleepy Jenny before climbing into bed. I set the alarm for early enough to allow me to have a leisurely morning before I would need to pick Damien up at the airport.

Before leaving the Los Angeles area earlier in the day, I talked with both The Colonel and Sophia, and had learned that the alleged arms dealer, Nikola Petrov, had gotten into a scuffle with his CIA watchers in Manila and had not survived. A suitcase full of mildly radioactive medical waste had been safely recovered. The fact that it would not have been much danger to anyone in the context of a dirty bomb had little bearing on the seriousness of the overall situation. It occurred to me for a minute that these would-be terrorists or bomb makers might be more stupid than dangerous, but then I also knew that stupid people with guns, explosives, and a grudge, could be very dangerous indeed.

As far as we were aware, Bobby Booth did not yet know of Petrov's demise, and CIA was taking steps to continue the charade of the back and forth negotiations between the two of them in order to buy time and prevent Booth from going to ground. The Booth brothers were planning to get together for some sort of meeting soon. The Colonel hadn't been kidding when he said that shit was happening fast. The next day promised to be a day of mission planning for the three of us at Tommy's place.

"I think the Minneapolis idea is solid," Tommy said. We had been kicking ideas around for hours and a plan was starting to take shape. "Nothing else we've talked about holds up better."

"You're right," I said, "I agree it's gotta be Minny. Which means we only have a few days to prepare."

"That's par for the course," Damien said. "This whole fucking show has been a race, you know? I was just thinking how much it seemed like it's been less than a week since we were out at the Salton Sea, then I realized that it really has been. But I vote for Minny too—that's the only real option."

"The way things are going," I said, "who knows when the brothers will be even within a few miles of each other again. So at least now we know what we're working with and where."

Based on the information the FBI had been able to get from their informants inside Darren Booth's New Confederates group, along with bits of intel from Bobby Booth's more radical splinter group, it was believed that the brothers planned to hold a meeting while they were both in Minneapolis to attend the massive annual gathering of the NRA. Our newly-clarified task was to wipe out the leadership of both groups in such a way that their destruction appeared to be the result of an internal squabble that had suddenly escalated. The Colonel had explained that he and The Council had several reasons for wanting things to go down that way. One was that, while they did want the American people to be vigilant, they thought it might cause too much of a freak-out to have an actual dirty-bomb plot splashed across all the front pages. The other main reason was that they thought it would be good for the mainstream public to clearly see the instability and ultimate self-

destruction of a radical group such as the New Confederates. We kept that requirement in mind while hatching our
plan.

Tommy stabbed his finger at a spot on our enlarged
map of The Twin Cities.

"The convention center is here. The Savoy House Hotel
is right across from it. Attached by one of those walkways
over the street, I think. The city has a ton of those things—
skyways they call 'em—so people can get from building to
building without having to go outside in the tough winters
they have there. I've spent time there. They really come in
handy when it's twenty below outside. The Savoy will
probably be jam-packed for the convention. We need to
know if the Booth brothers will be staying there. And if
not, where."

"Hang on," Damien said, "I think we might have that."
He rustled through several of the files in front of him until
he found the desired paper. He read through it quickly.
"This is from one of the last reports on Darren Booth.
Looks like he has three rooms booked at the Savoy. Says
here that it's likely he'll be with his regular girlfriend and
two of his inside crew."

"Fantastic," Tommy said, "so we've got at least one
Booth right there. We need to know if little brother will be
there too. I'll call Sophia and ask her to see if we can get
anything on that."

"Ask her if she can find out where in the hotel Darren
has his rooms," I said. "What floor, what room numbers—
whatever she can find out. And ask her to let us know what
capabilities she'll have for that hotel. We need to know if
she'll be able to tap into the surveillance cameras, alarm

systems, parking lot barriers, whatever. The other thing I'm thinking of is anything she can get on the NRA meeting itself. Guest speakers, police presence, celebrity appearances—anything she can get."

Tommy stood up, carefully steadying himself.

"I'll go call her right now. Then I'm going to lie down for a while. This is all exciting, but I think I've overdone it a bit. I'll rest up so I can be in shape for dinner later."

He went off to his bedroom, leaving me with Damien and a table full of folders, papers, and coffee cups.

"Seeing as how we don't have any time to spare," Damien said, "I think I should head on up to Minneapolis tomorrow to get the lay of the land. I'll try to get a room at that hotel and scope out whatever I can."

"I think that's a great idea," I said. "Take lots of pictures. Check out all the entrances and exits. And if you can, find out if there's still a Chinese place called "Eastern Dragon" in the Nicollet Mall."

"What do you need to know that for?" Damien asked. "I didn't see that in the files. Is that where we think the brothers are going to meet?"

"It's not in any of the files," I said. "But I'm telling you, man, they have the best pork lo mein I've ever had."

Later, after freshening up at our hotel, we drove back over to pick up Tommy at his house and the three of us went downtown to dinner at the Capital Grille.

"I'm sorry I can't be more hands-on with you guys on this whole thing," Tommy said, after we'd ordered our dinner. "But I'm glad to be in on the planning at least. This idea we've cooked up seems like something out of the movies, but if anyone can pull it off, you guys can."

"You're a big part of the plan, T," I said, "wouldn't want to do it without you. I won't say it'll be a piece of cake, but we'll pull it off."

"Yeah, we'll pull it off," Damien said. "It'll be something to write home about. Just one more thing that I can't tell anyone about, that is. Oh well."

"Does it bother you," I asked, "to not be able to tell anyone?"

"No, not really," Damien said. "I mean, shit, yeah, it does sometimes, but don't worry about me. I'm not going to tell anyone. It's just funny that we do and see some crazy stuff and then have to move on like it didn't happen."

"Well, why the hell do you think Dean and I drink so much?" Tommy said. All three of us laughed out loud. "I highly recommend it."

"Yeah," Damien said, "when you're right, you're right I guess. Anyway, it sure does pay well."

"Hey, when I first met you," I said, "you had a girlfriend. I remember you told me that you guys were on-again, off-again. You never seem to mention her."

"Off again," Damien said. "We had some good times, but I guess we weren't really a match. She told me I don't express myself enough. You know how it goes. Anyway, she had ODG. That irritated me, so it's all good."

"ODG," Tommy said, "that's a type of asthma, isn't it? That isn't very nice of you."

"No," Damien said, and laughed, "maybe you're thinking of COPD. No, ODG is Overly Demonstrative

Gesticulation. She would move her arms around wildly when she talked. You know, like an Italian person, but more so. We'd be having a conversation, in a restaurant maybe, and she'd be flinging her arms around to make some point. I started to think people were always looking at us, but I suppose it was all in my head. Don't tell me you've never heard of ODG. Come on now."

"No, sorry," Tommy said. I nodded with him and added an "oh shit—me too" face. "I guess I better add that to my growing list of code words younger people use that I don't understand."

After dinner, we drove Tommy back to his house in the Queen Anne neighborhood and accepted an invitation to help him with a bottle of Blanton's Bourbon Whiskey. We were settled out on his deck in time for the sunset.

"A toast to Tommy's deck," I said. "One of my favorite places in the world. And welcome, Damien, to the Brotherhood of the Deck."

"Thanks, guys," Damien said. "I mean it. I really do appreciate having you two to talk to, very much, so thanks for that."

We drank our toasts and sat for a few minutes, admiring the sunset and the city skyline spread out below and to the south. The Space Needle stood between us and the concentrated cluster of downtown buildings that reflected the orange light of the setting sun.

"I've never been a joiner," I said, "and I've had only a very few close friends in my life. Tommy here, of course. And I guess I'm stuck with you now too." I raised my glass at Damien. "Which is great. I'll take it.

"All this talk about friends reminds me of a funny story.

A long time ago, back in Cape May, I had these two friends who were best friends with each other—Gina and Trudy. You must have met them at least a few times, right?" I looked at Tommy, who shrugged in a non-remembering way. "Anyway, they were both from well-known local families. I knew Trudy from high school, and then later I worked with both of them at a restaurant in town for several years. So Gina and Trudy were the best of friends, had grown up together, and did lots of stuff together.

"They had been so close for years, and spent so much time together that sometimes they almost acted like a couple. I mean, they weren't ever a couple, that's not what I'm saying, it's just that they could do that secret look across the room that told the other one that it was time to leave the party, or we're outta time—whatever—like a married couple might do. And I'm sure that they could do 'the look,' but the thing I always thought was really cool is that they also had their own code word—'QRS.'"

"QRS?" Damien asked.

"That's right, QRS."

"Yeah, okay, QRS," he said, "but what did that stand for?"

"See, that's the thing," I said, "it didn't stand for anything. It had no meaning without context. It was just a thing they would work into a conversation. Like if they were at a party and they were talking to two guys, and Trudy wanted to tell Gina that she wasn't into them, she might say something like, 'I heard this really cool band on the radio the other day, but I can't remember their name. I think it was one long word, but all I can remember is QRS...' It didn't matter that it wasn't a sensible thing to say, it just had to show up. Then Gina would understand that Trudy wasn't into that guy and they needed to make tracks. Now, it wasn't all about ditching boring guys. It just meant 'I'm saying this thing about that thing, but I can't actually say it.' To the two of them, in the moment, it would have meant something and would have made sense.

"There was a whole bunch of us who hung out together, and a lot of us worked at this restaurant. When we were hanging around in the back of the dining room late at night, waiting for the last customers to leave, we'd all be having a beer or a glass of wine and blabbing about what we did last night, or who we had seen on the beach that day. One night I heard Gina and Trudy talking, and several times I caught a reference to 'QRS.' I finally got them to explain it to me. They didn't mind telling me because I was a good, platonic friend. I wasn't anyone they would be trying to sneak away from, so they trusted me with their secret. It was all about the context. I think it's cool when two people have a special communication like that. I think as close as I've ever come would have to be this old stiff right here." I gestured to Tommy, who attempted a small bow while remaining seated.

"That's a good story," he said. "Maybe we could figure out our own code like that. Not 'QRS' though. Probably not 'UCK' either, because that would show up too often in our conversation and throw us both off."

"Right, and right again," I said. "Couldn't be 'QRS.' If it was, every time I heard it I would think of Gina and Trudy and miss the message."

"You guys compartmentalize so well," Damien said. "I

envy that about you. It takes me a couple of days, and more than a few nightmares."

"Hey," I said, "don't think I haven't had my share of nightmares. Not always, but plenty. That means you're human, which is a good thing."

"The work we do," Tommy said, "it's like cleaning toilets. It's an important task that needs to be done by someone who'll do it right and be able to do it again next week. Most people don't like to clean toilets."

"I don't like to clean toilets," Damien said.

"Well, you're lucky, then," I said. "You don't have to clean toilets. See—it could be worse."

"I don't know, I never minded it all that much," Tommy said. "If you have a good pair of rubber gloves and one of those brushy things—not so bad."

"You guys are fucking nuts," Damien said. "Why do I even try?"

We all laughed and drained our glasses in the last toast of the evening. Damien reminded me that he was off to Minneapolis in the morning, and after making sure that Tommy had everything he needed, we left him and headed off to our hotel. There would be plenty of time the next day for Tommy and me to work on our assault plan again while Damien and Sophia gathered the information we needed.

15

It wasn't until after dinner with Tommy the next day that information started to come in from Damien and Sophia, but when it did, it came in buckets.

Sophia was the first to call. Through a combination of sources, she had been able to put together that Bobby Booth would be renting a townhouse for his visit to Minneapolis. The place was in the southern suburbs of the city, very close to the gigantic Mall of America, about thirty minutes away from downtown. Booth would be traveling by car, attending the conference with two of his men. They had a tentative plan to meet up with Darren Booth at the hotel Saturday afternoon.

As far as the Savoy House Hotel, she informed us that she should be able to access much of the security system. "They recently upgraded to a new digital camera system," she said, "and the good news for us is that they haven't yet loaded the latest security patch. I took the liberty of fooling around a little. It looks like I should be able to take cameras offline—or switch feeds around if you need that. In addition to the hallway camera on the upper floors, they have a few to cover most of each floor of the attached parking structure. Darren Booth has three rooms reserved on the sixth floor, all in his name. I sent you a rough diagram—have you had a chance to look at it yet?"

I brought up the drawing on my laptop and we looked at it together. The guest rooms on the upper floors were all laid out in an L-shape, with one long hallway being about three times the length of the shorter hallway. It was the end of the shorter hallway on each floor that had the connector to the parking garage.

"Can you make changes to existing reservations?" I asked.

"That should be a piece of cake. Their reservation system has been around for almost ten years and is pretty standard. Not hard to break into. Why—do you want me to have an extra cookie left on Damien's pillow when he gets there?"

"Not exactly," I said, "but feel free to do that if you want to, he deserves it. No, here's what I want you to do..."

I gave her my instructions and asked her to confirm back with me if and when she was able to get it all done.

Soon after hanging up with Sophia, Damien called and reported that he was on the ground in Minneapolis and had been able to get a room at the Savoy House. I put the call on speaker so Tommy could take part, and filled him in on the prior conversation with Sophia. He had spent several hours wandering around, familiarizing himself with the hotel.

"With the convention coming up, I didn't think I was going to be able to get a room, but the third time I called must have been just after somebody cancelled. Makes it easier for me to wander around and check the place out. The hotel is eight floors total, with the attached parking building only coming up to six. Part of the fifth floor of the parking structure, right where it connects to the hotel, is a construction zone. I chatted up one of the maids and asked about it. They're building one of those skyways from that point over across the street to the Drummond Bank Building. Most of the skyways are at the second or third floor, so this one will be unusually high. Has something to do with the bank building having some tall atrium inside. You can still go through to get to the garage, but they have that yellow 'construction zone' tape all over the place. There's basically a hole in the side of the hotel at that point where the new walkway will go, so we probably shouldn't go out there in the dark."

He went on to confirm what Sophia had told us about security camera placement in the hallways and in the parking structure.

"It's definitely one of the older city hotels," Damien said. "But they appear to be planning a major renovation that will kick off after the conference. Little posters are starting to pop up telling guests about planned improvements, and clearly some minor work has started. I've seen contractors going in and out of several rooms, you know—with those big carts full of paint and spackle, or a new sink. Maybe that's something we can use. But the rooms are fine, and I guess the main attraction is the proximity to the convention center, which takes up the whole block across the street."

"That's all good work," I said. "I want you to stay there

and keep doing what you're doing and learn everything you can about the area. Have you had a chance yet to go through the stuff Sophia sent us?"

"Just a quick look. I'll spend more time on it this evening."

"Fine," I said. "If you haven't already seen it, she found out that Bobby Booth will be renting a townhouse down in Bloomington—near the mega-mall. See if you can find where that is and if it's currently empty. If it is, maybe there's a way we can exploit that before Booth and his people arrive Friday. Communicate with Sophia if you need to."

"Got it," Damien said. "I've been thinking a lot about our plan, and I have some new ideas. If what I'm thinking of adds up, we're going to need some fast help from The Colonel. Let me chew on it for a while, check out that place, and I'll get back to you guys."

"Do that," I said. "Go ahead and get your ideas to The Colonel as soon as you're ready, and copy Sophia and me. Today's Wednesday. The best intel we have on the Booth brothers' pow-wow is that it could be Saturday afternoon. That means we have to do our thing before then or who knows what'll happen. They might meet up and go their separate ways, which we don't want. That gives us not much more than about sixty hours. We are really going to have to pull this one out of thin air."

"Ah yes," Tommy added, "my favorite kind of operation —plenty of time—no trouble at all. Piece of cake."

"I don't know about piece of cake," I said, "but we need to be in the zone for the next few days, that I can tell you. Damien, Briggs is back cooling his heels in San Francisco.

As soon as I hang up I'm going to call him and tell him to get out there to you as soon as possible. Sooner even. I'll come out myself on the earliest flight I can get tomorrow. Let's talk again before midnight tonight. Be prepared to tell me more about what help or equipment you think we'll need so I can get that to The Colonel."

"Over and out, then," Damien said. "I'll speak to you later." And he rang off.

Mentioning The Colonel must have conjured him up, because right after my quick call to Briggs, asking him to make tracks to Minneapolis, Tommy's cell phone rang. He put the thing on speaker and we exchanged brief pleasantries with the boss.

"NSA has picked up some communications that would appear to be of concern," The Colonel said. "What we're putting together is that the younger Booth has been reaching out to like-minded friends of friends with connections in Ukraine. If that is true, we can't help but see that as a serious escalation, because there are many people in that part of the world, known, unknown, and known-unknowns, who we believe really could put their hands on significant amounts of radioactive material. Now, we still don't know if Booth is aware that his friend in Manila has been killed, but in any case, the danger level has risen significantly. It appears Booth is planning to fly to Berlin early next week, so we must assume this is part of an effort to reach out to a Ukrainian contact. I want you to continue with your planning for this weekend in Minneapolis. It is now even more urgent for you to make sure that neither Booth brother leaves that city except in a box or a bag. That order comes from the top."

"From the top?" I said "Do you mean...?"

"Yes," The Colonel said, "I mean exactly what you think I mean. The top. How are you doing with making it look like they took each other out?"

Tommy and I exchanged looks.

"I think we have that covered. We're working on a plan to stage a big standoff, but we'll need you to get us some help with a couple of things. Some equipment, and also some help afterwards with controlling the crime scene and the narrative."

We discussed with The Colonel what we needed, and then, after going over some other details, we ended the call.

"Your standoff idea is really good," I said. "As long as we can pull it off, I think it'll be right on the money."

"It'll work," Tommy said. "You guys will get it done. Pretty gruesome I guess, but that's the world we live in. Those Booth brothers and their people—those are bad dudes. They are going to reap what they have sown."

"That they are, T, that they are. They have asked for everything they have coming to them, and we deliver."

"I'm sorry I won't be there to help out in person," Tommy said. "But I know we don't have time to wait for me."

"You'll be in on the next one," I said. "I have a feeling there'll be plenty of next ones."

We sat in silence for a minute, looking at the table full of papers and coffee cups. By unspoken mutual agreement, we decided it was time for the first drink of the day. We grabbed a fresh bottle of bourbon and went out to the deck to greet the sunset.

16

Kevin Briggs and I both managed to get to Minneapolis by mid-afternoon on Thursday, and had taken rooms at a major downtown hotel that was just a few blocks from the convention center and the Savoy House, where Damien was camped. After an early dinner at a nearby expense account steakhouse, the three of us convened in Briggs' suite for a strategic planning session. With a large pot of strong coffee from hotel room service in hand, we were ready.

I used my laptop to bring up our secure email application, and together we read through several messages from Sophia and The Colonel that had come in within the past few hours. The latest we had on the Booth brothers was that Darren was expected to check into the Savoy House that evening—late Thursday night. Younger brother Bobby was en route with his two guys and should arrive in the area by late afternoon or early evening the next day.

"Tell us what you were able to find out about the rental house," I said, looking at Damien.

"Easy to get to," he said, "right off 494 near the airport and the mega-mall. It's one of about thirty units in a cul-de-sac. New construction, maybe in the last year or so, and based on the signs of life I saw last night, I'd say there can't be more than a half-dozen units occupied. Intel from Sophia told us which unit he had, but I had a brainstorm and The Colonel was able to help out with a few phone calls. After a call from Homeland and an in-person visit from local detectives, the rental agent was happy to move Booth and his friends to a different unit. He just called and told them there was some problem with the plumbing in the first one. Apparently it wasn't an issue."

"How did Homeland finesse that with the local cops and the rental agent?" I asked.

"Nobody batted an eyelash, far as I could tell," Damien said. "Somebody with an impressive title from Homeland called the county police with a short story about some agents needing to keep an eye on a few people coming to town for the convention. No trouble expected, just routine surveillance, etc. The locals were happy to drive over to introduce me to the rental agent, who was glad to help out. The great thing is that I was able to rent the unit just next door for our own base down there. Now our unit shares an alley with the one Booth will be in, with the side doors to the garages only about twenty feet apart. I didn't try to get a key. I thought it best to avoid the whole warrant conversation, but I don't think picking the locks will be any problem. The fact that I paid a month's rent in cash to use the place for a few days might have had an effect on the rental guy's enthusiasm to help out and keep quiet."

"Nice. Really good work," I said. "And the stuff you

asked The Colonel for, when are you expecting that to arrive?"

"By midnight tonight," Damien said. "That's what he told me. By car from Virginia, personally delivered by a two-person team that he was able to borrow. They'll help us set it all up." He gestured across the room to Briggs. "They're meeting you and me at the rental place, so we should head down to Bloomington after this. As long as these guys show up on time with the gear, I figure we can get in by two or three tomorrow morning, get the place all wired up, and get out before sunrise. Their instructions are to help us again with manpower and equipment retrieval on Saturday, and then they'll disappear after that. We should be able to get Bobby and his guys up to the Savoy pretty much whatever time you order them—like room service."

"And this gas we're going to use," Briggs said, "what do we know about that? Is it something you're familiar with?"

"I wouldn't say that," Damien said, "but I've read about it and seen some demo videos. The CIA calls it 'Fentox-Nine.' It's a one-to-one binary that comes in a little kit with two canisters. Fentanyl is part of the cocktail, but that's about what I know of the ingredients."

"I've seen a report on it too," I said. "I think it's similar to the gas used by Russian Special Forces after those Chechen terrorists took all those people hostage in a movie theater. They pumped that in to knock everyone out before their assault. It did knock everyone out, but it also killed a lot of them. Hopefully it's been improved since then."

"Let's hope so," Briggs said, "we don't want to accidentally hurt anyone we're trying to kill."

Damien and I groaned at the joke while I poured out more coffee for all of us.

"The Colonel's contact told me it should be reasonably safe," Damien said. "We have to follow it with a stabilizing injection within thirty minutes. They should be very pliable after that—but alive."

"Okay," I said, "so after those agents get here from Virginia and help you with the install tonight, you work out how long you'll need Saturday morning. We want everything ready to go at the Savoy by, say, two hours before dawn. Squeeze in some sleep when you can; this is going to be a tight operation."

Damien and Briggs both nodded their understanding.

"The convention officially opened today at noon, and breaks up sometime late afternoon on Sunday. Sophia's report says there will be several celebrities in and out over the weekend. Gus Lindbergh will be doing his radio show from the floor of the convention hall on Saturday afternoon. Sam Hargity will be doing some special segment for FIX news. Both of them are on Sophia's list of secret donors to The New Confederates. Who else was it? Gimme a sec…" I took a minute to look through some papers. "Yes, here it is. Laura Cotter, the conservative writer, she'll be around too."

"You mean the really tall blond broad?" Briggs asked.

"Well, that's not a very nice way to refer to a lady," I said, "but yes, that's who I mean."

"I saw on some newsfeed," Damien said, "that her and

Gus Lindbergh are having an affair. Maybe they'll be engaging in a tawdry liaison at the convention."

"If so, then good for them," I said. "Anyway, look, I only mention those people to point out that there will be some celebrities around, and we should try to avoid them, mostly because they're the most likely people in the area to have reporters after them and maybe their own security people. Aside from that, they have nothing to do with our mission. If some of them are supporting the NC, I don't know—hopefully, their karma will catch up to them someday. If we're lucky, none of them will even be staying at the Savoy, so it won't matter."

"What else?" I said. "Was Sophia able to get the rooms we wanted?"

"She was only able to get one," Damien said. "It's a suite across the hall and down one door. She told me she couldn't get the rooms on either side of Booth's because the place is just too busy. On the bright side though, I was able to determine that one of them—on the right of Booth's—will be empty because of the redecorating work. Also, I've noticed that the upper club floors—where we are—are more quiet. I figure that's because those floors have more of the regular travelers that frequent the hotel, and they're keeping to themselves, either working or watching TV. The lower floors have a lot more traffic, especially the mezzanine, which has the walkway over to the convention center. The bar and restaurant are just off the lobby on the first floor. They're pretty busy too. The restaurant seems well respected in the area and brings in some diners who aren't staying there."

"Okay, okay, yeah, that all makes sense," I said. I knew

Damien would take 'casing the joint' very seriously, and he was impressing me. "And you have the van and everything else you'll need?"

Damien looked across at Briggs.

"Got the van," Briggs said, "and everything else. Checked and double checked. We are ready to rock and roll."

"Cool," I said. "We'll have time tomorrow afternoon for a last review. Remember, suppressed weapons only for all of us on Saturday. Let's assume that at least some of them will be armed, and that they will not have suppressors. When we use their guns, we'll have to improvise with a throw pillow or something. We'll figure it out."

We wrapped up the meeting soon after that. Damien promised to text key updates to me as he and Briggs went through their overnight activities. We set a time for the next day's final status and planning session, and I left the two of them alone to prepare for their long night ahead.

I went down to the hotel bar to have a few and to kick around ideas for one of the last puzzle pieces of the whole job—how exactly I was going to get into Darren Booth's hotel room on Saturday morning. I knew I could kick down the door and storm in if I really had to, but what we really needed for our plan to work was for him to invite me in quietly, like someone he wanted to see.

Friday evening, our final planning meeting behind us, Damien, Briggs, and I decided to have dinner together in the main dining room of the Savoy House. The place was large enough, and busy enough—especially with all the convention people coming and going—that we felt we would be anonymous.

The two of them had already briefed me on their night action at the Bloomington rental unit. The two-man team from CIA headquarters in Virginia had arrived on schedule. The four of them together had spent ninety minutes inside the house next door that would soon be occupied by Bobby Booth and his crew.

"You're confident you've got it all set up right?" I asked.

"Yes," Damien said, with Briggs nodding his agreement. "We've got that place wired up pretty good. Those two guys really know their stuff. Should all be smooth as a Swiss watch."

"Let's hope so," I said. "And preferably more accurate than some of the Swiss watches I've had."

"If they arrive on schedule, we'll make the delivery by five a.m.," Damien said.

We were finishing up our dinners, and hadn't yet seen anybody we recognized, when Darren Booth walked in with a female companion. He was a tall, slim man, maybe in his late thirties, neatly dressed in jeans, a white dress shirt, and clean but unpretentious cowboy boots. We all agreed it was him. Looking at him in the flesh for the first time, I didn't get the impression that he looked like an evil person, but then again, I wasn't sure I knew what evil looked like anymore. In any case, we had a job to do.

His companion would have been described similarly, but with sensible looking flats rather than cowboy boots. They had the look of a long-term couple. The hostess took them to a table for two, and I noted that Booth held his date's chair for her as she sat down. Just as they were being seated, a pair of men entered the restaurant and went to sit at the bar, but stopped first for a few words at Booth's table. They had the same general look as Booth and were dressed in the same fashion. I realized they must be his two men who came along for the ride, probably with a body-guard function. We watched them settle at the bar and pick up menus.

The main dining floor was broken up by an assortment of wide columns and half-walls, all decorated with what appeared to be fake ivy or some similar-looking fake plant. From where we sat, we were able to unobtrusively observe the Booth party by looking at their reflection in a section of mirrored wall near our table.

It couldn't have been more than five minutes after the Booth party was seated that a door opened by the side of the bar and I saw several men come out of what must have been a small private dining room. Gus Lindburgh himself emerged from the room with his small group and started to walk through the restaurant towards the hostess stand and the exit. He paused briefly to shake hands with the bartender and say a quick hello to a few people at one of the cocktail tables. His path took him within feet of Booth's table, and I thought I caught an exchange of friendly nods. It occurred to me that even if Lindburgh was a covert supporter of Booth's racist activities, he would certainly not want to be seen with the man in public.

"This may be crazy," I said, "but I have an idea. Take your time and settle the check. Don't be alarmed if you see me talk to either Lindburgh or Booth. Watch for my text."

A quick look over at the Booth party via the mirrored wall told me that the waitress had approached their table and was talking with them. I stood up and moved towards the hostess stand, stealing several glances to make sure Booth hadn't seen me. My loop between the tables brought me almost up to the hostess stand just as Lindburgh finished signing an autograph. I slipped in beside them just as the hostess thanked him and they all moved towards the entrance. A glance towards Booth's table gave me a slight electric thrill as I saw him watching the group, including me now, arrive at the door. I thought I saw his two friends at the bar were looking as well.

I positioned myself such that I was the first one to reach for the door handle, grabbing it and holding the door for Lindburgh and his friends as we all went through and out. Once out in the lobby, I ended my charade of being part of the entourage. I broke away from the group, pretending to make a phone call as Lindburgh and the others went off towards the skyway and the convention center. As soon as they were out of sight, I went back into the restaurant. With only a slight glance at our table, where I could see Damien and Briggs starting to gather themselves to leave, I walked straight towards Booth's table, noting that he had seen me and was watching me come towards him. As I neared the table, I held up a finger in a "may I have a minute?" gesture, which he returned with a nod. Out of the corner of my eye, I could see his two friends at the bar watching me closely.

"Good evening, Mr. Booth," I said, "Mr. Lindburgh wishes you both a good evening as well. He trusts you understand that he was unable to stop and chat just now. My name is Scofield."

"Thank you, Mr. Scofield," Booth said. "Please tell Gus that I completely understand. No offense taken."

Great, I'm in.

"He will be glad to hear that, Mr. Booth," I said. "And Mr. Lindburgh has something for you—ah—a package." I made a show of looking around the room before leaning in to the table. "To help support the cause. May I bring it to your room tomorrow morning?"

Booth's face lit up. The thought of money soon to come could do that to a person. His lady friend flashed a bright smile. Booth looked over to his friends at the bar and gave them a small hand-motion, telling them all was okay.

"Sure, that will be fine," he said, "we're staying here—606. What time?"

"Will eight-thirty be acceptable to you?"

"Sure," he said. "Just knock on the door. I'll make sure I'm up."

"That will be perfect," I said. "Room 606 at eight-thirty. It will just take a minute. I'll drop that off and then you can have your day. I'll see you then. Apologies again for the interruption and have a wonderful evening." I smiled at his date and walked away just as the waitress returned.

I stopped at the bar on my way out and arranged for a bottle of their best champagne to be sent to Booth's table.

From the lobby, I texted Damien, and met up with him and Briggs outside on the street a few minutes later. I filled them in on my encounter with Darren Booth.

"Whew, I think I pulled that off," I said. "Now we have a way to get into his room tomorrow. I mean, without kicking the door down or blowing it up."

"To be sure," Briggs said, "you are a master bullshitter. I am impressed. You could be a real con man."

"Oh that's nothing," I said, "you should see Tommy in action. He has honed the art of bullshitting to a fine point. He could sell water to a fish."

It was a warm summer night in Minneapolis, and we took a pleasant walk around the downtown area before splitting up for our own rooms in hopes of a few hours of sleep and to engage in whatever our individual "pre-action" rituals might be. The two of them would soon be headed back out of town for the rental house and a reunion with the men from Virginia. They had a long night ahead of them, while I would have the comparative luxury of sleeping until about three-thirty.

After a three-way call with Tommy and Sophia, I checked in with Jenny. I hadn't spoken with her for two days. She was surprised to learn I was in Minneapolis. I told her I needed to close out a case I was working on and, if all went well, hoped to be able to get back to St. Louis by the end of the weekend.

I used the spare bed to lay out the clothes and equipment I would need for the morning. Along with my freshly cleaned pistol, I set out spare magazines, and the matching suppressor. The big .45 was one of my favorites. I was confident in its ability to spit out large, fat doses of grievous bodily harm without waking the neighbors.

After double checks and triple checks, I felt I was as ready as I could be for whatever the next day would bring.

18

I t was just after two in the morning and the coffee maker in the Bloomington rental house was churning out thick, dark, go-juice.

Damien, Briggs, and the two men from CIA—Ethan and Carl—were gathered around a laptop on the kitchen counter. The screen held a dim view of a fully-dressed man sleeping on what appeared to be a queen-size bed. Carl hit several keys and the picture changed to a different man sleeping in a different bed. The second scene looked more normal, in that there was a pile of clothes next to the bed and the man was under the covers. With a few more keystrokes, a view of a third bedroom appeared with a third man sleeping in a third bed. That man was also under the covers. The CIA man who called himself Ethan stepped away to pour coffee into a Styrofoam cup.

"I guess that one guy just sort of passed out," he said. "Probably didn't even brush his teeth. The other two must've had it more together."

"I'm just glad they finally went to sleep," Briggs said. "I was starting to think they'd be up all night."

"Alright, then," Damien said. He pressed a button on his watch to start a timer, looking in turn at all of the other three men in the kitchen. "Let's start this thing."

Carl brought up a different screen on the laptop and typed in several commands. He also looked at his watch. "Here goes. Since we know they're all in the bedrooms, I won't set off the ones in the kitchen or the living room. We'll give it three minutes."

He typed something, pressed enter, and the screen changed again to a graphic of three dials. The men in the kitchen could see right away that a needle on each of the dials started to move slowly in a counter-clockwise direction.

At the same time, in the house next door, the circuitry inside three small metal boxes received the signals. Inside each box, electrically-actuated valves attached to the necks of two six-inch aluminum canisters opened, sending the contents of each canister on its way towards a small mixing chamber, then from there into a second chamber that housed a tiny fan. The fan mixed the two gasses, resulting in a spontaneous chemical reaction forming a potent aerosol, which was then sent through the perfora-tions in the exterior housing and out into the room. Mounted under the beds that held the three sleeping men, the aerosol quickly diffused throughout the closed rooms, soon reaching the necessary concentration levels.

Carl made a few adjustments on the laptop, arranging things so that his screen showed live feeds. He turned up the sound, such that Damien and the others could now clearly hear the snoring and breathing. Carl pointed to the part of the screen showing the man who had fallen on the bed without undressing. The guy seemed to gasp in his sleep a few times, and to struggle to move his arms and legs, almost like someone trying to fight off a monster in a nightmare. After no more than ten or fifteen seconds, he settled down and seemed to fall into a deep sleep.

"What you just saw," Carl said, "even though he was already asleep, was his body first noticing the Fentox-Nine and reacting to it. The heavy breathing is good. Let's see the other two."

Based on his breathing pattern, the next man appeared to have already gone deep under. Carl enlarged the view of the third man just in time to see him spasm a few times before settling down into his own steady breathing.

"Turning off the mechanisms now," Carl said, after another minute. "Let's keep an eye on them for ten minutes before we go in. When we do, we keep our masks on while we open a few windows and air the place out. Masks don't come off until the meter goes under twenty PPM. Latex gloves for the whole time we're inside. Got it?"

"Got it," Damien said. Ethan and Briggs both echoed their understanding. "We're doing good so far, and right on schedule. Ethan and I will go over first."

Fifteen minutes later, Damien picked the lock on the side door of the neighboring house for the second time in twenty-four hours, then he and Ethan stepped inside the empty garage. Ethan pulled two compact full-face gas masks out of a backpack and handed one to Damien.

Damien keyed his transmitter and spoke to Carl, still in the kitchen next door: "Everyone still asleep?"

"Like babies," Carl said. "I'll keep watch and let you know if I see anything."

As Damien threaded the suppressor onto the muzzle of his Beretta M9 pistol, Ethan got a small case out of his pack and checked its contents.

"I'll lead the way," Damien said, "one bedroom at a time, very quiet, and you can give the injections. Once we get all three of them, we'll go back and open windows."

Ethan nodded and they went through the inner door and into the kitchen. The man in the first bedroom, the fully-clothed one, was out cold. Ethan jabbed a small injector into the man's neck and depressed the plunger. The injection was a dose of a powerful sedative that was configured to complement the specific gas they had just used on the men. Once the injections were given, the men would remain unconscious for about eight hours, with reasonably stable breathing and heart rates. The CIA man noted that when they woke up, they would certainly have wicked headaches and nausea.

Within a few more minutes they had completed their work with the other two sleeping men. Damien used his transmitter to give Briggs and Carl a status report, explaining that he would open the windows and turn the AC fan to the highest setting. He and Ethan would then use their meters to monitor for gas levels before the other two men could come over to join them in the Booth house.

After eight minutes, the hand-held meters that both Damien and Ethan carried indicated the gas had dissipated to a safe level in all three bedrooms. They gave it an extra five minutes before taking off their masks and calling over to the other two men. All four gathered in the kitchen.

"There's hardly anyone in the neighborhood," Damien said, "but to be on the safe side, let's close the windows and blinds and keep the lights dim, at least at the front of the house. We need these guys fully dressed as though they were going to walk out the door themselves. Wallets, keys, whatever. I'll keep any cell phones or laptops myself. Briggs and I will secure any firearms that might be here. Carl and Ethan, you can collect all your equipment, and then if you could just help us move these guys around, you'll be off the hook with our many thanks."

With that, the four men moved off into the house to start their work.

Damien and Briggs quickly determined that all three of the men had come to town with automatic pistols, which they bagged up, noting which pistol went with which man. Getting the three guys dressed, and with shoes on and pockets loaded with their personal items was a challenge, but fortunately none of them was particularly heavy. The three unconscious men were downstairs and lined up on the living room floor within thirty minutes. Ethan and Carl completed the dismantling and collection of the gas units, along with all their surveillance equipment, and packed it all into a duffle bag. They opened the blinds partway and returned the air conditioner to its normal setting.

After bringing a collapsible wheelchair in through the garage, and three trips across the alley and into the neighboring garage, the three sleeping men were safely laid out inside the unmarked panel van that Briggs had rented the day before.

Briggs passed out plastic cans of cleaning wipes, and the men made a quick but careful pass through each house, wiping down all surfaces. They locked up the house as they left.

After profuse thanks and handshakes all around, the men from Virginia went off to their car on the next street. Damien and Briggs took a last pass through the rental house before locking it up and leaving. Briggs was driving the van; Damien followed in the car belonging to the Bobby Booth crew. Once out on the highway, Damien called in his report to Dean, still in his hotel room. Dean, Damien, and Briggs would all be on the same comm channel for real-time transmissions, while signals both to and from Tommy and Sophia would be delayed by as much as five seconds.

It was three-forty on Saturday morning. The summer sky was clear and the stars were shining bright over the Land of 10,000 Lakes.

As the two vehicles approached the highway exit that would take them along surface roads for the last six or seven blocks to the Savoy House, Damien keyed his mic and spoke to Sophia: "Just entering the downtown area. How does police activity look?"

"Very quiet morning," Sophia said, after the brief delay. "Some kind of factory fire going on north of downtown, but I'm not hearing anything in your area."

"Great, stand by," Damien said. "We're only a few blocks from the parking lot."

Five minutes later, Briggs turned the van onto the road at the side of the Savoy House and pulled up to the curb just before the parking lot entrance. Damien jogged up and climbed into the passenger seat, having squeezed the Booth car into a spot a block back. Damien signaled the go-ahead to Sophia.

"Wait one," she said. "Checking for any real traffic first."

Two minutes later, she sent the signal to Damien indicating that she had frozen all parking lot cameras. If anyone on the hotel staff happened to be looking at the monitors, they would now be seeing still images of the parking garage, while at the same time Sophia would be able to observe any activity on the live cameras.

Briggs drove the van into the lot and they slowly wound their way up to the sixth floor, where they parked as close as possible to the short corridor over to the hotel.

At the same time, I entered the parking area on foot and followed the van at an easy run. As I passed the area of each floor where the walkway over to the hotel opened up, I noted the construction signs Damien had mentioned after his initial reconnaissance.

I keyed my mic and spoke briefly to Damien: "Right behind you. Just gotta get my backpack from the car. Meet you at the van in two or three minutes."

Taking the stairs from the fourth floor up to the fifth, I stepped out of the cement stairwell and back into the parking area. On my right, between the stairwell and the first of the parking spaces, was the "big hole in the side of the hotel" that Damien had warned about, where they were preparing to add the new skyway. A sort of cantilevered

platform had been built to extend outward over the sidewalk below by six or eight feet. Workers had set up a
length of two by twelve lumber, supported by sawhorses at
each end, as a makeshift safety gate, and there was bright
orange CAUTION tape everywhere. On the other side of
the safety board, plastic sheeting had been rigged up over
the opening to keep the weather out.

Turning from the construction zone, I walked the thirty
feet over to where I had parked the rental car the night
before. After retrieving a backpack from the trunk, I went
quickly back up the stairs to meet Damien and Briggs at
their van.

"I just checked with Sophia," Damien said, "and she
doesn't see any activity in the area, or in the hallway. I told
her to go back to live feeds for the parking floors below us,
but she'll keep a still shot of the inside hallway up."

"Good work," I said. "Let's deliver these packages, then."

Briggs opened the rear doors of the van, got in, and did
a quick check on the unconscious men inside,
pronouncing them to be still alive and stable. He handed
down the folding wheelchair. Bobby Booth was the first
one into the chair, and after a quick look around and a
moment of careful listening, I led the way down the
connecting corridor to the hotel, where I used a key card
to open the door. Seeing no activity in the short hallway, I
held the door while Briggs pushed in the wheelchair.
Damien used another key card to open the door to suite
603, and we all went inside, where we worked together to
move the unconscious man from the wheelchair to the
floor. I cracked the door for another careful look and listen
before we all went quietly back out to the van. Ten minutes

later, all three members of The New Confederates were laid out on the floor inside the suite.

Briggs drove the van several blocks away from the hotel and left it, after wiping it down carefully. He returned in a Mustang, that, like the van, had been procured with a false ID and while wearing a disguise. He parked the Mustang in the spot recently vacated by the van, and returned quietly to suite 603.

"It's almost five now," I said, "and I don't need to knock on Booth's door until eight-thirty. We may as well grab a bed or a chair and get some rest."

19

My watch told me it was a few minutes before eight-thirty when the three of us gathered just inside our hotel room door. I had cleaned myself up and smoothed my hair into place. I was neatly but casually dressed in jeans, a white oxford dress shirt, and a summer weight silk blazer in light blue. I hoped I was dressed appropriately for my role as executive assistant to a famous and wealthy celebrity.

I carried a soft-sided leather bag, with the top unzipped.

"Hopefully he opens the door without any trouble," I said, "and asks me in. I'll have to see how it goes. I have cash in here if I need to flash it to him. I'll zap him as soon as I can and cover the girl if she's in the room. Briggs, you hang here until one of us signals you. Damien, I want you to stay in here at first, in case he looks around when he lets me in, but then come up to his door and be ready. Let's do this."

I left the room and walked over to the door of room

606 and gave a soft knock. When I saw the light change through the peephole, I held up the open leather bag, flashing the bundles of bills inside it. Darren Booth opened the door right away, looked quickly around the hallway, and motioned for me to come in. As I entered the suite I heard a door close, and realized that his lady friend must have retreated into the bedroom.

"Good morning, Mr. Booth," I said. "Thanks for agreeing to meet me. This is a very nice suite—much nicer than my room. I'm a bit jealous."

"Yeah, there was some mix-up when we checked in," Booth said. "They had to move me into this fancy room. I don't know why, but I didn't argue. Coffee?"

"That's nice of you," I said, "but no, I won't keep you. Let me get this out on the table for you." I gestured to a small table against the wall and we walked the few steps over to it. I reached into my bag and pulled out several bundles of bills, then reached in again and added a few more to the pile on the table. "Could you check that please? Should be thirty there."

As he reached for the money, I pulled a Vipertek stun gun out of the leather bag and shoved it against his side, triggering the charge. He went rigid; his body shook with the high voltage flowing through it. After two three-second bursts from the device, I let go and caught him as he collapsed, helping him to the floor. I quickly took a small self-contained injector from the pocket of my blazer and jabbed it into his neck, administering a powerful but non-lethal sedative. He was unconscious within seconds.

I worried that the brief struggle with Booth had made

too much noise, but a glance across the room told me that the French doors to the bedroom were still closed.

I drew my pistol from inside the leather bag as I stepped quickly over to open the door for Damien, who came right in with his silenced Beretta in hand. As he entered, I saw that his eyes went immediately across to the bedroom door. I spun around just in time to see Booth's girlfriend come out with a pistol in her hand. She saw Booth laid out on the floor, looked wide-eyed at Damien and me over near the door, then she raised her gun and shot me.

While I recoiled backward against the wall, Damien reacted with lightning speed, putting three hot bullets into the lady's upper torso before she could get off a second shot. She collapsed into a heap on the carpeted floor, her gun falling beside her.

Damien turned back to me. I gave him a thumbs-up, rubbing the spot on the right side of my chest where the bullet had hit. The Kevlar vest under my dress shirt had stopped the bullet, but as anyone who had ever been saved by a "bullet proof vest" knew, it was still, at a minimum, like taking a hard punch.

Damien spoke into his comm unit: "Briggs, someone got off a shot. All okay here but let's take a full minute to listen." Briggs would know to put his ear to the door inside our room across the hall. We needed to listen for anyone running out of their room, or yelling into a phone—any indication that they had heard a shot. Damien walked quietly over to where Booth's girlfriend lay to check her for signs of life. He looked over at me and shook his head. He came back across the room and spoke quietly.

"We're lucky she just had a twenty-two. Hopefully nobody heard it. She must have been really paranoid or maybe just really good."

"Yeah, I'll say we're lucky," I said. "Ruined my new blazer and a good shirt though." I moved to the door, and after a look through the peephole, opened it an inch. I heard nothing, so ventured a quick look around the hallway, still hearing and seeing nothing. I let the door close most of the way, but held it back from latching.

"I'm guessing either nobody heard that or at least they didn't know what it was. Get Briggs over here and ask him to bring my backpack along with everything else."

As Damien spoke into his comm unit, I stowed the pile of cash back into the leather bag. With a towel underneath her to avoid getting blood on the carpet, I dragged the dead girlfriend through the bedroom and into the bathroom, placing her in the tub. Back in the living area, I moved one of the side chairs from its place along the wall, positioning it to obscure the small bloodstain she had left there. The door opened and Briggs entered carrying a duffle bag along with my backpack. I took the backpack from him and put it out of sight in the bedroom. Briggs pulled two white lab coats from the duffle and tossed one to Damien.

I took my comm unit from the backpack and used it to have a quick exchange with Sophia.

"Booth's guys are beside each other," she said, "about at the middle of the other hallway. One of them got room service earlier and the other went downstairs for a while but came back. Far as I can see, they're both in their rooms now. A few civilians have gone downstairs in the last half-hour, but things are looking pretty quiet now on your floor. Hey —I haven't had a chance to tell you—call from The Colonel an hour ago. One of the people who's been passing us intel on Darren Booth was found dead last night. He said it was really a mess. Booth and his guys were the last people seen with him. That's all, just know who you're dealing with."

"Got it, thanks," I said. "It's already in play, but we'll keep that in mind. We don't have time for judge or jury, but we can take care of the third part."

I told Sophia I was about to call Booth's men to the room, and asked her to give me a signal on my comm when she saw them in the hall. With the unit on silent mode in my blazer pocket, one ping would mean one man in the hall and two would mean both were on their way. As I signed off with her, I saw that Damien and Briggs had put on their white lab coats.

I put my back to the door of the suite and surveyed the room, then walked around for a minute, directing the scene. "Let's get Booth laid out right here. Damien—you'll be the doctor kneeling next to him." I gestured to Briggs. "You kneel here but be ready to shoot. I'll be standing over there by the coffee machine. If we're ready, I'll call his guys." They both nodded. Damien knelt on the floor next to Booth while Briggs checked his pistol.

I picked up a phone from one of the side tables and punched the numbers to connect to one of Booth's men, who answered right away.

"Good morning," I said, "this is David Scofield. I saw

you in the bar last night when I met briefly with Mr. Booth. I came up to give him something this morning and he seems to have had some kind of seizure. Could you get your friend and come right over to help? The hotel doctor is just looking at him now. Lana? Oh—she's helping the doctor right now but she asked me to call you. Great, the door is open. Please hurry."

"I'm sure you'll get the Oscar for best actor," Briggs said. He knelt on the floor beside Booth, a few feet away from Damien. Both of them had their backs to the door. I took up my position halfway between the door and the medical scene.

"I'll settle for best technical effects," I said. "Okay, we're on. Try not to miss."

The comm unit in my pocket gave off two distinct vibrations, telling me that both of Booth's men were on their way down the hall.

The door opened and one of them came in. I was briefly alarmed that somehow Sophia had been wrong, but then the second man came in as well. I heard the door latch close; both men looked quickly around the room. Their faces held a mix of suspicion and confusion, but they had themselves under control.

"I was here for just a minute or two and he basically fell over," I said. "I really don't know what happened."

"Where's Lana?" one of the men asked.

I gestured towards the closed bedroom doors and he seemed to accept that with a nod.

Just then Briggs turned partly away from Booth to wave over the man closest to him.

"I need you to help me lift him onto the couch," he said to the guy.

As the man came close and started to lean over, Briggs turned quickly towards him, pumping a quartet of copper-jacketed nine millimeter bullets into the man's chest at a range of no more than two feet. The man fell backwards in front of his friend. One of his legs kicked a few times before he lay still.

As the first man died, I lifted the pistol that I'd been holding behind my back and did the same for his shocked friend, who was standing between me and the door, just as he started to reach for something under his shirt. The big slugs punched into his chest within inches of each other, and he crumpled to the floor at a right angle to the first guy.

Damien and Briggs both stood and stepped away from Booth. I listened at the door for half a minute before cracking it open an inch and listening again. All was quiet.

"Let's get the other guys in here," I said.

I went up the hallway, to just before the junction with the longer hall where the elevators were, to keep watch. I pretended to talk on my phone while Damien and Briggs used the wheelchair to bring the other three men over to Darren Booth's room. Ten minutes later we were all back inside the room. A quick search of the bedroom had turned up a Glock 9mm that we figured must have been Darren Booth's. Damien had gotten out the three pistols belonging to Bobby Booth and his men and laid them out on the floor next to the still-unconscious men.

"We're depending on our support plan here," I said, "and we know this isn't going to stand up to a real forensic examination, but let's do what we can to make it look good for the cameras."

"I was thinking," Briggs said, "instead of something from the couch, is there a spare pillow at the top of the bedroom closet we can use? Might look a little better and we can just take it with us." He went into the bedroom, emerging thirty seconds later with a regular looking pillow. Damien and I nodded in approval. After a brief huddle, we commenced to playing out the scene.

Damien and I stood Bobby Booth up against the wall. Briggs pressed Darren Booth's gun against the folded-over pillow from the bedroom as a makeshift suppressor and shot him dead. We then did the same with his two men, using Darren's gun for one and the girlfriend's twenty-two automatic for the other.

The last to go was Darren Booth, leader of The New Confederates. I shot him three times with Bobby's gun, again using the pillow method for a degree of quietness.

After carefully checking that all members of the two Booth parties were thoroughly dead, we moved them around into an approximation of an encounter that had gone from meeting to standoff to gunfight. I dragged Lana out of the bathroom, using the towel again to prevent a blood-trail, and put her back on top of her original blood-stain. Everyone's gun was either gripped in their hand or dropped beside their body. The pleasant, old-style hotel suite had become a killing floor.

I used the towel to wipe up the blood from the bathroom floor and the tub, put it into a plastic trash bag, and then into the duffle when I was finished with it. We packed up anything of ours that didn't belong in the room, adding in the mangled pillow, and retreated back across the hall to our own suite. Damien and Briggs took off their white coats and packed them away. I stowed the leather bag and the blue blazer into my backpack, putting on a dark wind-breaker with "SECURITY" emblazoned on the left breast in white lettering.

"You guys go first and get the hell outta here," I said. "I'll give it a minute after you're out the door and then I'll follow. My car's on the fifth floor. I'll call you as soon as I'm clear and we'll meet later as arranged. See you in a few hours."

After a listen at the door, and a visual check of the hall-way, they left the room and went down the short hall towards the door and the ramp that led to the parking structure. I followed a minute later, using the stairwell at the end of the ramp and taking the steps quickly.

As the cement stairwell brought me down to the fifth floor, and I turned to enter the parking area, I smelled cigarette smoke and heard voices. As I came up beside the long board that had been set up to cordon off the construc-tion area, I saw two people leaning against it, and realized that my sudden appearance had startled them. Both of them had a distinctive and instantly recognizable look. Gus Lindburgh was a large and tall man, mostly bald, and heavyset. Laura Cotter was a six-foot woman with long blond hair and a slim, almost emaciated frame. They were sharing a cigarette while leaning against the long board, but, and here I had to do a double-take, they were on the outside of the board.

How can people be so dumb?

"Oh!" I said. "I'm sorry if I startled you folks. Just getting off my shift. Please be careful there."

I saw Lindburgh's eyes go to the SECURITY label on my jacket. He gave a slight nod and followed that with a dismissive wave. I turned to walk to my car as they went back to their conversation and cigarette.

After stowing my backpack in the trunk and starting the car, I started to pull out of the space into the main aisle. I could see that they were still both there, leaning against the board, deep into their conversation. I didn't see or hear anyone else in the area.

Gus Lindburgh and Laura Cotter, what a royal pair. Opportunity knocks.

I lifted in my seat and twisted around to my right to be able to look over the back seat and out the rear window as I had learned to do many years before when I was a valet parker for a ritzy restaurant. I stepped on the gas. The car closed the distance in two seconds. The rear bumper hit the long board squarely, shoving the two surprised people forward into the construction zone. Like a spatula sliding a burger across a hot griddle, the long straight board moved the two of them quickly across the cement floor and launched them through the flimsy plastic sheeting and off the edge into space. I had gauged the short trip backward well, with the rear tires stopping about four feet short of the edge. I hadn't heard any screams.

I whipped the car forward and around the corner, pulling into a large open area of several unoccupied spots. Leaving it running, I got out and dashed back to the construction area. The long board was there on the floor, though now sticking several feet out into the air. I pulled it up to lean against the wall, and also righted the two sawhorses that had supported it. Walking up to the end of the new cement shelf, I pushed the loosely-hanging plastic aside enough to look down. They had hit the sidewalk close enough together that it looked like their arms were reaching out to one another in death, almost as though they had held hands while they jumped. A large puddle of blood was forming under them, and I realized that someone's head must have broken open with the impact.

"Well, that is a shame," I said out loud, shaking my head. "The good ... they die young."

The honk of a car horn somewhere on the parking level below tore me out of my fantasy, and I shook my head to snap myself back to reality. As I moved the gearshift into reverse, I saw Lindbergh and Cotter still together behind me. He was holding out his hands to light another cigarette for her. With a last look back at the happy couple, I sighed heavily, and then backed slowly out of my parking space before pulling forward and towards the exit. Winding down through the several parking levels, I drove out of the lot and then out of the city. I took a ramp to enter the interstate and drove southeast towards Rochester, home to IBM Headquarters, the Mayo Clinic, and the world's largest ear of corn. Once there, I would reunite with Damien and Briggs for debrief and whatever came next. I was looking forward to a hearty breakfast and some good strong coffee.

B ased in the headquarters building in Washington, Supervisory Special Agent Dorothy "Dottie" Benz, of the Homeland Security Urgent Threat Department, had been working on location in the Twin Cities Field Office for the last two weeks. She had been within hours of leaving for the airport, bound for a pit-stop in DC, followed by some well-earned downtime with her husband at their vacation house in Key Largo, when the director had called her. Now, weaving her way through the lobby of the Savoy House, she saw one of the local agents waving to her from beside the elevators. She had gotten to know Agent Joanne Belli well over the past few weeks and liked her, but had also come to respect the local agent's instincts and professionalism.

"Morning, Joanne," she said. "You get a call from the big man too?"

"Yep, I sure did," Agent Belli said. "I guess you'll be missing your plane—sorry about that. Our office is at your disposal of course." They got in the first open elevator and she pushed the button for the sixth floor. "I haven't been up to the room yet, but a local detective I was talking to told me it's quite a bloodbath. I hope you've had breakfast. The director only told me to meet with you and assist. You know what's going on?"

The elevator doors opened to the sixth floor. After flashing their IDs to the uniformed police securing the hallway, the two Feds stepped aside for a brief conference. As Agent Benz summarized the content of her ten-minute call from the Director of Homeland Security, the junior agent's eyes grew wide.

Lieutenant Bill Tanner, the senior homicide detective with the Minneapolis Metropolitan Police Department, had been in room 606 of the Savoy House for fifteen minutes and had already made a significant dent in a travel pack of Rolaids. His doctor had warned him to go easy on the spicy foods, coffee, and hard liquor, but hadn't said anything about rooms full of bullet-riddled bodies. He made a mental note to tell the doc to add that to his list of standard advice.

Thirty minutes earlier, some anonymous caller had phoned the city police tip line to report what had sounded like gunshots on the upper floors of the hotel. Another thirty minutes from the time the tip was called in, a thorough room-to-room check had revealed the carnage in 606. That suite had been one of the last rooms checked by virtue of the fact that it was located in the shorter hallway of one of the top floors, and was one of the farthest rooms from the elevator.

The first officers on the scene, along with an EMT, had confirmed that no ambulances were needed, before sealing up the room and calling the homicide division. The city medical examiner had not yet arrived. Now, Lieutenant Tanner, two other detectives, and a photographer, were the only people in the room. The uniformed officers guarding the door had orders to keep everyone else out.

"What are your initial reactions?" Tanner asked.

Detective Gonzales spoke up first: "Initial reaction? Some kind of standoff gone bad, but why? I don't see any drugs and I don't see any money."

"Agree on some kind of standoff deal," Detective Boyd said, "and yeah, no sign of drugs or money. That could mean that there were one or more other shooters here who took something away, or maybe not, and this was all about something else."

"Okay, yeah," Tanner said. "Anything's possible. Just seems like a lot of killing happened here to not be about drugs or money. Everything's about drugs or money these days. You know another thing I see? Or don't see, really? No bullet holes in the walls. Everyone here took multiple hits. So, what, maybe thirty shots fired and none missed? I've only ever been in one gunfight, and seven out of eight missed."

"Good point, Lieutenant," Detective Boyd said. "I guess they could have all been experienced shooters, but that doesn't seem likely."

"I don't know how unlikely it is," Tanner said, barely holding in a laugh. "There's a fucking NRA convention next door. Ninety percent of the hotel guests are probably packing cold steel. There's another weird thing that I can't figure. The tipster who called this in said that he'd heard gunshots, yet, here we are, and we can't find a single person in the hotel who admits to hearing anything like that. Doesn't make a whole shit-load of sense, does it?"

Just then, Lieutenant Tanner held up his hand to the other detectives as he felt the phone buzz in his pocket. He saw from the caller ID display that the call was coming from the office of the police commissioner.

"Tanner here," he said.

"Good morning, Lieutenant Tanner, this is Commissioner Mayhew. I don't think we've met in person, but I've heard a lot about your good work."

Tanner could tell that the commissioner was on speaker.

"I'm here in my office with Chief Barnes, and we need your help with something. Chief?"

"Morning, Tanner," the chief said. Tanner recognized his boss's voice. "That thing you're working on there, seems like it's connected to something big and we're going to have to do our part."

"Tanner," said Commissioner Mayhew, "these jurisdictional things are tough, but we know you'll do what needs to be done. Right now there's someone on hold who wants to speak with you. When I hang up, you'll be on the line with Gerry Cunningham. You may know that he's the Director of Homeland Security. And thanks, Tanner. Fill the chief in later."

Tanner heard several clicks on the line and then a new voice came on. "Lieutenant Tanner?"

"Yes, sir," Tanner said, "Mr. Cunningham, I mean Mr. Director. This is Tanner."

Tanner listened for several minutes, nodding here and there but making only brief comments.

"Yes, sir, I understand. You can count on us. We'll help out however we can. I'll have my men let her in as soon as she gets here."

He ended the call and looked at Boyd and Gonzales, who had been waiting impatiently to find out what was going on.

"Motherfuckers," he said. "That was the Director of Homeland Security. This is all part of some big terrorism thing. Some bigwig agent will be here any minute to take it from us."

Boyd and Gonzales both made their own colorful comments as the three of them looked around the room trying to make sense of the whole thing. A uniformed officer knocked on the door, getting the attention of the three detectives.

"Lieutenant Tanner, two agents from Homeland Security are here."

"Let 'em in," Tanner said. He walked towards the door as the two well-dressed federal agents entered the room. If the two women were affected by seeing seven dead bodies lying all around the room, they didn't show it. Tanner introduced himself, along with Boyd and Gonzales.

The two Homeland Security agents introduced themselves as Agents Benz and Belli.

"I just had a very interesting call from your director," Tanner said, "Mr. Cunningham. Apparently, I'm supposed to hand all this over to you. I don't like it."

"We just found out about this ourselves, Lieutenant," Agent Benz said. "The director has been making a lot of calls this morning. And I get that you don't like it—I wouldn't either. As a matter of fact, I worked homicide in DC for twelve years before I joined Homeland, and it happened to me more than once. Nobody likes it. But I'll still need you to tell me that we'll have your full cooperation. Can we count on that, Lieutenant?"

"Yeah, sure," Tanner said. He gestured to Boyd and Gonzales. "We'll play ball with you. This is a giant mess anyway."

"Let me be clear," Agent Benz said, "as long as we're all on the same team here. What you see here in this room is the end of a long investigation. You've already got plenty of pictures, right? And you probably have your initial impressions of what happened here. I need the crime scene and everything in it. That includes the bodies. I need approval of any press release and approval of any report you file. Aside from that, you guys can take the credit for solving the case. Never mind the fact that it seems to have solved itself this morning."

Tanner was brightening up a bit, along with his two detectives. He shrugged and then nodded at Benz.

"Here, look," Agent Benz said, "let me show you a few things." She held up her phone to the three detectives in turn to show them a man's picture, and then pointed to one of the dead men on the floor. "This guy right here is Darren Booth, from Alabama. He is—was—the leader of The New Confederates, that white supremacist group you might have seen on the news. And this guy over here, see the resemblance?" She showed them another picture on her phone. "This is his younger brother, Bobby Booth. We've been watching them both for some time. Bobby wanted the group to be more militant, and we believe he was working on a plan to set off a serious bomb in a major U.S. city. That lady over there has a record as long as…"

Agent Benz held the city detectives in rapt attention as she related a mostly accurate, though somewhat sterilized summary of the Booth terror attack situation. As she was wrapping up, six more agents from the local field office arrived to secure the area and start their work. Shortly after that, the sanctioned medical team arrived to start processing and bagging the bodies. Two unmarked vans entered the parking structure, wound up to the sixth floor, and pulled up next to the door leading over to the hotel.

Lieutenant Tanner and Supervisory Special Agent Dottie Benz exchanged contact information, and the detectives departed. A half-dozen uniformed city police officers stayed behind to assist with securing the area while the Homeland team did their clean-up work.

"Do you think there's even a chance," Agent Belli said, as the team was finishing up, "that what looks like what happened here is actually what happened?"

"Not much," Agent Benz said. "No, that dog won't hunt. I've seen some gunfights in my day, but this is the first one where everyone involved took three or four slugs to center mass and fell down nice and neat. But what the hell … that's why we're here. A whole bunch of terrorist dirtbags got together and killed each other. Local cops foil a potential attack. What's not to like?"

"Yeah, I guess you're right," Belli said. "Ours not to reason why…"

"You said it sister," Agent Benz said, "Ain't that the truth. Hey, you as hungry as I am? The director called this morning just when I was about to order room service. Let's get some lunch. We can talk about the story you're going to leak to the press."

21

B artlett's overtaxed reservoir of self-control was the only thing standing between him and a major freak-out.

"Somebody's definitely fucking with us," he said. "I'm telling you, they're on to us, big-time."

"I don't know," Sykes said, "maybe you're right, but I'm not so sure. Who would 'they' be anyway? The only agency we have that just kills people is the CIA, and they don't operate domestically. Least they're not supposed to. The papers and the police report say they all killed each other in some kind of big standoff. A Mexican standoff."

Bartlett paced the office while holding the phone to his head with one hand and chewing on the nails of his other hand. *How did I get myself into this shit. I can't believe we were actually going to kill people with some stupid bomb! Hold it together. Hold it together.*

"First Booth's cousin—this Puckett character—gets gunned down with eight other men. I mean, who killed them? I guess that wasn't the CIA either, was it? Then this thing in Minneapolis and Booth is dead. And you even told me that guy in the Philippines just sort of disappeared. Who is killing all these people? That isn't supposed to happen."

"Well, we don't really know that Petrov is dead," Sykes said. "But that's overseas, so could have been CIA. Someone like him, I don't know, seems possible to me that he could have had a lot of irons in the fire and any number of people after him."

"Right, right, dammit, I get all that," Bartlett said. "But surely you can't deny that somebody seems to be working against us here. We need to stop all this. I just run a construction company, for Christ's sake."

"Keep cool Mr. Bartlett," Sykes said. "Things are going to work out and you are going to be very rich. Let's keep our eyes on the prize. I agree that events seem to have been stacked against us lately. I'm just not so sure it's some kind of coordinated plan."

"Well, how about if you and your friend West find out, then?" Bartlett said. "My father-in-law is paying you two a lot of money, and all our asses are on the line here. Didn't you tell me you had a friend in the DEA in California?"

"I did," Sykes said, "I do. And he had told me a few interesting tidbits. That raid that the DEA pulled on Puckett before he ran off to that Salton Sea place—Puckett lost two guys that night, and so did the DEA. What's interesting, my friend tells me, is that there were two others in on that raid who weren't DEA. Like, some other agency helping out. Another thing my friend told me is that three of Puckett's people were tracked to some building downtown the next day, and were wiped out in another big blow up. Again there was some pro in from out of town, is what he told me."

"So who the hell are these people? They must be FBI or ATF, then, right?"

"Could be, and that would make sense normally," Sykes said, "but my friend didn't think so. He told me they seemed more military than federal, like black ops or something like that. Anyway, one of them was killed, one was shot up, and one we don't know about. May not mean anything, but I've already sent West out to see my friend and find out whatever he can find out. If there's someone out there working against us I want to know it as badly as you do. Stay put for now and I'll let you know what I find out."

22

A fter all the action in Minneapolis, Damien, Briggs, and I spent a day and night regrouping in Rochester. We joined a conference call with The Colonel, Tommy, and Sophia, during which we all got caught up on recent events.

"Good work, everyone," The Colonel said, "you may very well have prevented a major terrorist attack. There will be another tomorrow of course, and another the day after that, but it looks like our team was able to nip this one in the bud. I'm working with my counterparts in the other agencies to see if we can find out what—if any— higher-ups were behind this Booth plot. It's possible they were acting alone, but I don't personally buy that. If I'm right, well, there will be more to do. I'll chase it till I'm satisfied. For now though, I think it would be a good time for all the rest of you to take a few days off. As always, keep your phones handy and we'll talk soon."

A little R & R seemed like a great idea. I was anxious to get back out west to Seattle and hang out with Tommy for a while, but not so anxious that I didn't first want to stop into St. Louis to spend a day or two with Jenny. The next morning, Damien, Briggs, and I went off in separate directions. As I headed south out of Rochester, I took a few minutes to locate the famous "World's Largest Ear of Corn," and marvel at that creatively painted water tower. With a few photos of the thing safely stored on my phone, I continued on southwards through Iowa and into Missouri, rolling into town in time to take Jenny out for a quiet Sunday night dinner.

Much later that night, relaxing on the sofa together, Hazelwood curled up at one end, Jenny sipped a glass of dry white wine while I enjoyed a twelve-year old scotch in a heavy rocks glass with a few ice cubes.

"It's really good to be home," I said. "Dinner was really nice—let's remember that place."

"That's the third or fourth time I've heard you call this place 'home.' I like it. You may keep doing that."

I felt my face starting to flush. I had a feeling it wasn't just the scotch.

"Well, you know," I said, "I mean, it's your place…"

"Stop, just stop," she said. I could tell it was all she could do to keep from laughing at me. "Don't worry about it. I'm not trying to capture you. I know you need your space. I'm just saying it's nice to hear, that's all. Home is an idea, not just an address. Let's just enjoy what we have and it's okay if you slip and call it 'home' sometimes. You, me, and Hazelwood."

Hazelwood looked up, but I didn't think it likely that it

had anything to do with the mention of his name. He usually looked to me like he felt at home. I was jealous of his perfect attitude. I decided for at least the tenth time in my life to come back as a housecat.

"Okay, Jen-Jen, you got it. You, me, and Hazelwood. As long as you don't mind if I slip and call it home sometimes, let's enjoy it."

"Well, at least one of the three of us has to work in the morning," she said. "So I'm off to bed. You and Hazelwood can sit up and talk for a while. Your task for tomorrow is to figure out where you're taking me for dinner."

We had already discussed that I would be flying off to Seattle on the second day to spend some time with Tommy, who was still recovering from his injury. After refreshing my drink, I turned on the TV and browsed through the movies on demand, settling on an old John Wayne western with lots of scenes in Monument Valley. *Need to add that to my bucket list. Also—need to start working on that bucket list soon.* Hazelwood signaled his approval of my movie choice by moving onto my lap.

23

I deplaned in Seattle in the late afternoon, after an uneventful but pleasant flight. I had opted for a booze-free trip, looking forward to tearing into a good bottle later on my favorite teak deck. Tommy had insisted that he was in good enough shape to pick me up, but nevertheless I was mildly surprised to see him waiting for me, unescorted, as I exited security.

"Sure, my daughter would've brought me," he said, "or you could've gotten a car, but it's good for me to get out. The doc says I need to keep using the arm. He wants me to push myself a little every day. I'm probably at about seventy-five percent. This business of being shot is getting harder as I get older."

"That's great, T," I said, "I'm only at about eighty-five percent, and I haven't even been properly shot lately."

"The day is young, the day is young. Hey, after the last time you were here with Damien, I caught shit from Sophia for not getting together. I hope you don't mind that I made plans for us to meet her for lunch. We don't have to go all the way into town, just to that place you liked by the marina, not far from my house."

Forty minutes later, and after both sharing big hugs with Sophia, we were sitting and chatting with cold beers while waiting for lunch to arrive. With all of us knowing that many details of the Minneapolis operation made for unsuitable mealtime conversation, we covered that topic only superficially. Without her usual hoodie, I could see that Sophia had dyed her hair again since the last time I'd seen her, and the short, jet-black bob suited her face perfectly. She wore faded jeans, with the tears at both knees that some people would have paid extra for. I knew she had come into significant money over the past year, and was therefore not surprised to see her carrying a small but elegant Chanel bag that I didn't for a moment consider to be fake. The nose ring was gone, but the torn collar of her white t-shirt, along with the sleeve tattoo on her right arm assured me that she was still the young and smart-ass super-hacker that I knew and had come to depend on so much.

We made comfortable small talk about current events in Seattle and the rest of the world. Sophia told us about a trip she had taken with a friend to an exotic Pacific island a few weeks before. Tommy told a tasteless but very funny joke that had something to do with the Pope and the smartest man in the world somehow ending up on a plane together.

The three of us laughed out loud, tamping it down to a giggle as the food arrived. We ordered another round of beers and ate mostly in silence for a while. It was Sophia who restarted the conversation.

"I wanted to tell you guys something that I just found out this morning. After Stillman was killed, and Tommy was in the hospital, I got impatient with not knowing how you were doing. I'm sorry, but I hacked in and looked at your medical records. I just wanted to make sure you were okay."

"Thanks for telling me that," Tommy said, "but I understand. Don't worry about it."

"Well, thanks," she said, "but I only mention it because there's something else. I put a flag on your records. Just a routine security thing, nothing very hard to do. That way I would get an alert if some unauthorized person tried to look at your stuff. I mean, someone not as good as me anyway. The thing is, I think someone got in early this morning and might have been able to see your info."

"Couldn't it have been one of his doctors? Or a nurse?" I said.

"Or someone from an insurance company?" Tommy asked.

"I can't say for sure," she said, "but I don't think so, because any of those people would look at your records in a certain way. It's like, any of them would come in through the front door. I think someone broke in the back door. Look, I don't mean to freak you out. I just wanted to be sure you were aware. I had a call with The Colonel earlier and I told him about it. I'm sorry again, Tommy, but that was the right thing to do."

"Sure, right, I agree," Tommy said. "I appreciate your letting me know. So what does this mean to me? Someone might know that I was shot, or that I take the purple pill for acid reflux?"

"Yeah, all that possibly," Sophia said, "but the way I see it—the thing that concerns me most—is that whoever was looking could have been looking for your home address. And could have found it."

"Ah, okay," Tommy said, "so that sounds like probably the worst case. With the best case being…?"

"Some hacker just messing around," Sophia said, "looking for credit card information, or dirt on a movie star. Who knows? And frankly that's the most likely scenario. Someone messing around and nothing will ever come of it. I just thought I needed to tell you. I don't know if I know everything you've got going on."

"Actually you do, you do," Tommy said, "but I get your point. So, thanks for the heads-up. I'll be careful. Next time I talk to The Colonel, I'll be sure to bring it up. Thanks for looking out for me, Sophia."

Tired from my trip, I was glad to finally get out onto his deck and into the Adirondack chairs later that day. It was a warm summer evening after a hot summer day. The sunset was a stunning burst of red, orange, and gold. We opened a bottle of good Kentucky Bourbon and poured it out freely.

"I was shot too you know," I said. "I didn't want to worry Jenny. I told her I banged into the corner of a table. Amazing what a bruise you can get just from a twenty-two kicking Kevlar."

"Ah, you said you hadn't been 'properly shot'—now I get it," Tommy said. He held his glass up and looked through it, admiring its kaleidoscope effect on the colors of the sky. "Like being kicked in the chest, yes. I know it well. You've seen a lot of bad guys and a lot of guns in the past few weeks and come out clean. I'm glad. Here's to you. I'm sorry I had to sit here on my ass."

"Stop with that T," I said. "We all have to sit one out now and then. You'll be in on others." Figuring he'd get a good laugh out of it, I told him about how I had imagined backing up the car the other morning and shoving Gus Lindbergh off the ledge to his death.

"Well I'm glad you didn't really do it," he said. But then couldn't hold back his laughter. "But I have to admit—the world would be a better place."

"I know, T, I know. I more than almost wish I had done it, but it might have blown the job. You know, short story. One day last week I was filling up at a gas station and I decided to use their restroom. The place was surprisingly clean—like whoever worked there actually cared. It was one of those little restrooms for both men and women. I felt bad that someone before me had gotten piss on the seat. I didn't do it and it wasn't my problem, but I still took a paper towel and wiped it off. Don't worry, I washed my hands three times after, but I guess what I'm trying to say is that every once in a while, somebody has to step up and wipe up something gross. That's what it would have been with Lindburgh and Cotter. Wiping off the toilet seat."

"Whew," Tommy said, "that's some pretzel logic, but I get your point. Just don't get too caught up in being a vigilante or anything like that. Fun idea though."

"How 'bout what Sophia was saying at lunch," I said. "I'm a little concerned about that. What do you think?"

"Yeah, I'm a little concerned too," he said. "I guess it

would be dumb of me—or either of us—to assume that we haven't made some enemies along the way. Must've pissed some people off."

"No doubt," I said, "but for someone to dig up your real name and address, I don't know, that kind of freaks me out. If someone was pissed about us wiping out Puckett and his gang, I could see that if they wanted to do some detective work they might start by looking at who got hurt in that raid. And if that happened, and if they had a connection in the DEA, it wouldn't be too hard to figure out that you and Stillman weren't DEA. After that, who are you and what were you doing there? They might think someone had been out for payback, and then decide they wanted to pay back whoever it was that was giving them payback. Don't look at me like that, T. It isn't so crazy."

"No, it's not," Tommy said, "But let's not get carried away too fast. We'll call The Colonel tomorrow and hash it all out. Meanwhile, we'll be careful and watch our backs. The house is alarmed and we're heavily armed. This is probably nothing, but we'll operate like it's not nothing, okay? Now earn your keep and pour me another friggin' drink."

24

The next day opened with a call to The Colonel. He was concerned about Sophia's report of the possible data breach, but was pragmatic about it.

"I agree this could be much ado about nothing," he said, "but let's be careful and take it seriously. I'll reach out to some friends and see what they can find out about anybody snooping around. It may be that there's a leak at the DEA, or it may just be someone with a grudge against Tommy who stumbled on a possible way to find him. Or it may be, again, nothing. Meanwhile, Tommy, I want you to be armed and ready at all times. Look, if someone were after my ass, I can't think of anyone I'd rather have watching out for me than you two, so for as long as Dean is out there with you, I think you should be safe. After that, maybe we can get Damien or Briggs to hang around for a while until we fox this out. Check in with me every day."

"I just had a thought, Colonel," Tommy said. "You just said how if you thought somebody was after you, you'd like to have Dean and me around. Well, here he is now. What I mean is, as long as we're both here together, we could go out like tourists for the day and just see what we see. You know, see if anyone shows himself."

"Use yourself as bait?" The Colonel said. "Is that what you're getting at?"

"Yeah, I guess that's what I'm thinking," Tommy said. "I know it's a long shot, but why not at this point? I've been wanting to take a drive anyway, so really all I'm saying is we'll put on an extra watch. What do you think, Dean?"

"You know, when you first brought it up," I said, "I thought it was wacky, but after thinking about it for a minute, I really don't think it is. I'm here, let's treat it like a mission and do this. Colonel?"

"I don't think it's a bad idea," The Colonel said. "Just take it easy and be as careful as you've ever been and let me know if you see anything at all. Both of you, be on combat alert."

After discussing a few more items, we ended the call and Tommy and I got ourselves together for a day out.

It was late morning by the time we broke free of the Seattle Metropolitan area. We rode the auto ferry across Puget Sound and then headed west along the northern coast of the Olympic Peninsula. We skirted the edge of the Olympic Mountains before turning southward to follow the coast along the Pacific Coast Highway. We took turns driving the same Mercury Marauder that I had crossed the country in the year before while working on the BEQ affair. Despite already having two other cars, Tommy had decided to keep it. It had plenty of power and made for a very comfortable ride. We stopped frequently to admire the scenery, keeping an eye out for any cars that stopped near us or seemed to slow down to check us out. After a while, we started to get comfortable with the idea that nobody was looking for us, and allowed ourselves to fully enjoy the day and the beautiful natural surroundings.

We were starting to feel quite hungry for lunch by the time we approached the Queets River. Tommy told me he knew a tavern nearby that he had frequented in the past when he had spent some time out this way.

"If my memory is on straight," he said, "it's just up ahead on the left. Place called 'Larry's Lucky Penny.' It's a tavern —sort of a roadhouse kind of place—with good food and cold beer. Guy named Larry runs it, if it's still the same owner. His wife Penny handles the kitchen. They're Michigonians."

"Michiganders," I said.

"That too, for all I know," Tommy said. "What's the difference?"

"Michiganders are people from Michigan. Michigonians is something you just made up."

"I used to be a New Jerseyan," he said, "now I'm a Washingtonian. Why are they Michiganders?"

"I don't know, T," I said, "I guess because they liked it there. Anyway, I hope they're open because I'm starving."

We rounded a bend and there it was—lo and behold— a big old neon sign proclaimed our arrival at 'Larry's Lucky Penny.' There were seven or eight cars already there in the lot. We parked the Mercury and went in, obeying a sign that told us to seat ourselves. We found a booth against the front window of the place. A man came over who looked like he was probably the owner or the manager.

"How are you folks doing?" he asked. He thought for a moment and did a slightly exaggerated scratching of the chin routine. He spoke to Tommy. "You haven't been in for some months, but I remember you. How are you? Todd, right? No—Tom—is that it? Didn't you live around here some ways back?"

If for any reason I had been inclined to doubt Tommy's comment that Larry Bonnard was from Michigan, any such doubt would have been out the window five words after he had opened his mouth.

"You are still sharp as a tack, Mr. Bonnard," Tommy said. "And how is your wife Penny? Does she still make that incredible pineapple upside-down cake?"

"She does, when the mood suits her. She knows I like my sweets. I might even be able to rustle you up a piece, if you save room, that is."

"We'll see," Tommy said. "If my memory of your wife's cooking is accurate, there won't likely be any room for dessert. So your wife takes care of the cooking and baking. What do you do around here to keep busy?"

"Oh, I'm busy alright," Bonnard said, "I manage the crew and help them with the cleaning and that. Watching out for the property keeps me running round."

He stepped aside as a waitress came over to take our order, but checked on us several times during and after our meal. It was after our plates had been cleared away and we were having coffee when he brought his own cup over to join us. While we talked about the weather and other current events, both Tommy and I noticed that he appeared to be looking out at the road quite a bit.

"Is everything okay, Larry?" Tommy asked. We both turned in our seats to look out at the road beyond the parking lot. "Something going on out there?"

"Oh, I'm sorry," he said, "I didn't mean to be rude. It's just that … it seems like every time I stop by your table I see the same car pass by. Just then it pulled into the lot, almost like whoever it is was looking for something, and then drove away again. Just a weird thing. Probably someone looking for the road back to Seattle."

"Did you happen to notice what kind of car it was?" I said.

"Yeah, sure. It was a 2016 Ford Taurus, with the performance package. Color was 'Oxford White,' but you can call it white."

I looked at Tommy with wide eyes.

"I guess I didn't tell you," Tommy said, "Larry and Penny came out here and opened this place after he retired from Ford out in Detroit. Put in a few decades, right, Larry?"

"That's right, thirty-six years in. Got out right about when Billy Clay took the reins."

We chatted for a while longer before settling the bill and getting back into the car. As we spent the second half of the day wandering along the coast and touring through little towns, we kept an eye out for the white Taurus, spotting it several times.

"Yeah, I'm willing to bet that he's following us," I said. I had been watching out the rear window for much of the past hour. We had turned roughly eastward back towards

Seattle and the sound. The sunlight was starting to fade and there was more than a hint of fog misting the air. "I think we need to take him out here on one of these winding roads. Let's not let him follow us back to the city."

"I agree," Tommy said. "We need to do it before it gets any darker. I think I know a good place. Let's see, we passed the town of Elma just a ways back. The Capital State Forest is over there somewhere, and I think there's a road into it coming up ahead on the left. That would be a good place to ambush him, but we need to make sure he's close enough to notice when we turn in there."

"Hopefully he's not too smart to take the bait," I said.

"I just saw him," Tommy said, "he's maybe a half mile back and I don't see anyone else."

A few minutes later, we rounded a bend and the road became a straightaway that stretched ahead as far as we could see. Tommy pointed to a small sign ahead on the left side of the road and started to slow down.

"This is perfect," he said, turning the Mercury into the road that had opened up to the left. "You can see so far ahead right here that he'll know we must have turned in here."

Tommy steered the big sedan down the new road, which had frequent curves in either direction. I stretched over the seat to retrieve several long guns from their hiding place under a blanket on the rear floor. I laid the AR-15 assault rifle lengthwise across the back seat, where Tommy could get to it quickly, and pulled a shotgun into the front seat for myself. A Mossberg 12-gauge pump, loaded with six rounds of double-oh buckshot, I figured it would go a long way towards stopping a car.

"I think he turned in after us," Tommy said. "I saw a flash of white back on that last stretch."

"As soon as you take a curve where there's a long straight stretch right after," I said, "stop and I'll jump out."

After we took the next curve to the left, we could see immediately that there was another curve to the right coming up, but after that the road stretched out straight for a mile or so. Tommy braked hard and pulled over. I jumped out and ran to the tree line on the opposite side of the road as he drove away quickly.

I picked a large pine about ten feet from the shoulder and concealed myself reasonably well behind it. My hope was that the guy would turn the corner and immediately focus on the Mercury way up ahead of him.

Tommy had driven a half-mile up the road before slowing down to a crawl. I heard the Taurus approaching before seeing it, and then there it was, coming around the curve and into the stretch. I steadied the barrel of the shotgun against the tree and fired at the left front tire.

The car veered wildly and then pulled sharply to the right as the driver must have tried to correct its course. I stepped away from the tree, pumping the shotgun's action, and fired twice more into the front and rear tires as the car passed. I could hear the engine rev as the car again jerked sharply to the right and flipped over.

The Taurus rolled fully two times before coming to rest upright just off the right shoulder, rocking back and forth for a moment before settling on the slanted ground between the road and the thick line of pine trees. The engine died. In the sudden quiet, I heard the approaching sound of another car and looked up to see that Tommy had turned the Mercury around and was coming back towards us at high speed.

The sound of a car door opening brought my attention back to the Taurus in time to see the driver side door open. I was still at least a hundred feet away, approaching at a fast walk with the shotgun ready, when I saw a man step out. I could tell he was banged up and probably in shock. He wavered and stumbled, a large pistol in his right hand. He saw me and appeared to steady himself against the car door, aiming the pistol towards me.

I dropped to the ground as the distinctive boom of a .357 magnum revolver filled the air, once, twice, three times. I was grateful that he either wasn't a very good pistol shooter or was just too disoriented from the crash to effectively draw on his skills. Still, the sound of the heavy gun demanded respect. He fired a fourth time, and fortunately for me, that screaming bullet followed its friends well over my head and off into the forest. I started to bring my arm around to point the shotgun at the guy, when a different sound—a high-velocity rifle this time—filled the air.

The driver of the Taurus dropped his revolver and fell back against the car, sliding along it and down to the ground. I looked across the road and saw Tommy, out of the Mercury now, holding his AR-15.

"You okay?" he called to me.

"Yeah, okay," I said. "What kept you?"

"I saw you lying down and figured you were taking a nap over there."

I got up and we both walked towards the Taurus, guns

at the ready, meeting at the body. Tommy checked him before standing up and shaking his head.

"Dammit, bad break. Would have been good to question him."

We both looked up and down the road, seeing no other people or cars in either direction.

"Can't hang around here too long," Tommy said. "You search him and I'll search the car. At least we can get his wallet and cell phone. That'll give us something to go on."

I got a wallet out of the guy's pocket and found a cell phone nearby on the ground. I saw that the phone was locked with a passcode, and started to look through the wallet as Tommy finished up with the car.

"Guy's name is—was—James West," I said. "That's either real or these are very good fakes. I don't see anything official. No gun license. I can't open the phone, but I assume Sophia will be able to."

"Nothing interesting in the car," Tommy said. "Food wrappers, maps, local paper. There's a small backpack, but nothing personal in it. Most of a box of .357 shells. That's a nice gun, looks like a Smith & Wesson model 19—you want it? Let's take it with us anyway. Not good to leave a gun lying around. Okay, does that cover it? Let's get outta here. We can call this in on the way back."

"Sounds good," I said. Then I had a thought. "You know what, this stiff's going to get caught up in the system, and who knows what'll happen to him. Let's get his finger-prints before we go."

"Damn if that isn't a good idea," Tommy said. "How do we do that?"

"Well, I don't suppose you'd have a kit in your car by any chance, would you?"

"Oh sure, like I drive around with a fingerprint kit. I've got a typewriter and a crock pot too, in case you need them."

"I just thought, oh hell, I don't know," I said, "you are a senior federal agent. Stranger things have happened."

"Hey, my middle name is 'Danger,' not fucking 'Office Max.' I shoot people, I don't fingerprint them."

"Alright, my bad. Dumb idea," I said. "What do you have in the trunk? We could rub a pencil on a piece of paper and get a pile of graphite. That might work."

Tommy was rooting around in the cavernous trunk of the Mercury.

"Aha!" he exclaimed. "We can get his prints after all. Pull his arm up on that tree stump over there." I looked at him beaming with satisfaction as he held up something he'd pulled out of the trunk for me to see. A machete.

"Oh great, that'll do it," I said. "Tommy comes through once again. Bring it over here. Wait—while you're in the trunk…"

"Yeah, what else do you need?"

"We could use a plastic bag."

25

On the second morning after the eventful drive through the countryside west of Seattle, I lingered over a leisurely breakfast at my hotel on Union Square in San Francisco. The flight into California had been smooth, but it had been a late night and a fitful sleep, and the strong coffee was welcome. I tried telling myself that the negative effects of all the bacon I put away would be cancelled out by the fresh fruit and whole wheat toast that I had also eaten, but eventually conceded the weakness of that reasoning. My meeting at The Buena Vista was scheduled for 1:00 that afternoon, so I had some time to kill.

After breakfast, and after catching up on communications in my room, I left the hotel and went out into the sunshine, where I whiled away several hours with some sightseeing and light shopping around Union Square and Chinatown. After that, I made a brief pit stop back at the hotel to drop off my shopping bags, then took the fifteen-minute walk to where I picked up the Powell-Hyde Cable Car Line. I rode the car north and mostly downhill to the turnaround at Beach Street, not far from the famous Fisherman's Wharf part of town. From there, it was less than a block to The Buena Vista. The famous café had been a San Francisco landmark for decades, and had found itself on any number of "Top Ten" or "Must Do" lists for visiting the city. I had been there for lunch or for a drink on several past occasions.

I got there about ten minutes early. The local lunch crowd had mostly dispersed, giving way more to the tourists, who were not constrained by a set lunch hour. I didn't know much about the person I was meeting yet, but a look around gave me the feeling that I was the first to arrive. I took a small two-seater table next to the window, with a view of the bay. I folded my *Wall Street Journal* in half and set it on the edge of the table, sticking out like a diving board, and waited.

Two days before, out in the forest west of Seattle, Tommy and I had done what we could to tidy up the scene of the shootout with James West. As we drove away, we were confident nobody would find any connection to us, but the police wouldn't have too much of a hard time identifying the body. Though we had taken West's wallet, phone, and both hands, we left his head, and it was likely that an area airport, or the rental car counter, would have images that could be tied to his arrival and the procurement of the

Taurus. The ID in his wallet didn't look fake, but then neither did the various fake IDs that we routinely used ourselves. We called The Colonel as we drove away and filled him in on the events of the afternoon.

"Well, let's hope that takes some heat off you for the immediate term," he had said. "I'll get on to Homeland again to get their help with the crime scene. Are you going to be able to get hold of a fingerprint kit on the QT?"

"Yes," Tommy had said. "I have a friend who'll help me with that with no questions asked. Then we'll get the prints to Sophia, along with the phone and wallet."

"All good, except probably not Sophia," The Colonel had said. "I've got her pretty busy with everything I've dumped on her plate in the past week. Let me see what help I can pull in on that and I'll get back to you tomorrow. Oh, and don't forget to get rid of those hands as soon as you get the prints. I don't want to have to explain that to anyone."

"Got it," Tommy had said. "We will make sure they are disposed of in a permanent and respectful manner."

The 'permanent and respectful manner' had turned out to involve a weighted canvas bag and an evening drive out to the floating bridge across Lake Washington. As we drove back into the city after our strange errand, we opened the car windows and enjoyed the warm summer air that flowed in.

"It was really nice of that guy to stop and give us a hand yesterday," Tommy had said. "He seemed nice. Really a disarming fellow."

I groaned, but also couldn't stop myself from laughing a

little. I was trying to think of a good reply to my friend's terrible puns when we were both saved by the ringing of my phone. It was The Colonel.

"Can you get a flight out to San Francisco tonight?" he had said. "I've managed to get us a resource from the NSA who should be able to get us a positive ID and background on that West guy. Where he's been recently, who he's been calling—whatever we need."

"Sure, I'll get it together right away. Tommy can run me down to the airport," I had said. "Who am I looking for?"

"You'll be meeting with an agent by the name of Sam Gage. Works out of DC, but is house-sitting or something in San Fran. I just sent you an email address, so get in touch and try to meet in the city tomorrow. Take the prints and whatever else you have on this guy West. Gage will know what to do."

Now at the Buena Vista, in San Francisco, I stole glances at the door whenever I heard it open, in between my gazing out the front window at the street life and the occasional passing cable car. I didn't know what this Gage character looked like, but he had told me via email that he knew what I looked like, and had asked me to do the thing with the newspaper. It all seemed a little bit corny to me, but then I figured it was probably normal procedure for a super-secret NSA spook.

As our meeting time approached, I watched a number of customers as they came into the café. A group of three middle-aged ladies, a few couples, an older man, and two giggly girls who looked like they were probably just old enough to drink. I didn't see anyone who looked like they might be Sam Gage—whatever it was he looked like. I bided my time watching the people come and go.

A well-dressed and professional-looking woman came in and glanced around as though she might also be there to meet someone. She wore a tailored pantsuit in a dark gray pinstripe over a light blue button-down shirt. Her shoes were black and shiny and I guessed they were patent-leather loafers. She was very slim and petite overall, with blond hair that was long and thin and pulled back into a tight ponytail. Her face was pretty in a youthful, tomboy way, with dimples that implied it would readily break into a wide smile. She carried what looked like a slim soft-sided briefcase in black leather in her right hand.

I looked at my watch, noting that it was ten after one. *Alright, where is this Gage?* I turned to look out the window again at the cable car turnaround, where the operators were outside the car pushing it around the rotating platform in a well-rehearsed routine.

"Mr. Boudreau? Dean Boudreau?" a voice said. I turned back sharply to see that it was the professional woman with the ponytail speaking to me. She saw my surprise and smiled. I stood up.

"Yes, that's me," I said. "And you are…?"

"Sam Gage," she said. "Sam as in Samantha. I can see I've thrown you off a bit. I'm sorry." We shook hands.

"Of course, Sam," I said. "Nice to meet you. Yes, you're right. I was thrown off. It's just that, you know, you're a…"

"Your observational abilities seem to be in excellent working order," she said, and we both laughed. "May I join you?"

"Of course, yes," I said. I gestured for her to sit, and also signaled for the waitress. "I'm sorry, I don't usually say things that sound that dumb. I'm starting to think my boss may have been having a bit of fun with me. Anyway, it's very nice to meet you. I just got here about fifteen minutes ago but I waited to order. Will you join me in an Irish coffee? Coffee and whiskey together in the same glass is generally not my thing, but you know, when in Rome, right?"

"Agreed and agreed," she said. "That'll be fine. I don't usually drink when on duty, but I think in this case I should, if only to help maintain my cover. We don't want to draw attention to ourselves by not having an Irish coffee in this place, now do we?"

We exchanged small talk for a few more minutes while waiting for the drinks. Gage told me that she lived in Virginia, just outside of DC, but was working remotely while house-sitting for a friend who was off on a two-week trip to Europe. We showed each other our identification as nonchalantly as possible.

"When I was first told about you," she said, "I thought I recognized your name. I hope you won't mind that I did a little digging. Just for my own curiosity before meeting. I live outside DC now, but I grew up in the Philadelphia suburbs, and still have family there. I was in the area when all that happened, what, little more than a year and a half ago. You know it was in the *Inquirer* and all the local papers. Is it okay if I ask about it?"

"Go ahead," I said. "I don't mind. Seems like that was another lifetime, but I guess you're right—just two Decembers ago."

"Was it really all just mistaken identity? Five guys and none of them realized they were breaking into the wrong house?"

"The police were pretty sure about that, yes. They figured one of them had been in charge of directions and had gotten it wrong. The others didn't question it. It was some gang turf thing. They weren't the sharpest knives in the drawer, there was no doubt about that."

"No charges were filed, right? Not even manslaughter."

"No, none," I said. "It was all pretty clear. They broke into my house, with guns, and attacked us. Pennsylvania's good about that."

"I'm sorry," she said. "I have to admit I read the crime scene report. It was fascinating. You got all five of them, in what, like three minutes? The cops must have been asking for your autograph. And you were hit too, weren't you?"

"And stabbed," I said, "but neither was really bad. Hurts like hell when it happens though. I don't recommend it. And it was only two minutes. When you're in a gunfight, believe me, two minutes is a long time."

"Your friend who was there," she said, "I read that she wasn't hurt, physically anyway. How is she?"

"Brenda's okay," I said, "but the relationship didn't make it. Which makes sense, given everything, you know."

"Yes," she said, "that would have been a lot to get through. Well, enough about that. I'm glad you're on our side."

Our drinks arrived while we were talking and we took

a quiet moment to enjoy a few sips. The crowd in the café had thinned to the point that the tables on either side of us were empty. It was much too early in the day for the fogbank to come rolling in through the Golden Gate and into the bay, and the afternoon sun streamed through the glass door and window at the end of the bar.

"Now then, to the matter at hand," Gage continued. "It seems your boss and my boss go way back together. I was asked to meet with you and to provide whatever assistance you need. I understand you're working on a pretty hot situation that may involve domestic terrorism. I was briefed on the case as it stands so far."

She sat back and sipped her Irish coffee. I got the feeling she was studying me, looking at me like she'd never seen one of me before. She looked around and then leaned in closer again, this time with a mischievous grin.

"You're one of the 'double-Os,'" she said, "with the license to kill. I've heard about your team, but you're the first I've met."

Though I knew she was being humorous, I was still somewhat taken aback by the comment. On the other hand, I thought to myself, she was with the NSA—*the watchers*. She could probably dig up every phone call I'd ever made and what brand of toothpaste I used without much trouble.

"Well, that's just something from the movies," I said. "We're just trying to help deal with the bad guys—same as you. We're all on the same team. At least most of us who work for a living."

"So what's this all about?" Gage said. "How can I be of help?"

"You said you've been briefed on this case so far," I said. "Does that include Minneapolis?"

"That bit with the Booth brothers? Yes, I have been filled in on that. Very good work by the way. I was glad to hear that none of you were hurt."

"Thanks," I said. "So you probably know that we're hopeful we stopped a potential attack, but now the follow-up is to find out who was really pulling the strings at the top. I know my boss is working on that, with the FBI I presume, but right now we think we may have a more immediate problem."

"Someone was following your other team member—Tom—is that right?"

"That's right," I said. "It was our tech person who figured out someone might have gotten some personal info on Tommy, and then we actually found someone following us around the Seattle area. Fortunately, we figured out what was going on in time."

"Oh good," she said, "so what—do you have this person somewhere?"

I took a quick look around before looking back at Gage. Her face flashed with understanding of what I was about to say. I leaned in across the table.

"We tried," I said, "but it didn't work out. He won't be causing any more trouble. But … we got his prints, wallet, and phone." I pulled a bulky manila envelope out of my bag and pushed it across the table to her. "The ID looks real, but you decide. My guess is he's not—ah, wasn't—any kind of trained operative. The phone is locked, but I assume that won't be an obstacle for you. We'd like to know who he is, where he's been, and who he's been talking to. We hope that will lead us to someone else, and maybe then to someone else—you get the idea."

"Have you considered the possibility that he could have been working alone?" She put the manila envelope into her leather bag. "Doesn't seem like much of a stretch that guys like you and your friend Tom have made some enemies somewhere along the road. Also, is there any hint that this guy could be related to this terrorist attack and the Minneapolis thing?"

"At this point," I said, "we figure anything is possible, including those two ideas. We just don't know yet. That's where you come in. One thing's for sure: we can't have people following us around like that. How long do you think this is going to take?"

"I'll get right on it this afternoon," she said. "Two days, maybe less. Where do you plan to be?"

"This is what I've got going on," I said, "so I can hang around through tomorrow and tomorrow night. I'll let you know if I need to leave town."

We stood up and she started to gather herself to leave. We shook hands again.

"I suppose I should say 'Watch your back,'" she said, "but I bet you always do. I'll get to you as soon as I can."

"I always do," I said, "but thanks anyway. And for your help. I look forward to hearing from you."

"Oh, by the way," she said, "next time you talk to him, tell my uncle I said 'Hi.'"

"Your uncle?" I said. "I don't know your uncle, do I?"

"Oh yes you do," she said. "My uncle Cameron. I call him 'Uncle Cam.' Cameron Bixby is his name. I think you usually call him 'The Colonel.'"

With that, she turned and walked out, leaving me silent and more than a little bit stunned.

Yes, that clinches it. The Colonel was having a bit of fun with me.

26

The Tonga Room, in the basement of the Fairmont Hotel in San Francisco, is one of the city's great hidden treasures, as well as being one of the country's finest surviving monuments to Tiki style and décor. While I'd been sitting there at the bar for the last ninety minutes, the interior light and sound effects had cycled several times through night and day, clouds and rain, and even lightning. The centerpiece of the sprawling room was the rectangular "lake", which I knew to be a repurposed former indoor swimming pool. A faux wooden boat sat in the middle of the lake, and was all done up in a Tiki-hut style, serving as a stage big enough for the quartet that was finishing up a set of well-known standards.

I had declined the traditional ceramic cup in the shape of an Easter Island statue and the associated paper umbrella, but in a nod to my surroundings, as well as perhaps an attempt to appease the Tiki gods, I was at least drinking rum. The remnants of my tropical-themed dinner had been cleared away, and I was just polishing off the last

sips of my rummy drink, when my phone vibrated. It was
my third evening in the city and about thirty hours since
having met with Agent Gage at the Buena Vista. Signaling
to the bartender that I would be stepping out to the lobby
to take the call, I pressed the button to answer as I walked
to the nearby door.

"Dean here," I said.

"Gage here," a voice said, "but call me Sam. I have information for you. Are you still here in the city?"

"Still here," I said. "Actually I just finished dinner at the
Tonga Room. Cool place—do you know it?"

"Been there once," she said, "and yes, really cool place.
I'd come join you but I can't get free tonight. Can you meet
me for breakfast or coffee tomorrow?"

"That'll be fine," I said. "Tell me when and where."

Agent Gage gave me the name of a place and we agreed
on a time and then ended the call. I went back into the bar
and wrote it all down on a Tonga Room cocktail napkin. I
settled my tab and drained the last few drops from my
glass. Outside on the sidewalk, I looked across at the Inter-
continental Hotel and briefly considered going in and up
to the famous Top of the Mark bar for a drink. Finally I
decided the idea could wait for the next trip to the city. I
turned and started on the six-block walk back to my hotel
on Union Square, glad for the slight breeze of the warm
summer evening.

At the agreed-upon time of nine-thirty the next morning,
the cab let me off at the restaurant. I went inside and easily

found Agent Gage at a table for two in a quiet corner. She waved to me as I approached. Coffee came right away; our breakfast came soon after that.

"One of my team members was in between assignments," Gage said, "so I was able to draft her to help out. Strictly need to know, so don't worry that anyone else got looped in. Anyway, that's how I was able to put together as much as I was since we first met."

"Have you communicated with The Col...," I stopped myself, looking around at the other tables. "With your uncle?"

"Yes, as he requested," she said. "I sent him a summary late last night. Same stuff I'm going over with you now."

"Alright, well I really appreciate your help," I said. "Let's hear it. I hope you don't mind talking while we eat."

"First things first," she said. "Based on the fingerprints you gave me and the contents of the guy's wallet, it appears he really was one James West, forty-two years old. He's been living outside Louisville for most of the past year but seems to have spent much of his life in Texas. No college and no military, but he did do a stint in the Texas State Police, and then later the DEA out of El Paso. I'm just giving you the main points. The report I'll send you has more detail. By the way, the Washington State Police were having a field day with the crime scene out west of Seattle, until someone from Homeland stepped in and took it all over. Seems Mr. West was missing his hands, but they were able to ID him through his face and the car rental records."

"That's a terrible thing to say while I'm eating breakfast," I said. "Homeland, huh? Thanks to your uncle no doubt. More coffee?"

"Sure," she said. I poured out some more for both of us. "Once we knew who he was, we were able to use his credit cards and the record of his phone calls to reconstruct his last few days. He flew from Cincinnati to San Diego on Monday, where he spent one night at a hotel before taking the Coast Starlight train from Los Angeles up to Seattle. He rented a Ford Taurus in Seattle and spent most of two days there before running into you and your friend."

"Any indication of why he went to San Diego?" I asked.

"Patience, I'm getting there," she said. "Yes, we think so. Before he left Kentucky, he called a local San Diego number several times, and then called it twice more after arrival. One can then surmise that the idea behind the San Diego trip was to meet with someone there. We were also able to determine that the local number he was calling— the person he was trying to meet with—is registered to a man named Denny Straight. What might interest you is that Denny Straight is himself a DEA agent, but on suspension pending an Internal Affairs investigation. Seems he has a long record of disciplinary problems, and someone finally decided to take steps.

"I talked with your friend Sophia yesterday evening about this. I don't know the half of how she can do what she can do, but she was able to get into his file. It may not be proven yet, but he's at least suspected of passing information about pending actions—raids, for example—to one or more big players in the drug scene down there."

"That's really interesting," I said. "I'm thinking about that big DEA raid down at the piers not too long ago. It was supposed to take down a meth gang led by a guy named Puckett, who we now know had his hands in gun running and who knows what else. Maybe this guy Straight had a line in to Puckett and put him on his guard."

"I knew about the raid," she said, "and I've come across the name Puckett in my investigation, but I didn't know the raid was on him until you just told me. That is very interesting indeed. And yeah, I bet Straight dropped a dime on the DEA. That adds up. Probably for a wad of cash. Now, my uncle has briefed me on what your team has been working on for most of the past two weeks, so I have the general outline. The largest amount of recent calls from James West's phone, by far, is to a man named Bernard Sykes. Also from Kentucky and also with lots of Texas history, also former DEA. Very similar biography as West. Tell me what you think of this."

She drank some water and I poured myself a little more coffee. The dishes had been cleared away and the waitress had left a check. The place had mostly emptied out. She leaned in and continued.

"Sykes and West obviously had some kind of close relationship, and talked frequently on the phone. Both of them, but Sykes more than West, also spoke numerous times with the late Bobby Booth. Booth's phone is dead now, but we can see from his call history that he recently spoke several times with Clarence Puckett out in San Diego, and then again a few times to that same number, but somewhere out in the desert south of Palm Springs."

"Right, we caught up with Puckett and eight of his people out at the Salton Sea," I said. "Rescued a deep cover DEA man in the bargain."

"My uncle did tell me about that," she said. "So Sykes and West were working on some level with Bobby Booth to try to get guns, explosives, or something like that from Puckett. But Puckett goes into hiding after that botched DEA raid in San Diego. You track him to the desert and then that's the end of Puckett. A little more than a week later, Bobby Booth and his brother meet with that unfortunate incident in Minneapolis. Within forty-eight hours, this guy West flies to San Diego hoping to get a clue from our crooked DEA agent, Denny Straight."

"Man, talk about the plot thickening," I said. "Sykes and West probably saw what was happening to all their friends and started to sweat. West flew out and talked to Straight, and they started to think about how Puckett's gang was just wiped out. That led Straight to start nosing into who the non-DEA guys were who'd been in on the raid. He must've called in some favors, found out who Tommy was, and then guessed that it was his group—us—that was behind the job at the Salton Sea. If that's the way it went, then the next thing that happened is that West hopped on the train up the coast to Seattle to stalk Tommy. This is making my head hurt, but it just could be."

"Have some more coffee," Gage said. "The caffeine will help. Yeah, I think that's probably what happened. Which leaves Straight as a loose end."

"And possible loose cannon," I said. "You're sending all this to your uncle, right?"

"As soon as I get home after this meeting," she said. "I'll summarize the ideas we've been hashing out. We're not done yet though—there's more."

"I bet," I said. "Like, we know that Bobby Booth was a violent racist with a crazy plan, but what about Sykes and West? Were they just two more loonies from the same bin, or were they part of something bigger that we haven't seen yet?"

"Now you're talking," she said. "I vote for the second option. The agency friend I mentioned did some digging into Sykes for me. He's put in over twenty calls in the past two weeks to a construction company called Consolidated Barrier Corporation. More specifically, to the owner of that company, a man named Gavin Bartlett. James West called Bartlett a few times also, but it looks like Sykes was the main contact. And there's something else. It looks like West and Sykes were some kind of temporary employees for Bartlett's company. Just about six weeks ago they both started drawing salary checks, but in oddly high amounts. Like maybe they were hired for some special project."

"More and more interesting," I said. "If that's true, then we have Sykes and West, who, well—West at least—appear to be some kinda muscle or enforcers maybe. They get on the payroll of this Bartlett company, and then they get involved with Bobby Booth and his plan to stage a terrorist attack with help from Clarence Puckett. And part of the whole thing is apparently financed by the CEO of this construction company. But why? How does he fit in?"

"That's why you're buying me breakfast," she said, "because I have a theory. Bobby Booth wanted to stage a terrorist attack that would be set up to get blamed on immigrants, right?"

"As far as we know. Muslims, Latinos—looks like he hated everybody equally."

"You got it, and what's one of the biggest things on people's minds these days, or on the news anyway, politically speaking?"

"Hmmm, well, healthcare is a biggie, but I'm thinking you're waiting for me to say the wall. There's a lot of talk about whether or not we need a giant wall along the border with Mexico."

"You got it," she said. "Healthcare is important, but let's talk about the wall. Think about it—it's safe to say there are millions of people on the fence about this wall, no pun intended. What if Bobby Booth's plan had been successful and suddenly it was all over the news that terrorists— Latinos particularly—had been behind some deadly attack? I think some of those millions of Americans wouldn't stay on the fence for long. There would be demonstrations in the street demanding that this wall be built."

"Okay, that makes sense," I said. "I'll buy that. And so this Gavin Bartlett guy...?"

"Bartlett is the owner and CEO of Consolidated Barrier Corporation, one of the largest construction companies in the country specializing in large-scale concrete and steel barriers. It's a wall building company."

I had never been any good at whistling, but I sat back and tried to whistle anyway.

"Man, that's a lot to take in," I said, "but almost everything you've said is just laying out facts. The rest of it sounds like a reasonable theory. You need to get that to your uncle as soon as possible. The next move has got to be to get to Sykes and find out what we can from him, and then from him to Bartlett."

"Don't forget about Denny Straight down in San Diego," she said. "He might fill in some blanks for you."

"When we climb the ladder," I said, "do you think it stops with Bartlett, or does he have other backers?"

"Not sure yet on that," she said. "There are a few things that I need to dig deeper into before I can say more. Few pieces still missing from the puzzle. I'll talk to my uncle later today and I'll run that and everything else by him. Let you know when I can. Will you be staying in the city?"

"I can't really say until I talk to The Colonel later myself, but I have a strange feeling that I'll be ending up in Kentucky before too long. Fortunately, there's a lot of good whiskey there."

We stood up to leave. I put money on the table to cover the check. Outside, on the sidewalk, the clear, sunny day felt like it was going to be a hot one.

"I think you mentioned you sold your house in the Philly burbs, didn't you?" Gage said. "Where is home for you these days?"

"You know, that's a fair question," I said. "I did sell the house, but I still have a condo in Philadelphia. Lately I've been thinking that 'home' is my other condo in St. Louis. Not because of any attachment to Missouri, but because there's someone there—Jenny. Things have been going pretty good. Even have a cat."

"That sounds nice," she said. I thought I saw a flash of disappointment cross her face, along with a slight delay in her reply. "It's good to have someone. She's a lucky gal. What's the cat's name?"

"You're the NSA, can't you find that out?"

She laughed, pulled her bag up over her shoulder, and started to walk away.

"I'll work on that one," she said. "I'll be in touch. Be nice to have lunch or something again. Maybe another time."

I nodded and gave her a smile and a wave. *Another place,*

I thought to myself. She turned and walked away towards wherever it was she was going. I started off in the opposite direction, thinking I'd enjoy walking for a while and get some good thinking done before picking up a cab back to the hotel and checking out to go wherever it was I was going.

27

The schedule for my immediate future was decided for me when I got back to my hotel and checked my email. Aside from a personal message from Jenny, there was a request from The Colonel asking me to meet him the next day at Tommy's house in Seattle for a briefing and planning session. I checked out of my hotel within the hour and drove south out of the city to the airport. A substantial flight delay made it close to midnight before I landed in Seattle, so I texted Tommy that I would get a rental car and down-town hotel for the night, and would see him by late morning.

It was ten o'clock the next morning when I arrived at Tommy's house. Colonel Bixby was already there, having spent the night in a different nearby hotel. I found the two of them having coffee at the dining room table. File folders, legal pads, and various writing implements were scattered around.

"Guys, first of all," The Colonel said, "the fact that we're meeting here privately should not suggest in any way that I don't have total confidence in the rest of the team. It's just that this whole Booth thing has veered into some really strange territory, and for the moment I want to keep the circle very small. Starting here because you two are the team leaders. We'll add people if and as needed.

"You both know that I was able to secure the loan of an NSA field agent—who happens to be my niece—for a limited period of time. The purpose is to leverage that agency to help connect the dots relative to phone calls, travel, financial history, and whatever else we could find on this man West, and whoever he might have been working for or associated with. My niece—Agent Gage—was able to put together quite an interesting file in a short time. Dean, I sent the summary to Tommy last night, so he knows what you know. What are your initial reactions?"

Tommy was the first to speak.

"Well, my first reaction is that it all seems too insane to be true, but there appears to be a real case for it. I wish it weren't true, but I guess it is. Where do we go from here is the puzzle."

"I agree with that," I said. "Looks like one of those times where you just can't make this stuff up."

"Yes," The Colonel said, "that is certainly true. Let's go through the whole thing together one time just to make sure we're on the same page and see what questions come up."

He opened one of the folders in front of him and passed

around several papers. The three of us spent the next forty minutes going over what we already knew and where we felt the evidence led. We talked it all back and forth and inside and out. We agreed that there was no denying the fact that the Booth terrorist plot went higher up the tree and off onto a branch that we hadn't foreseen.

"Okay then," The Colonel said, "It looks like Sykes and West were some kind of hired guns working to help Bartlett with his bombing plan. Bartlett stood to benefit in spades, but I don't see him as being the mastermind. No, that had to have been his father-in-law. He was the puppeteer."

"Colonel," Tommy said, "Sykes and West are no-brainers. Even Bartlett. They're guilty as charged. But the other guy—the puppeteer as you say—I'm just trying to wrap my head around that. Is The Council really sure about all this?"

"Unfortunately," The Colonel said, "the evidence is solid. I know it's incredible. Like a bad movie except that it's real. The Sen…shit, I don't even want to say it. We need a code word for him so we don't have to use that word in communications.

"QRS," Tommy said. "Call him 'QRS.'"

"QRS?" The Colonel said. "What the hell is that?"

"I like it," I said. "There's a story, but I'll spare you. It would have no meaning to anyone who would happen to see it or overhear it."

"Fine," The Colonel said. "QRS it is then. Now here's the thing though, keep that, ah—QRS, under your hat for now, and take no action apart from research. I'll be working with The Council to figure out what to do about him." He checked his watch. "As a matter of fact, I have a secure call with them in just over an hour. When I have more to report, I'll let you know right away. Guys, I know I don't have to tell you that this is strange new territory." He held up his hands and shook his head, as though asking for an answer that none of us had.

"Dean, I want you to get out to Kentucky and start checking out Sykes. Get comfortable with the area, where he lives, where he drinks—you know the drill. Same for Gavin Bartlett. Don't move on either of them until I give you the green light, but recon the perimeter and be ready. Think about what equipment you might need. I suggest you get to Kentucky via Pittsburgh, so you can stop in at our apartment there. Rent a car and drive the rest of the way. If there's anything special you need that we don't have at the apartment, let me know and I'll do what I can to get it to you.

"Meanwhile, I'm going to send Briggs down to San Diego to check out this DEA agent, Denny Straight. I don't see him as a big threat at present, but it is a loose end that we can't leave loose. Briggs has a background in interrogation, and also a degree of talent at making certain events resemble accidents. Even if Straight is bent, he's still DEA and we can't be seen as having any connection to whatever harm might come to him."

Tommy and I knew that the "apartment" was actually one of three highly-secure and climate-controlled storage units the team maintained around the country. The one outside Pittsburgh, like the others, was stocked with an assortment of modern weaponry, ammunition, explosives, electronics, and all manner of tactical assault gear. Between the varied array of goodies stashed there, and a trip to the local home improvement store, it was hard to imagine any threat that couldn't be dealt with effectively.

"How is your physical therapy going?" The Colonel asked, directing his attention to Tommy. "Don't sugarcoat it. Are you ready for light duty?"

"I am," Tommy said. "There's still intermittent pain, but it's down to a level that all I need is a few Motrin. I don't have a hundred percent range of motion yet, but the exercises are helping. I can drive and do most other daily things. Just can't do much heavy lifting, and I need to hold off on rappelling down the sides of any buildings for a while. I can run and I can shoot—been to the range a few times already."

"That's great," The Colonel said. "Glad you're doing well. I want the two of you to work on your plan and then stay in close touch when Dean gets out to Kentucky. If you're both needed out there, you can fly out too. Up to you if you would also go via Pittsburgh. Sophia's schedule should be freed up by now, so she'll be available to help you with whatever you need. Also, we are still free to call on Agent Gage as needed."

We talked for another twenty minutes, kicking around ideas for a plan going forward, before The Colonel gathered his files and left, bound for his hotel and then a flight to DC.

Tommy and I sat silently for a minute, and then walked out onto the deck, where we stood looking out at the city for another minute. I looked around at whatever I could see of the street and the neighborhood, as though spies might be hiding in the bushes or under the cars.

"A United States Senator? Holy shit T. We have gone

through the looking glass with this one. No wonder I drink."

"Right-oh and right-oh," Tommy said. "The world has shifted on its axis. But, you know, the more I think about it, if I had to pick a senator that could get himself up to something like this—Wilfred O'Donnell would probably be the one. An asshole of historic proportions. QRS."

We tidied up and went out for a long lunch at one of Tommy's favorite places along the shore of Lake Washington. During lunch and the ride back to his place afterwards, we continued to work on a mission plan. It was late afternoon when The Colonel called, giving Tommy a randomly-generated code for a secure conference call. It took us a few minutes to fire up the scrambler software on Tommy's laptop, and then, after some clicks and beeps, we were again chatting with The Colonel. The electronic compression of our voices made the three of us sound like robotic versions of ourselves. The call was brief.

"You have a green light to take the usual action against Sykes and Bartlett," The Colonel said. "Robbery or assault will be fine. No need to send a message. As to QRS, you DO NOT have the green light for the usual action. Repeat —do NOT take the usual action against."

"But Colonel," I said, "surely he can't be allowed to get away with what he's tried to do..."

"You are correct," The Colonel said. "We do not want him to get away with it. My order to you is to not take any direct action to kill him. Also, we do not want the investigation that would certainly come along with the accidental death of such a highly placed figure. However, The Council and I are in agreement that it would be good for him to die as soon as possible. Therefore, please work on a plan to encourage him to take his own life."

Tommy and I exchanged wide-eyed looks.

"Boss," Tommy said, "this gizmo is making everyone's voice sound wacky. Just to make sure I'm getting this right —no murder, and no accident, but we want him to off himself as soon as possible. Is that about the size of it?"

"Yes," The Colonel said. "I'm aware of how it sounds, but you have it right. Think about it and come up with something that'll work and look good. You have my orders. We'll talk again soon." A series of clicks followed by a steady tone told us that the call had ended. Again we sat looking at each other in silence.

"Okay, I'll bite," Tommy said. "How do you get a senator —especially an old and powerful senator—to kill himself?"

"Hmmm, that is an interesting question T. Only one thing comes to mind."

"Well let's hear it man," Tommy said. "The suspense is killing me. How do we get this guy to want to kill himself?"

"We need," I said, "to make the alternative too horrible for him to contemplate."

B y the time I had deplaned in Pittsburgh and picked up a rental car, it was close to dawn. I checked into a hotel near the airport in search of a few hours sleep and a hot shower. Later, after breakfast at a nearby diner, I found my way to the storage unit facility that housed our "apartment." Our unit was in the indoor section, protected by a heavy padlock and a state-of-the-art palm print reader. As usual, I was pleasantly surprised when the technology worked and the door clicked open to let me in.

The unit was the size of a medium-to-large shed that might be found in a typical suburban back yard. A number of trunk-sized lockers and lidless storage bins lined most of the floor space around the edges, with shelving and hanging racks lining the walls above. I set an empty duffle bag on top of a small work table in the center and started to shop for the items I thought I might need to carry out the plans Tommy and I had worked out.

I decided the only firearm I would need was a powerful

and reliable combat pistol. Because the one I'd been traveling with was quite large, and thinking that I might need something with better concealability, I opted to set it aside for a while. From one of the racks on the wall I chose a Heckler & Koch 45C, also in the heavy .45 caliber. With its excellent matching suppressor, compact size, and ten-round magazine, I felt it would be more than adequate for the mission at hand. To my collection, I added two spare magazines and plenty of ammo.

The last item added to the duffle bag was a pair of standard M112 demolition blocks, otherwise known as C4 plastic explosive. I put them into their own smaller satchel along with a half-dozen electric blasting caps with radio adapters.

With a final look around, and a check of my mental shopping list, I zipped up the bag and took it out of the unit, resetting the locks carefully. I stowed the bag in the large trunk of the rented Dodge Charger, and left the complex.

It was almost noon when I pointed the car in a west-by-southwest direction to cross Southern Ohio on my way to Louisville, Kentucky.

My growling stomach was demanding dinner as I took the exit near Louisville for a place called Simpsonville. It appeared to be a substantial town with a choice of hotels and restaurants about twenty-five miles due east of the city. While studying the map earlier, I had determined that a base of operations in Simpsonville would put me within thirty miles of several places that I would be checking out in the coming few days.

After checking into a clean-looking chain hotel, I ventured out to a local bar and grille that I had passed on the way in from the highway. It was done up in a faux-Tudor style, complete with the brightly-painted jockey statues outside, and was doing a booming business. Knowing that eating out where the locals go is always good travel policy, I went in and found a seat at the end of the bar. The prime rib special that the bartender raved about would not normally have interested me, but the combination of his rave review and the fact that they still had an end-cut available convinced me to give it a try.

When dinner arrived, it was in fact quite good, though much more food than any one person should eat. It was served with a huge baked potato that was well prepared and delicious in its simplicity. I had not been offered a choice of vegetables, but was very happy with the side of broccoli that arrived. It was tender enough, but still with some crispness and a bright green hue. The chef's heavy hand with the garlic might have bothered some other diners, but was just fine for me.

Such a meal demanded a sturdy red wine, and fortunately, despite being in the heart of bourbon whiskey country, the bar had a good selection of California big reds. I ended up with a 2015 Ravenswood Zinfandel, which complemented the roasted beef nicely. The bartender assured me that, in the unlikely event that I didn't finish the bottle, it would be fine for me to take it back down the block to my hotel.

During the meal, and while savoring the wine afterwards, I considered my plan for the next day. The address I had for Sykes was close to the city, though still on the east side of it. There were two locations for CBC that I wanted to check out, both to the south, closer to Bardstown. My information was that one of them was in what we thought to be a typical suburban corporate-zoned area, and the other was some sort of special facility about ten miles farther south from there. The first location was probably where Gavin Bartlett had his main office; the other was something entirely different, somewhere I needed to get a close look at. That would cover Sykes and Bartlett. The remaining target, QRS, to the east and closer to Lexington, would be the toughest. I was going to have to get as good a look as I could, and study the overall area, before I'd be able to figure out the final approach.

After the trip out from Seattle, and then the drive from Pittsburgh, I was starting to realize how dead tired I was. I settled the check at the restaurant and took the last third of the bottle of Zinfandel back to the hotel. After unpacking, doing a routine weapons check, and using my laptop to catch up on communications, I got out a map of the area and poured a glass of the wine. With a map in front of me now, I took a few minutes to review the ideas that I had considered during the long drive and during dinner. With a plan in mind for the next day, I settled into bed to flip TV channels for a few minutes before turning out the light and promptly falling asleep.

I was up early the next morning. After a short run to loosen up the joints and get my blood pumping, I took in a light breakfast at the hotel buffet. By ten o'clock, I was in the car and ready to begin my reconnaissance. The August heat was already reaching out across the land. The sky over Kentucky was a brilliant and clear blue. It was going to be a scorcher.

With a folder full of information from Agent Gage, along with various maps and a pad full of my own notes on the passenger seat, my first target was Bernard Sykes. Checking my notes for the address we had for him, I set off in that direction.

Twenty minutes later, I drove down Sykes' street and located the house number I was looking for. I pulled the Charger onto a side street and parked, picking a spot where it looked like I could sit for a while without being noticed or bothered. My notes indicated that Sykes was renting the converted loft apartment over the garage of the large house down the block and across the street. The dark blue, recent-year Ford Explorer in the driveway was consistent with what the file on him said he drove. After a quick look around the street outside the car, I steadied a compact "super zoom" Nikon camera against the door-frame with my right hand, draping my left forearm lightly over it, with the moveable display pointed up so I could see it clearly. I panned across the house and driveway several times, getting a feel for the area in general, and clicked off a dozen shots to be closely studied later.

The Explorer that I assumed belonged to Sykes was the only vehicle in the driveway. Either the landlord was away, or perhaps their own car was inside the garage. While panning the camera again across the front of the main house, it was then that I noticed a "For Rent" sign on the window. *Could the whole house be for rent?* I made a mental note to get someone to try to find out if the main house was presently occupied. The neighboring house on the left side also showed a "For Rent" sign, but there were several indications of habitation, including a car in that driveway.

Setting the camera on the seat, I started the car. Then I froze in place when I happened to take a last look over at the house and caught sight of a man coming out the door at the top of the outside staircase and start down towards the driveway. I quickly grabbed the camera, repositioned it, and took a half-dozen shots as steadily as possible. *Well, I'll be dipped in shit*, I thought to myself. *If that isn't Sykes himself, then I'm Peter Pan.*

Reaching the bottom of the stairs, the man paused in the driveway, patting his pockets as though making sure he had everything he needed for some errand. He was casually dressed in faded but well-fitting jeans, and a polo shirt that was neatly tucked in. I found his light jacket to be a bit incongruous, considering the ninety-plus degree heat, until I remembered that he was probably on guard and likely carrying a gun. Before getting into the Explorer, his careful look around the street reinforced the idea that he was very much on his toes. His quick check of the area included a look down the street where I was parked, but he didn't appear to see me or show an interest in my car.

As he started the Explorer and pulled out of the driveway, I made no effort to follow him. I already had the addresses I needed for my other targets. My plan for Mr. Sykes was to confront him, interrogate him with an aim towards confirming some aspects of the case that we already suspected, and then to eliminate him. A violent ending would be fine, but it was important to my plan that his demise not be discovered immediately.

After he drove away, I waited several more minutes before leaving the area myself. I invested ten minutes more in winding through the neighborhood, getting to know it. It was a quiet several blocks, mostly pleasant and well maintained, but with seemingly half the properties either for sale or for rent. It must have been an area hit hard by the last mortgage crisis, and was still going through a slow recovery process.

Before getting back on the main road in search of my next destination, I took a break at a coffee shop to check emails and send out a few texts. One message I sent was to Sophia, asking her to find out the status of the main house adjacent to Sykes' apartment.

Forty minutes later, on the edge of a sprawling island of corporate buildings in the Kentucky countryside, I pulled up across the street from a complex of buildings emblazoned with the "CBC" logo of Consolidated Barrier Corporation. Seeing there was no outside security gate, I drove into the main parking lot and made a tour around as though looking for a good spot to park, before driving out. I noted several helpful signs, pointing, among other things, to "Receiving," "Research and Design," and to "Corporate Offices." Other roads to the side and behind the CBC property, leading to other businesses, allowed different views of the complex. I paused in several places to take pictures before getting back on the highway.

The next stop on my Kentucky research tour was another CBC facility that shared space with a small regional airfield. After pulling into the long drive that served as the entrance, I drove past a building that looked like the main office for the short-range commuter airline. Past that was a variety of related support buildings, along with several that appeared to be configured as office space. I followed a series of rectangular signs pointing the way to the CBC building, across the sprawling property and on the other side of the single runway. The road took me along the perimeter of the airfield, no doubt by design, in order to keep any automotive traffic clear of the runway at all times.

I saw no signs of any security patrol as I drove up to and past the repurposed aircraft hangar that was the CBC building. The building was a giant rectangle, I guessed at least two-hundred feet long and seventy or eighty feet wide, situated parallel, lengthwise, to the runway. There were several doors, with what looked to be the main entrance built into part of the huge sliding door on the end. I estimated those sliding doors to be about thirty feet tall, with the wall of the building reaching up another ten feet beyond that.

There were two cars outside, pulled up near the building apparently without regard for marked parking spots or painted lines. I considered that, from the look of the two cars, whomever they belonged to was just dropping in for a time—perhaps to check on something or pick up something—as opposed to someone actually spending their workday in the building. It seemed to me that someone who reported to work there on a regular basis would park with more care.

I completed the slow pass by the building before continuing around the perimeter road and back towards the airfield office and main grouping of buildings. There were three other hangars of various sizes, all displaying signs of active involvement with storage or repair of different small aircraft. One building wore the signage of a major oil company and had a matching truck parked outside. There was a long structure, simply built but brightly painted and well-maintained, that had been divided up into four or five retail establishments—a typical small regional airport making some extra money by renting out space and facilities.

The last building I passed on my way out was done up like a giant red log cabin. There were a dozen or so cars parked outside, and as I neared the place I saw it was a restaurant. The noon hour had passed and, realizing how hungry I was, I decided to stop in for some lunch and a cold beer. The interior was decorated in a very busy but appealing way, with a huge collection of airport and air travel memorabilia. While waiting for my food to arrive, I walked around the main room looking at the many framed pictures that described the history of the airfield and the surrounding area. I found one large photo particularly interesting, and studied it carefully for several minutes. It was a clear aerial view of the entire property, showing the perimeter road and some amount of the surrounding territory. I noted that a neighborhood of twenty or more single homes abutted the airfield quite close to the old hangar that was now the CBC building. An arterial road went through the neighborhood, with two smaller roads branching off towards the wooded border of the airfield. I made a note that one of those roads might be a good place to park when I came back after dark to get a closer look at the CBC building.

On my way out of the restaurant after lunch, I paused in the foyer to look at the display of maps, brochures, and slim magazines proclaiming the wonders of various area attractions. A picture of a woman on one of them caught my eye. Taking a closer look, I realized the woman was none other than Louise O'Donnell-Bartlett, wife of Gavin Bartlett, and daughter of Kentucky Senator Wilfred O'Donnell. I leafed through the magazine quickly, skimming the material inside. The article mentioned her husband, the CEO of a major state corporation, along with her legendary father, and described how she had gotten involved in being a spokesperson for the latest "Visit Kentucky" campaign, coordinated by the state tourism board. An inset on one page urged readers to go to a certain website and watch the ten-minute video, hosted by her, showing off the many wonders of the state. I took a copy of the magazine with me as I left.

The last reconnaissance stop of the day was to the historic town of Woodford Oaks, on the edge of Lexington. An hour after my lunch at the airport restaurant, I exited the Bluegrass Parkway and entered the quiet and leafy enclave of beautiful old houses. I turned onto Bluegrass Boulevard and followed it as it wove through what amounted to a paved, shaded pathway under some of the largest oak trees I'd ever seen. The long arms of the ancient trees reached across the road towards each other, high up above the power lines. The homes all had generous yards, with the houses set well back from the sidewalks. Many of the homes were huge, but even the smaller ones were stately in their presentation. It was a peaceful and elegant setting, with the thick shade providing relief from the blazing summer sun.

A few houses after the intersection at Lexington Avenue, I came up to the senator's house on my right—646 Bluegrass Boulevard. The corner property was enclosed by a brick wall, maybe eight or ten feet high, and mostly covered with ivy. As I passed the driveway, secured with its matching iron gate, I was able to get a glimpse of the house that stood thirty or forty yards inside. It was a brick house of just two floors, and like the surrounding wall, was thickly covered in ivy. It was not large enough to be called a mansion, but was imposing in a well-manicured, old money way. I passed the wide driveway and then was looking at the brick wall again, which continued up to and around the corner. I took the right turn onto the side street and followed the wall about two-hundred feet to where it ended at the next property, making a ninety-degree right turn to continue along the rear of the senator's yard.

The next property along the side street was bordered by an ornate cast iron fence painted in shiny black. The house that sat on the grounds well inside the fence was indeed what anyone would call a mansion. While the fence and the yard were clearly well-maintained, the property otherwise appeared to be deserted. More majestic old oak trees dotted the lawn, with gnarled limbs approaching the roof of the house and even extending over the brick fence and into the next property, like the protective arms of a benevolent giant. As I passed the closed gates of the drive-way, I slowed down to read an oval sign that stood to one side, realizing it was one of those "historic landmark" signs. The house was called "Rutherford Manor," but I couldn't make out the paragraph of smaller print under that. The fence around the mansion ended halfway down the block, and the next property was open, with another huge and very old house sitting well back from the road. A second, briefer sign proclaimed the house to be "The Rutherford Museum."

I turned right again at the next corner and saw several smaller buildings adjacent to the ones that made up Rutherford Manor Estate. There was a pathway winding towards them from the sidewalk. I passed several signs on knee-height poles, and slowed down to read one of them as I passed. It was shaped like an arrow, and read "Manor House Tours."

The huge mansion, along with the related Rutherford buildings, made up a well-preserved historic estate that occupied most of the block. As I drove past the property, I decided I would probably have to go through it in some way to get to the senator's yard and house. I did a full circuit around the next block, reversing my route. While I again passed the Rutherford Estate and then the senator's house—in the opposite direction this time—I snapped away with the camera, hoping to get a few usable shots to examine later and add to my understanding of the area.

Less than five minutes later, I was back on the Blue-grass Parkway, headed west towards Simpsonville and my hotel. I had dozens of pictures to download and study, maps to consult, and drawings to create. My head was swimming with ideas and I needed to tame them and trim them down and into a cohesive plan.

Kentucky in August was a hot place to be as the Charger ate up the pavement, but the color of the sky had changed slightly, offering a teasing hint of cooler evening. I handed the task of driving the heavy car over to my mental autopilot as a plan for the coming days began to coalesce in my mind.

The breakthrough came to me in a dream.

I was sitting at a sidewalk café on the outskirts of a park with a small river running through it. A dozen metal tables were arranged around a stone patio. Most of the tables were filled with people picking away at huge piles of cheddar cheese goldfish. I knew that I was in the Kentucky countryside but yet I could see the St. Louis Gateway Arch in the distance.

A waiter with a black apron was making his way towards me through the tables. When he reached my table he was suddenly my girlfriend Jenny, who handed me a menu. I saw immediately that the menu was blank.

"Are you ready to order, Mr. Boudreau?"

"My menu is blank," I said. "What do you have?"

"All we have is what we once knew about ourselves, but now doubt," she said. "It comes with a side of goldfish. So does everything else."

"But what is everything else?" I asked the waiter/Jenny.

"There is nothing else," she said. "It will be right out. Would you like a drink to go with that? We have everything."

I looked around at the other tables and realized that everyone was drinking from a bottle of Jim Beam Bourbon. I turned back to her and saw that she was now back to being the waiter again.

"Bring me a glass of everything," I said.

He laughed out loud as he moved his hand up to and across his face. I realized that he was about to peel a mask off his face. His entire façade was just a thin cardboard cutout of a person. His hand moved it away and then he was Jenny again. She tossed the cardboard aside and started to walk towards me, laughing. She, along with all the diners on the patio, suddenly looked up as a loud buzzing filled the air...

Wakened suddenly from sleep and yanked out of my strange dream, I grabbed my phone from the nightstand and turned off the alarm. I had experienced my share of dreams that were upsetting and downright terrifying, but this one had been merely strange and amusing.

"That's it!" I said aloud to the hotel room. *Dreams. Changing faces. That's how we do it.*

I started the little coffee maker and let it brew while I grabbed a notepad and worked on a list.

"How soon can you get out here?"

"Well, my bag is mostly packed already," Tommy said, "I'll just give that a final check and get my gun case together. Since money's no object, should be able to meet up with you by early morning."

"And you're sure you're okay driving, right?" I asked.

"Yeah, fine to drive," he said. "I just don't want to get into any fair fights for a while still. I'll email you a copy of my flight info when I have it."

"Fantastic, I'll be glad to have your help. I'll work on this some more today and we can talk it out over a good bottle when you're here."

It was early afternoon on the day that I'd woken up from the strange dream. The Colonel had given his approval to my general plan when I'd filled him in on the work in progress earlier. After that call, I had spoken briefly with NSA Agent Gage. She had given me some more interesting information and had agreed to try to get me whatever she could on a few specific items.

It had been a busy morning, but things were moving along. Tommy and I talked on the phone for half an hour, discussing our plans only in coded terms, but we would soon have the opportunity to drill down into the details more openly. Tommy noted the town and hotel I was in, then we ended the call with him agreeing to keep me updated on his travels.

My next and last call was to Sophia. We made small talk for a few minutes and caught up on the team. She told me she had been working closely with Agent Gage for several days and that the two of them were forging a good working relationship.

"How are you with Photoshop?" I asked.

"Pretty damn good," she said. "I actually taught a class on it at the local community center just a few months ago. You know, as a volunteer. What do you have in mind?"

I gave her an outline of the several images I was thinking of, promising to send her more specifics via email later, along with some images I had for her to work with. I asked if she knew of a comparable tool for video.

"You mean like if you have a video of Gary Cooper riding a horse," she said, "but you want it changed to be Tommy riding the horse instead? Something like that?"

"Right, that's about it," I said. "Along those lines. But, continuing with your example for the moment, what if I only had video of a horse with no rider, and I wanted you to put Tommy on the horse?"

"Hmmm, that could be tricky," she said, "but could be done. It would be best if you had a source video of Tommy moving in some way similar to riding a horse. I don't think Tommy likes horses."

"You're right, Sophia," I said. "I think he was thrown by a horse when he was a kid at summer camp, but that's okay. I won't tell him about the horse if you don't. But really, I think what I need will be easier. Like person A just sitting at a desk, say, but I want it to be person B. Easier?"

"Much easier," she said. "Yes. Get me whatever footage you can and I'll work on it. I'll figure it out."

"Now here's the thing though," I said. "The video thing will need to be turned around pretty quick. If I can get a source video to you by tomorrow, say, noonish, can you turn something around within twenty-four hours?"

"I should be able to do that," she said. "Get me what you can as soon as you can. Meanwhile, I'll start some practice templates today."

I gave her the URL for a website where she could find one of the source videos, and promised to email her a specific list of what I had in mind after our call, along with several other images I thought she would need.

"Oh, by the way," Sophia said, before she hung up. "I looked in to that rental house where your guy Sykes lives. Turns out he actually owns the whole property. If you said he's living over the garage, then my guess would be that he stays up there and makes some extra cash by renting out the main house. Does that help?"

"Yeah, that helps," I said. "It's just background information, but thanks. As long as the main house is empty, I can use it."

After my series of business calls, I settled down on the hotel room's sofa and put in a call to Jenny, back in St. Louis. Busy working, she only had a few minutes to talk, but she was very happy to hear from me and happy to hear that I thought I could be back in Missouri within less than a week. After my conversation with her, I sat for a minute reflecting on the absurdity of some of the situations created by trying to maintain a warm and trusting relationship while at the same time being a top-secret government assassin. I hated to lie to her, and tried hard to keep it to a minimum. I was aware that my success and survival over the past year or two was due as much to my advanced ability to compartmentalize my thoughts as to anything else.

All this and paid vacation too—what's not to like?

It was almost eleven o'clock at night when I approached the small airfield again. I drove up the entrance road as far as the main cluster of buildings to see how many of the businesses were still open and how many people were around. There didn't appear to be much happening at all: a minimum of lights on inside the buildings, the few streetlights illuminating the empty stretch of sidewalk. Just as I looped around to go back towards the main road, I passed a uniformed man sitting inside a white SUV that was marked as being with some security company. He returned my wave as I drove by. *The night watchman for the whole property*, I thought to myself. He could have been retired military, but didn't look old enough to be a retired cop. Probably just a guy who took a few courses and applied for the job. In any case, I did not want to have to hurt him, and so made a note to make sure to not attract his attention while checking out the CBC building.

Driving back down the lane to the exit, I again passed

the restaurant where I'd had lunch the day before, passing by just in time to see a worker tossing bags of trash into a dumpster sitting near the kitchen door. Aside from the several cars parked around the place, and the night watchman I'd just waved to, I didn't see any other signs of life.

I drove out of the airfield complex and followed a route around and into the neighborhood that I'd first seen in the aerial photograph on the restaurant wall. The roads through the area were curvy, and covered a heavily-wooded residential area equivalent to about a dozen square blocks. Somebody in one of the houses along one road must have been throwing a party; parked cars were lining the road for a block in either direction. I parked behind a line of cars, grabbed my backpack from the rear seat, and walked towards the sound of music. Seeing nobody in my immediate vicinity, I ducked down a short block that appeared to have no houses on it, looking to me like a part of a planned community that had been zoned and cleared but not yet built up.

I stayed close to the tree line as I approached a chain-link fence, and after a quick look back towards the parked cars, moved out of sight and into cover. At about eight feet high and with no barbed wire along the top, the fence was not hard to climb over. From the other side, another twenty feet of clear grass took me to the back wall of the CBC building. I moved along the wall to the corner, and then along the short side, passing the entrance, to the next corner. Retrieving a pair of light-amplifying binoculars from my backpack, I knelt to survey the area.

The main cluster of buildings was far across the property on the other side of the runway. Light spilled out from the door of one of the hangars, where just inside I could see a worker moving around a small propeller plane. I spotted the security vehicle parked near the office, but not the guard.

There were no cars anywhere outside the CBC building itself, and otherwise no sign of life apart from the light above the entrance and a few others mounted high up on the corners of the building. Stowing the binoculars, I took out another gadget The Colonel had acquired from his friends at Central Intelligence. About the size of a pack of smokes, it detected and analyzed any electrical activity within a range of about six feet, displaying plain-English information on a small screen. Several passes of the device around the door and a few feet to either side told me there was a loop of standard 120 volt wiring inside the walls around the door, doubtless to support the inside and outside lights, but none of the low-voltage wiring that would be required for an alarm system.

With that in mind, and with relief, I got out a standard lock-pick kit and was inside the hangar within a few minutes.

I found myself in a cavernous space, dimly lit by several lights mounted high up above. I switched on a compact three-hundred lumen flashlight, and soon located a bank of light switches to one side of the door. Flicking them up caused the inside of the hangar to be fully illuminated by a series of large, round fixtures mounted below a network of catwalks suspended from the ceiling. I had been inside hangars during my military service, and had always been in awe of their size. The old CBC building was no exception.

Looking at the space with my back to the door, I had no view of the opposite end due to the great size of the objects that stood inside.

I was at the edge of an open expanse of cement floor that extended from one side of the building to the other. From where I stood, the first object looked to be at least forty feet away. I estimated it to be about thirty-five feet across from side to side, and twenty or twenty-five feet high—a huge rectangle. It was clearly a section of a very large-scale wall. With the off-white color of the cement, along with the pebbled finish, it reminded me of one of those sound-barrier walls that gets put up along a new roadway to protect the tranquility of the adjacent neighborhood.

I was inside CBC's wall showroom.

Walking up to and around the first displayed wall section, I noted that it was about ten inches thick, and seemed to be made of a number of cement panels fastened together by some hidden connectors. It made sense to me that a modular construction method would be required by the great weight of the material. An old news report about a concrete jersey barrier crushing a worker's leg on the Jersey Turnpike came to mind. I remembered reading in that article that a ten-foot section of that common type of traffic barrier weighed about four-thousand pounds. With that in mind, walking around the wall section in front of me, I estimated it must have weighed at least thirty or forty tons, or maybe more.

I followed back along the side of the hangar, looking at the various types of wall sections on display. Some were similar to the first one, but with variations in the surface patterns or coloration, while others were more basic constructions of sheet metal or combinations of metal and other materials. There was one made of glass blocks, and several built with different colors and styles of bricks. Some of the smaller and clearly lighter walls were held in place by simple wooden supports. The larger ones, including the massive cement section that I'd first seen, were supported by steel cables reaching from the top corners of the wall sections up to sturdy anchors mounted to the hangar walls near the ceiling. Making use of a narrow steel staircase in one corner of the building, I climbed up to the catwalk to spend several minutes examining the cabling and anchor support systems, taking pictures with my phone along the way.

Back down on the ground, I explored several small rooms built out from the side wall. In one of them I found a stack of folding chairs, and carried one over to sit a few feet out from the section of cement wall. From my backpack, I retrieved a bundle, which I unrolled to reveal a wrinkled and deflated human form. I found the air valve on the left foot, and started blowing into it to inflate the thing.

The embarrassment I felt when I'd bought the inflatable sex doll earlier in the day at one of those adult stores along the highway had reminded me of my nervousness during an early under-age attempt to buy beer. Now, blowing the thing up with nobody around to see it and with absolutely no sexy thoughts in mind, I was surprised to feel the same embarrassment creeping in.

The design of the doll was such that it wanted to be fully extended when inflated, so I only filled it about three-quarters full before plugging up the valve. I used a roll of heavy tape to position it in the chair in an approximation of a normal seated woman. The hair on the doll's head was terrible quality for a wig, but would probably be good enough from a distance. After walking around and back and forth to look at the seated form, I made a few adjustments before getting out a small video camera and starting to film. With luck, I hoped to get some usable footage to Sophia.

The things I do for my country.

33

Tommy called me as soon as he got to the hotel the next day, and after giving him a half hour to get situated in his room, we met up in the lobby and went down the street for some lunch. The Tudor place with the lawn-jockeys outside had plenty of seating, and we gabbed away over sandwiches and cold beers.

"You seem to be moving well," I said. "How's everything healing? Still sore?"

"There's the occasional jolt," Tommy said, "but overall I'm pretty good. I have doctor's orders to not be shot again for at least six months."

"That sounds fair," I said. "I guess it's my turn anyway. By the way, I haven't spoken with The Colonel for a few days. Did Briggs ever go out to see that Straight guy in San Diego?"

"He did," Tommy said. "The Colonel thinks that should all be wrapped up now. It does look like Straight was the one who tipped off Sykes and West about me, and about me being in on the raid. Probably the guy who tipped off the others that you ran into the night after too. Briggs didn't think the circle went any wider than that, as least as far as would concern us."

I took a long drink of my beer and considered that for a minute. "Alright, if that's what he thinks, it sounds good. I'll take it. What happened with Straight?"

"That's a damn shame," Tommy said. "While he was talking with Briggs out on the back staircase of his apartment building, he tripped and fell down to the alley. It was only three floors down, but some workmen had been building a retaining wall, and there was steel rebar sticking up all over the place. To hear Briggs tell it, poor guy was heavily perforated."

"Ouch," I said. I took another bite of my sandwich. "Well, everybody's number comes up eventually."

Back at the hotel after lunch, we continued the discussion in my room, with maps and notes spread across the coffee table. I told him about my idea that Sophia was helping me with, and showed him the video footage I'd taken inside the CBC hangar.

"We're going to have to work really close to pull all this off in one night," Tommy said. He made a few faces before nodding. "I think we can do it."

"The NSA agent—Gage," I said, "told me that Sykes and Bartlett usually communicate via text, and that they've arranged meetings several times at the CBC building out at the airfield. She said it looked like Bartlett was deferential to Sykes. If I can get to Sykes early in the day—Saturday is what I was thinking—I can take him out of play and then use his phone to contact Bartlett and get him to meet at the hangar just after dark. After that, if all goes well we can get up to the senator's house by midnight or so. He's often said in public that he's an insomniac and likes to work late, and this Saturday would be good because he'll be alone in the house. His wife, along with Bartlett's wife, is taking part in a three-day tour around the state to kick off some kind of tourism campaign. I actually got that from a Kentucky tourist website."

"Sweet," Tommy said. "I like it. Gonna be tight, but I like it. Show me that drawing you made of the senator's neighborhood."

I unrolled a map that I'd drawn out on several sheets of paper taped together, showing a several-block area off Bluegrass Boulevard, the senator's house, and the historic Rutherford Estate. I pointed to several parts of the map while I narrated.

"Whenever he's in residence, there'll be a state police car out front somewhere along this stretch. There was nobody there when I went by, and no sign of life. If you follow past and take the side road, this is some old historic mansion. All these other buildings behind and spilling over to the next street are related. They must do tours or architecture classes and that sort of thing. Remember the old Physick Estate on Washington Street in Cape May? Something like that except a much bigger property that takes up most of the block apart from the target. I was thinking if I could come through that property and past the big house, maybe from there I could get over the fence, well out of sight of the state boys out front."

Tommy was eyeing my map, and appeared deep in thought. He was saying something under his breath that I couldn't quite make out.

"Is this correct? The Rutherford Estate? You sure that's the name?"

"Yeah I'm sure," I said. "I took a picture of the sign."

"I've helped my daughters with a bunch of their college papers over the years, and one of them—it was one of Julie's I think—was on the Underground Railroad. You know about that, right?"

"I guess I know what most of us learned in school. It was a secret network of people who helped escaped slaves get north to free states or into Canada. Through most of the 1800s I think. I guess it would have petered out after the Civil War."

"That's pretty much it," Tommy said. "Free blacks along with whites who didn't support slavery. They had special routes between towns, secret rooms in their houses or barns, tunnels between buildings, all of that. Helped thousands of people get to freedom. Anyway, when I helped with that paper, I found it all so interesting that I read a bunch of books on the subject. One of them was called *Routes of Freedom* by a guy named Jackson Hodge. Great book. I still have it on my shelf at home."

"Are you thinking this big estate next to the senator's house had something to do with all that?"

"That's what I'm thinking," he said. "Unless there's more than one Rutherford Estate on the western side of Lexington, this must be it. A major stop in the Kentucky part of the Underground Railroad. Lemme see if I can get Sophia on the phone. I bet she can get us some info really fast."

Sophia picked up right away. Tommy walked around my hotel room talking with her for several minutes. I heard him saying something about access to the Library of

Congress, along with making reference to the book he'd told me about.

"As soon as you can, thanks," he said, into his phone before ending the call. "She said she should be able to get back within the half hour."

While we waited for Sophia's call, I cracked a bottle of good Kentucky Bourbon and poured us out a stiff one.

"I guess we should be all done with this in a few days," Tommy said. "Whatta you got going on after that? Relax in St. Louis for a while?"

"Actually," I said, "The Colonel wants me to take on a special mission."

"Oh yeah, what's that?" He looked at me skeptically but with interest.

"I'm to eliminate everyone who's being loud in public."

"There you go again..." He laughed at me and took a drink. "So you'll be spending the next six or seven years in the northeast."

"Probably," I said. "There and Texas. Lots of loud people in Texas too. Everything's big down there. Even their voices."

"Right," Tommy said, "but at least they have all that great barbecue to go with it. If I'm going to have yelling people around me, I'd rather have Texas barbecue than Rhode Island chowder, that's for damn sure."

"You mean 'chow-dah'," I said. "Where've you been, man?"

We were saved by the sound of Tommy's phone ringing. It was Sophia, even though it had barely been fifteen minutes. They spoke for several minutes and Tommy thanked her profusely before hanging up. He gestured to my laptop, across the room on the corner of the bed.

"She said she's sending us an email with some files. See if you have that yet."

Two minutes later we were both looking at my screen. Sophia had sent us a digital copy of Tommy's book, *Routes of Freedom*, along with a few other attachments. Tommy commandeered the laptop and started scrolling through pages. He carried it over to set on top of the map I had drawn. After a minute, he gestured to me excitedly to look at the screen.

"Here, look at this. This is the Rutherford Estate in 1860, showing the whole surrounding area. This road here, "Bellevue Trail" it says, that must have become Bluegrass Boulevard. You can see the big mansion and all these outbuildings that go with it."

I looked back and forth between the screen and the paper map, comparing what I was seeing and making marks here and there on the paper. The digitized map on the screen was very old, but clearly had been professionally done, with distances noted in the fancy writing style of the period. The orientation of the Rutherford mansion house and the related buildings made sense to me, having just driven by them, but the senator's house had not been built yet. I pointed to one of the estate outbuildings that sat substantially apart from the others.

"Look at this one up here," I said. "I thought I saw a small wooden building—like the size of a large shed or something like that—when I drove through. If the angles of the brick walls are constant through the property, then this little building would have to be inside what's now the senator's back yard. I think that's the building I saw back there. Must have been cut off from the rest when the land was parceled out."

Tommy was scrolling farther into the book. He stopped at a point and gestured for me to look at the screen again.

"Here, let me just blow this up," he said. "There. I wish we could print this out and overlay it, but use your imagination. Grab your map and hold it up."

I did as he asked while also looking at some kind of diagram on his screen. He pointed back and forth to corresponding areas.

"What are we looking at?" I said. He saw my puzzled expression. I studied the screen and the map some more. "Oh, okay, I think I see it. This is some old pathway between the buildings. This one goes from the barn to the mansion. And...this one goes from the mansion over to that building that we think is now in the senator's yard. Is that what it is, then? Pathways around the property?"

Tommy was grinning from ear to ear.

"In a way, yes. These are pathways all around the property and between the buildings. But here, look closer and read the caption."

I leaned in to read the writing below the pathway diagram.

Original architect's drawing of tunnel network below the Easton Rutherford property.

I sat back and let out a whistle.

"Are you kidding me? There's a tunnel network below the whole thing? It looks like they go everywhere."

"Underground Railroad was not entirely just a figurative term," Tommy said. "There really were lots of tunnels.

The guy who built up this whole area—Easton Rutherford —made his fortune building small bridges and tunnels back in New Jersey. He would have known whatever there was to know about tunnel construction, and would have had all kinds of experienced people on his payroll."

"Holy shit," I said. "If that network is still intact, maybe I can use it to get inside the senator's house."

"Now you're talking," Tommy said. "It's worth a try anyway, but we'll have to get over there in the dark and recon the situation."

"Damn, I hate that you're right," I said. "Not because you're right, but because that means I'm going to have to go through a bunch of creepy tunnels. Well, it's a good thing I have a flashlight fetish and have some really good ones. I don't see any reason why we shouldn't do this tonight. It's about a forty-minute drive from here."

"Let's do it," Tommy said. "If those tunnels are usable, that'll be the ticket to get in and out of there without being seen. You don't have a problem with spiders, do you?"

34

It was after midnight when we entered the town of Woodford Oaks and made the turn to drive down Bluegrass Boulevard. Four blocks before the senator's house, Tommy made a right and then a left to continue the trip a block over and behind the vast Rutherford Estate that surrounded the target house. Having spent almost an hour looking at hundreds of online images of the estate, and using Google Earth to get the bird's eye view, we had settled on a good drop-off point and plan of ingress and egress.

After another three blocks, the forested border of the estate grounds began. Thick at first, the trees gradually thinned over the next hundred feet, before yielding to the more lightly-wooded grounds surrounding the estate buildings. Seeing no other cars or people in the area, Tommy pulled to the curb and stopped. He reached up a hand and flicked the switch to stop the dome light from coming on when a door was opened.

"Remember, this is just reconnaissance. Don't engage

with anyone. If you have to, try to make it look like some kind of simple break-in. If I get your distress signal, I'll do what I can to cause a distraction. Otherwise, I'll pick you up right here after I get your all-clear."

"Got it, T," I said. "I'll be fine. I just need to make sure I'm gonna be able to get in and out tomorrow night." I checked my watch and rotated the bezel to mark the time; Tommy did the same with his. "I've got twelve-forty. Shooting for twenty-minutes, max, but we'll see."

I got out of the car and moved into the trees. I watched the road as Tommy drove off. Much of the block I was on, as well as the next one over, was taken up by the estate and all its associated buildings and activities, so I was not surprised that it was a quiet area. Satisfied that no one had seen me, I moved farther away from the road, towards the building that we had identified as the visitor center. Retrieving a pair of light-amplifying binoculars from my backpack, I knelt to survey the grounds. I saw no sign of any kind of security patrol, which I thought was a bit strange, but I decided the estate was probably watching expenses and relying on the regular patrols of the local police.

My black cordura combat backpack, though not large or heavy, was filled with everything a man might need to break into a building. Aside from the night-vision binocs and my comm unit, it held all manner of lock-picking and door-opening equipment. A compact toolkit included two sizes of titanium pry bars, along with an assortment of screwdrivers and a small saw. Inside a special satchel at the bottom of the pack were some items that I hoped not to need—a half dozen balls of C4 plastic explosive and the electronic delay primers needed to set them off. Each about the size of a small tangerine, I would only use them down below in the tunnels if needed to get past some obstacle, or, in case of emergency, to blast my way out. In one of the pockets of my black cargo pants, I carried the electrical field sensor device that would help me determine if a door or window was alarmed.

The Heckler & Koch automatic rode under my left arm in a shoulder holster, with the matching suppressor in one of my pockets. This night, I carried the pistol for defense only, and sincerely hoped to not have to draw it.

With a final scan of the area, I dashed out towards the wall of the visitor center building, following the shadows of the huge old trees along the way. I crouched low and followed the side of the building to the corner nearest the old mansion. From there, and after another careful look around, I made the short run over to the mansion. I knelt low and kept silent as I got out the night vision binocs for a long look around. Either I was alone on the property or, if not, whoever else was there must have been deep inside one of the buildings, having coffee or maybe catching forty winks.

From where I was alongside the mansion, I was looking across thirty or forty feet of manicured lawn at the tall brick wall that formed the rear border of the senator's property. My plan was to break into the mansion and find my way to the basement. Once there, I hoped to locate an entrance to a tunnel that I further hoped would take me under the brick wall and into the adjacent property. I needed to do all that in such a way that I could come back through the next night and have neither of my subterranean trips be discovered. In the dark, beside the old house, I shook my head at the improbability of it all.

Avoiding the door that was clearly the main tour entrance, I ran the electrical sensor around another door that looked like it was probably an entrance to the kitchen or a storage room. Despite there being no alarm system, the door was solid and the lock was serious, though no match for the CIA's latest lock-picking tools. Closing the door behind me, I saw that I was in a narrow shelf-lined hallway that led into a large kitchen. I took a minute to stand quietly and listen, and then another minute moving from window to window looking out at the yard. The house smelled of paint and fresh woodwork, as though repairs or restoration were going on somewhere inside. The floors were dark and well-polished, and were solid enough that they made almost no sound as I walked from room to room.

My search for the entrance to the basement was made easier by the tour-oriented signs all over the place. My guess that the stairs down to the basement would be behind the door marked "BASEMENT" turned out to be correct. The only security was one of those velvet ropes like the ones found all over museums, along with a small sign indicating that the basement was for "Staff Only."

The stairs were ancient and creaky. The basement itself was musty and cool. It was a warren of different-sized rooms that doubtless would each have had some designated function during the home's glory days. With a powerful flashlight, I wound my way through, looking for anything that looked like it could be a tunnel entrance.

After ten minutes, I had no promising leads. *This is the original house. It's got to be here somewhere.*

I sat down in an old wicker chair for a brief rest. As I sat there thinking, I looked across the room at the fieldstone wall that must have served as part of the building's foundation. A dozen or more chairs like the one I was sitting in were stacked haphazardly against it, several deep. Narrowing the beam of the flashlight for a more precise look, I realized there was some sort of wood framing set into the wall behind the chairs. I contained my excitement for long enough to take several pictures of the chair pile before starting to move them away from the wall. With all the chairs out of the way, I could see the timber framing of what was clearly a door set into the stone. I realized I had originally missed it because the door, at about four feet square, went only halfway up the stone wall. There were no markings on or near the door, and the heavy iron hasp and loop fixture was secured by a relatively modern padlock.

My lock-pick kit was well suited to the standard lock, and I had it open in a few minutes. I had to use some muscle to pull the small, square door open, but I eventually got it open wide enough to be able to look into the darkness of the low corridor that must extend off under the lawn outside. As I moved the beam of my flashlight around, I could see that the walls of the tunnel were lined with brick in a very professional-looking construction.

I stepped back to think for a minute about the tunnel diagram we had studied, as well as the surface layout of the estate. If I had my orientation inside the basement right, the tunnel I was looking at would be going off in a straight line towards and then under the brick wall of the neighboring property. Somewhere around halfway, there should be a junction where this tunnel met another, going off towards where the old barn used to be. I figured that, from where I stood, it must be no more than fifty feet to the senator's wall, and then about that far again to its terminus —whatever that was.

I got out my communicator and tapped out a quick message to Tommy, telling him where I was and that I had located the tunnel entrance.

Once through the door, I was relieved to see that the tunnel itself was higher, if only about five feet. The extra foot of height made it possible for me to walk at a crouch rather than having to go on all fours. I moved slowly and carefully, using the flashlight to inspect the walls and floor as I went. The tunnel was in surprisingly good condition, and cleaner than I had expected. It occurred to me that portions of it might have once been part of a tour of the property, and if so, would have been carefully inspected and maintained. My crouching gait made it hard for me to estimate distance with much accuracy, but I guessed I was about halfway between the house and the brick wall when the tunnel opened up into a round chamber that formed a junction with another tunnel going off to the left. As I entered, several rats ran out of my way and down the other tunnel. Keeping the diagram in mind, I continued down the tunnel that branched slightly to the right. My flashlight revealed a shape up ahead, which, as I got closer, turned out to be a steel or iron gate. *Shit. This must be the property line.* A sense of deflation came over me, until something bright glinted in the light and I saw that the door was secured with another standard padlock. A small sign hung from the top of the cage-like door. The hand-painted lettering on the wooden plank had flaked away to some extent, but I could still read it.

PROPERTY LINE – DO NOT ENTER

Ignoring the sign, and making short work of the padlock, I continued through the door and down the tunnel. Counting off steps, my rough estimate told me I was somewhere around thirty feet past the brick wall when the tunnel again opened up into a small, round space. Aside from the tunnel I'd just come out of, the only other opening was a much smaller one. I judged it to be three feet across at most, and it was roughly square. I wondered why they would have made the tunnel smaller at this point, but could come up with no answer that made sense.

The smaller tunnel was just high enough for me to negotiate on my hands and knees with the small pack still on my back. Shortly, it opened up again into a round chamber that was substantially larger than the two I'd already seen. Someone, presumably the same people who had built the metal gate under the property line, had set up a kind of fence here—cast iron was my guess. It spanned the chamber, again with a door that was secured by another padlock. Beyond the fence, I could see there was a vertical shaft reaching up to somewhere above. Simple iron rungs, set into the wall of the chamber, disappeared up the shaft.

The padlock mechanism must have corroded over the years, and gave me a bit of trouble, but ultimately popped open with a raspy snap. Now on the other side of the chamber, I was able to look up into the shaft to see that it met what looked like wide wooden boards not far above. Using the metal rungs to make the short climb, I found the shaft narrow enough that I could lean away from the rungs and against the opposite wall with a degree of comfort while I examined the barrier at the top.

I soon realized I was looking at the underside of a wooden door. A trapdoor. It was made of oak or some other heavy hardwood, and was in good condition. There were some slight cracks between the boards, but no light showed through. Apart from the hinges on one end, I saw no sign of any locks or latching mechanisms. I tried pushing up on the end opposite the hinges, gently first, and then with more force. The substantial amount of "give" confirmed to me that there couldn't have been any metal hardware holding the door closed, but there was still some resistance. I pushed up and down several times, raising the door by as much as several inches, trying to interpret the odd sounds generated above when I did.

The sound was something I'd heard before, from the distant past of my youth. *A lawnmower. That's it!* The door I was pushing up on had a lawnmower sitting on top of it.

Bracing myself, I pushed the door up high enough that I could get my right arm up to feel around. I smiled to myself as I indeed felt the hard wheel of a lawnmower. After some feeling around, I decided the mower was situated such that I thought I could get it to roll out of the way with a good shove on the trapdoor—but I would have to risk making a little noise. As I lifted the door, I could hear the wheels rolling off to one side, and was pleased to hear only a mild thump as the mower hit a wall or some large object.

I pushed the door up high enough to stick my head out, cupping my hand around the flashlight to control the light as I shone it around. I saw an assortment of rakes, shovels, and other yard-work implements either leaning against walls or hanging from hooks. A work table was built in against one wall and appeared to have tools and other junk sitting on it and hanging above. I was inside a large shed. Something caught my eye and I looked down in time to see the mower slowly rolling back towards me. I reached out in time to shove it away.

I hoisted myself up out of the shaft and into the shed. There was a double door in the middle of one long wall, with a window on either side. Looking around at the inside of the structure, I could see that the shed wasn't one of the modern pre-fab ones that suburban homeowners buy and drop on the lawn; it looked very old and hand-built. The hardwood floor creaked as I moved around, but had a solid feel to it. The shed was at least as old as the main house, probably older, which might explain why it was built over the old tunnel from the estate next door. The tunnel had been all locked up, with access to the other end entrusted to the keepers of the Rutherford Estate. The entrance inside the shed had long ago been covered up and possibly even forgotten. Looking around carefully, I had the impression that the various tools, along with the mower itself, had not been used in ages. That made sense to me, since I found it unlikely that the senator, in his golden years anyway, would be taking care of his own lawn and grounds. The dark floorboards of the shed were liberally covered in a mix of ancient grass clippings, dirt, and bits of leaves. It was ideal flooring to conceal where someone had stepped. Whoever had built the trapdoor had done a finely detailed job, blending it in well with the rest of the floor.

Above ground now, I took a minute to get out my comm unit and type a quick message to Tommy, telling him where I was and that my recon mission was almost complete.

Now that I had made it this far, I needed to know that I would be able to get out of the shed and back in when I had to. After closing my eyes for a full minute to enhance my night vision, I looked out both of the windows to examine as much of the yard that I could see. The shed must have been near the extreme rear of the property, looking towards the back wall of the senator's house. The house was mostly dark, with a few fingers of light reaching back across the lawn from some fixtures on or near the front. I tried the door and found it to be locked from the outside. I knew I could force it, but doing so would likely give away the whole deal. I turned my attention to the windows, seeing they both had the basic sliding lock that kept the lower portion from being raised.

Wait a minute, I thought to myself. *I'm not on the outside breaking in, I'm on the inside breaking out.*

The window lock had not been moved and the window itself had probably not been opened in decades, but with a mixture of force and finesse, I got them both open.

I took off my backpack, and after a long look out the window at the yard and the back of the house, I climbed through and dropped to the lawn below, where I crouched beside the shed, watching and listening. Not detecting any reaction to my appearance on the lawn, I dashed straight across to the shadows at the back of the house.

I moved along the back wall until I came to a set of cement steps going down to what was obviously a basement door. With no intention of gaining entry, I took the few steps just to examine the door and the lock. Running the electrical sensor all around the doorframe did not indicate the presence of any low-voltage alarm system wiring. Noting that I could probably get into the house through that door, I moved along the rear of the house in the opposite direction until I came to the corner, and looked out towards the front yard. From where I stood, I could see up the driveway towards Bluegrass Boulevard, where what looked like a state trooper's car was parked across the road. The front of the house and driveway were very well lit. The back of the house was not. *Stupid.*

I had seen enough for the time being. I knew I would be able to get to this yard, and once here, should be able to get into the house through that basement door.

Keeping in the shadows as well as I could, I ran back across to the shed. After a moment of mental rehearsal, and not without some struggle, I was able to pull myself back up through the window and into the shed. After closing and locking the window, I was interested to see that the mower was now back to its original position on top of the old trapdoor. As I walked to the other side of the shed, thinking it over, I realized I was walking slightly uphill. With age and settling, the shed had become just barely tilted to the one side, enough to make the mower roll back over the trapdoor after it was closed. *Beautiful.*

With a careful look around at the shed floor, I found a small scrap of wood, doubtless left over from some old project. With the mower rolled back away from the trapdoor again, I jammed the piece of wood against one of the wheels to hold it in place. After grabbing my backpack and lowering myself back down into the tunnel shaft, I pulled the scrap of wood away from the wheel and tossed it to the side, where I could use it again on my next trip through. With the trapdoor fully down, I listened for a moment until I heard the sound of the mower's wheels as it rolled back to settle in overhead.

On my trip back through the tunnels to the Rutherford Mansion, I closed the steel gates but left the padlocks hanging unlocked. Back in the basement of the big house, I did the same, but carefully piled all the wicker chairs back against the wall to hide the lock and the door. I took a minute to send the pick-up message to Tommy, and less than five minutes later we were driving out of the neighborhood.

I described my trip through the estate and the tunnels, and my findings at the basement door of the senator's house.

"According to the gizmo," I said, "the door isn't alarmed. I find that strange."

"Agreed," Tommy said, "but remember, you're talking about a guy who has twenty-four hour police protection. Most of us don't get that. Were there many spiders? I hate spiders."

"Thankfully not many," I said. "A few rats, which don't bother me much. Anyway, a successful night. Showtime tomorrow as long as Sophia gets that stuff to us in time."

I could see Tommy nod in the dark car. It was a hot night, and as we took the ramp to enter the highway outside of town, he hit the button to open the sunroof. A cool wind poured out of the star-filled sky and into the car, surrounding us with the scent of summer in the country.

35

It was mid-afternoon when Tommy drove us up the street towards Bernard Sykes' apartment. After cruising by for a good look, it was our intent to stake out the place from a block away and wait for him to leave. I would then break into his apartment and be ready to take him down when he came in. Sophia had told me that the main house belonged to Sykes, and real estate listings told us that it was currently unoccupied. It was my plan to enter the house at ground level and then get into Sykes' apartment via the shared second floor deck.

"Look, the driveway's empty," Tommy said, as we came near the house. "I think opportunity knocks. I'll go around the block and come up again on the other side."

Tommy made a long, full circuit around the block and started the approach to the empty house again. The driveway of the house just before it was also empty, so Tommy backed the car into there as though to facilitate a U-turn, pausing just long enough to allow me to jump out and run back along the fence to the rear and out of sight.

I was at the rear of a narrow alley between the houses, completely paved over, and home to a number of trash cans. I estimated the houses to be about twenty feet apart at their closest point, with the alley being evenly split all the way out to the street by a five-foot high white vinyl fence. The trash cans were fairly new, clean, and didn't smell, all of which gave me the impression that the house I was outside of was as empty as the target house next door. I risked a look into one of the windows and saw a sparsely furnished interior with nothing on the walls.

Good. I haven't been seen yet.

After a long look over the fence, I set one of the smaller metal trashcans upside down and used the shaky platform to help me hoist myself over, dropping down into the alley on the other side. I moved to the small back yard, where a door opened up onto a patio just large enough for a few plastic chairs and a gas grill. Finding that the door was not alarmed, I got out my lock-pick set, entering the house and closing the door behind me a few minutes later. I stood still just inside the door to listen for a moment. The presence of a large sink, along with a washer and dryer set, told me that I was in the home's laundry room. Two units of plastic shelving took up part of the extra space, and were stocked with the typical assortment of toilet paper, paper towels, and cleaning supplies.

The next room looked like a small pantry, with plenty of empty shelves, and after that was the kitchen. The house had the clean smell and unnaturally empty feel of a rental unit waiting for the next tenant. As I moved from the kitchen into an adjoining dining room, I noted the smell of paint, and the sharp, distinctive scent of silicone caulk. It all made sense when I moved through the dining room and saw the evidence of ongoing work: a ladder leaning against the doorway, a folded canvas drop cloth, and an assortment of painting equipment gathered together in a corner. *The last tenant must have hung pictures and left some holes in the wall. Nothing going on here. Let's get me up onto that deck.*

I moved past the tools towards the next room, where I could see the bottom of a flight of stairs. Just as I passed the ladder, I heard something behind me, and reacted instinctively, reaching to draw my gun as I turned. My spin was just clumsy enough that my left elbow caught the side of the ladder, sending a sharp pain all through my arm. As the ladder fell against me, catching my arm between two of the rungs, I fell back through the doorway. I heard a pistol shot ring out. I sensed, as much as felt the bullet fly over me as I fell, and then another boom filled the house. The second bullet slammed into the wooden doorframe, and then a third boom filled the air, and that bullet ricocheted off a rung of the ladder inches from my face. Fortunately, the ladder was lightweight aluminum and didn't cause me much damage as we hit the floor together. With my left arm still stuck, I was finally able to raise my right enough to get off a shot back towards my assailant in the kitchen. I caught enough of a quick glimpse to tell me that it was Sykes. I didn't think I had hit him, but taking return fire had at least thrown him off balance.

Finally getting my left arm free of the ladder, I shoved it as hard as I could, like a lousy approximation of a spear, along the floor and into the kitchen. It wasn't much of a weapon, but from my vantage point on the floor I could see that it hit Sykes on the shin as he appeared again in the doorway. It was good for throwing him off for another second or two, and he ducked back out of sight with a loud curse. I used the few seconds to get myself into a crouch on the other side of the doorway that I'd just fallen through.

It was brilliant sunshine outside, and the light streaming through the kitchen windows cast shadows across the floor. I watched the ghostly shapes move across the floor just inside the kitchen and decided that Sykes must be pressed against the wall, just inside to the right. I took aim at the wall ten inches in from the doorjamb, five feet from the floor, and fired three times. He screamed and fell down, stretched across the doorway, but still managed to twist and get off another shot, putting a bullet into a paint can two feet from me. I took steady aim and put my next bullet into the center of his face. He jerked a few times, as though experiencing an electric shock, and then was still.

I approached him slowly, my gun still at the ready. He was not moving and appeared very dead. I gave him another slug in the chest, just in case.

That business aside, I went around to several windows, looking out at the street and the neighboring houses. Having planned to deal with Sykes later, with the suppressor attached to my pistol, I was concerned about having ended up in a full blown, banging gunfight in a suburban house in the afternoon. Fortunately, the area had a high vacancy rate and I didn't see any sign of a public reaction.

Returning to the body, I felt through his pockets until I found a wallet, and was relieved to find a driver's license confirming that the man I had just killed was in fact,

Bernard Sykes. I found a phone in another pocket, and was again relieved, since I had missed my chance to interrogate the guy, that it wasn't secured with an access code. I took a quick look through his recent texts and saw several conversations between him and "Bartlett."

I took out my own phone to call Tommy, noticing first that I had missed a text from him just minutes ago: *Heads up. Dark Blue Ford Explorer on street a block away.*

I called him and he answered immediately.

"Hey, what's up? I'm two streets over. Did you get my text?"

"I got it, but only just now," I said. "It's all over already. I never made it to the apartment. He was here in the empty house. You know what I mean—he was in here for some reason. There's a room full of painting and spackling stuff, so maybe he was just getting ready to do some work on the place. Get it ready for the next renter."

"Got it. What's your status? You hurt?"

"Just banged up, probably have some bruises, and I whacked my damn funny bone pretty good. Oh, and looks like I cut my arm too—shit. I was attacked by an aluminum ladder, but I think I owe it my life. I'll explain everything later. Anyway, I got his phone and it's not locked. Give me a few to check out his apartment, then I'll call you for a pick-up."

"Fine. I'll pull up down the street where I can keep an eye on the outside and wait for your call," Tommy said.

I didn't find any keys on Sykes, so guessed he had just wandered over and left his apartment door unlocked. I found a small sunroom on the second floor where a door opened up to the deck that connected the house to the apartment and garage. It was unlocked, as was the door into the apartment. Sykes must have been a better house-keeper than many men who live alone, because there were no dirty dishes in the sink, just a few freshly washed items in the drying rack. The bathroom was spic and span and the bed was neatly made. I spent ten minutes going through drawers and closets, finding nothing that we didn't already know as far as Sykes' plans or relationship to his confederates. I dumped out a few drawers and left others hanging open, thinking to give whoever came upon the scene the idea that he had been the victim of a robbery. Sweeping my hand between his mattress and box spring revealed another loaded handgun, along with a thick enve-lope that looked like it held five or more thousand dollars in cash. I dropped the gun and the cash into a small canvas tote bag I found at the bottom of the closet and took them with me. As I left, I pocketed a set of Ford car keys that I found in a dish by the door.

On my way back across the small deck to the main house, I looked down and noticed a pair of buckets and a long-handled push broom below in the driveway. *Ah*, I thought, nodding to myself, *he must have been planning to scrub the driveway or something. That's why he moved the car out onto the street.*

Back in the main house, I added the dead man's wallet, watch, phone, and the first gun to the canvas bag, before calling Tommy for a pick-up. I didn't bother collecting my spent brass, knowing I would be discarding the Heckler & Koch in another day or so.

Three minutes later, Tommy backed into the neighbor's driveway again and I jumped in. He drove us halfway down the block to the blue Explorer, where I confirmed that it was Sykes' car by clicking the unlock button and getting a flash of the headlights in response. A man was mowing his lawn a few houses down, and a lady had just passed by on the sidewalk with her dog, but neither of them seemed interested in us. I got out of Tommy's car and into the Explorer. I started it and followed Tommy as he drove away.

Once outside of the immediate area, we pulled into a drugstore parking lot and I joined Tommy in his car for a conference. We examined the cut on my arm and decided it could be patched up back at the hotel. The arm was feeling better, but several other spots on my body were complaining. I hoped it would be downhill after Sykes.

"So now we need to text Bartlett," Tommy said. "What time do you think they should meet? I'm thinking just late enough that it's dark outside, but not much later than that."

"Right, agreed," I said. "We don't want to freak him out."

I got out Sykes' phone and texted to Gavin Bartlett: *Need to see you. Can you meet at the hangar tonight?*

The response came within two minutes: *Christ, man, how about a little more notice? It's Saturday. How about Monday?*

I texted back to him: *I need to get you some information in person, then I need to get out of the area.*

The response came in less than a minute: *What the hell is so important?*

I looked at Tommy, thinking for a moment before speaking. "If we're right about the relationship between these two, Bartlett is probably irritated with Sykes and wouldn't mind if he just went away."

"Yeah," he said. "And probably more than a little bit afraid of him too. Play that up."

I texted back to Bartlett: *It's almost over. Meet me tonight at ten, I'll give you the info and then I'll get out of your life.*

Bartlett's response came right back: *Alright, I'll meet you at the hangar at ten.*

"The game's afoot," Tommy said.

36

It was shortly after nine when Tommy drove into the airport complex, with me following in Sykes' Explorer a minute later. The plan was for him to drive all the way up to the t-intersection by the airline office, and then make a left to go off in the opposite direction. That way, if the security guard was in a curious mood, Tommy would be the bait and lead him out of the way, while I quietly drove in and around the perimeter road to the CBC building. We were both wearing our combat comm units. Tommy's voice came through my earpiece just as I turned in from the main road.

"I see the security vehicle parked outside the office, but there's nobody in it. I'm guessing he's inside somewhere."

"Great, I'm coming in, then," I said. "I'll proceed across to CBC. You can wait at the rendezvous point."

"Will do, and be careful," came his reply.

I followed the road around and up to the CBC building, seeing no cars anywhere outside. Checking my watch, I saw I had arrived fifteen minutes before the scheduled meeting with Bartlett. Leaving the Explorer in plain sight next to the door, I easily picked the lock and went inside to prepare for the meeting.

It was a few minutes before ten when I saw a set of head-lights separate from the airport buildings across the field and follow the perimeter road around towards the hangar. As the car got closer, I was glad to see it was a Cadillac sedan. Gavin Bartlett parked next to Sykes' Explorer, got out, and went up to the hangar door. I approached quietly from behind. As he reached for the door handle, I shoved the Vipertek stun gun into the small of his back and hit the trigger. He went rigid and made a gurgling noise before falling to the ground in a heap.

I immediately dropped to one knee beside him and jabbed him in the neck with a dose of a powerful and fast-acting sedative. A "Mickey Finn" of sorts, but one that came dressed up as a needle. His eyes closed and he went limp almost immediately. I checked my watch, verifying that I would have plenty of time to get him trussed up. I opened the door and dragged him inside, thankful he wasn't a large man. With some minor difficulty, I got him seated into the folding chair I had set out and attached him firmly to it with duct tape. A strip of tape across his mouth served as an effective gag.

Twenty minutes later, after completing some further preparations, I stuck him in the neck with a dose of stimu-lant specifically tailored to counteract the knockout drug I'd given him before. He awoke with a start, wide-eyed and struggling futilely against the duct tape. I slapped him hard across the face to get his attention.

"Try to relax, Mr. Bartlett, and I might be able to take off that gag."

I held up my government ID in its little folding case, complete with a fancy-looking, gold plated, fake badge, close enough for him to almost read, before shoving it back into my pocket.

"You are in the custody of the federal government. My team has been investigating a domestic terrorist threat involving Mr. Sykes, Mr. West, the Booth brothers, and even your famous father-in-law. You are right in the middle of all of it." His eyes were already as wide as they could get, but he still tried. "Mr. Sykes was arrested this afternoon, and I used his phone to arrange this meeting. We have the texts and the phone calls you've exchanged over the past few weeks, we have calls between him and Bobby Booth, we have records of large deposits coming in to your company, and then payments going out—we have it all, Mr. Bartlett. The jig is up. There may be some options for you to get out of this, but that window won't be open very wide or very long. Now nod if you'd like to have a reasonable conversation about that."

His eyes were filled with suspicion, but he nodded vigorously.

I found the end of the tape that I'd folded over and yanked the strip off his face. He cursed loudly at the shock.

"Sorry, Mr. Bartlett, I find it's best to just yank it off quickly."

"Who are you?" he said. "You knock me out and tie me up—you can't just do that! I have a right to an attorney."

I slapped him across the face again and he looked at me in shock.

"I took the tape off so we could have a conversation," I said. "If you're going to yell, I have more tape."

He looked like he was going to yell again, but stopped himself, settling back and taking a breath. "Am I under arrest? I have a right to a phone call. I have a right to a lawyer."

I pulled a chair up to him and sat down, leaning in before speaking. "Do I look like a cop? No, you are not under arrest—yet. And as to your phone call and your lawyer, that's rich, Mr. Bartlett. Tell me something. The innocent people your friends were planning to blow up, were you going to get them a lawyer? As far as your rights, forget about it. You may, just maybe, be able to go back to your life if you cooperate with me. If not, well, things probably won't go well for you. Haven't you heard of the Patriot Act? Guantanamo Bay? Extraordinary rendition? No, Mr. Bartlett, you play ball with me or you're going to be filed away in a cold, dark cell somewhere and your family will think you ran off to Costa Rica with some young chica. You'll waste away on a diet of cold rice and beans. So I'll say this one time only—spare me any more of your bullshit protestations. You get me?"

"Yes, I get you," he said. "What do you want from me?"

"We want your father-in-law to resign and go away," I said. "We don't believe we can prosecute him, but we want him out of the picture. He can retire and keep his pension, so to speak. But I need your help with a little bit of play-acting to make that happen."

"I don't know," he said. He was shaking his head slowly. "I can't do anything like that."

"Excuse me," I said. I pretended my phone had vibrated in my pocket. I stood and walked a dozen feet away to act like I was answering and taking a call. I spoke just loud enough for him to hear me.

"Yeah, how did it go? Great—no trouble, then? Keep them separated and don't let them talk to anyone. No, definitely no lawyers. Right, yes, Louise is her name. I'm with her husband right now. Great—send a unit here to the hangar to pick him up. Soon as you can get here. Right, see you in a half hour."

I returned the phone to my pocket as I walked back towards him. I had seen his reaction when I said his wife's name.

"Who was that? You said my wife's name. She has nothing to do with any of this."

"That was the team that's been covering your wife and your mother-in-law on their promotional tour around the state. They were both taken into custody an hour ago. I agree with you, Mr. Bartlett. I doubt either of those ladies had anything to do with your sick plot, but we can't be too careful. Anyway, we can only hold them for a month without charging, so we'll see what shakes out. Of course they'll be in the general prison population."

Bartlett's face was red with anger and excitement; he was straining against his bonds.

I slapped him again while he was still trying to spit out whatever terrible diatribe he wanted to hurl at me. "I've got a whole bag of slaps—and worse—where that came from, so cool it. Remember the tape. Keep calm and quiet.

All I need you to do is to talk into the camera. Ask your father-in-law to help your wife out of this jam. Just need to read a few lines, and then we can talk about a deal. How's that all sound? Can you do that?"

"I can do it," he said. "I'll say what you want."

"Good," I said. "Good man. There's a light at the end of the tunnel for you, see? Let me get my camera."

I used my tablet to film him for several minutes, moving in and out and around him to capture different angles. I made sure the sound was recording properly when he read the few lines I had written out for him. When I felt that I had enough footage of him, I went over to a corner outside a small office and set the tablet up on a portable tripod.

"You did good, Mr. Bartlett. I'll make sure your assistance is taken into consideration."

I adjusted the camera to capture a wide view of Bartlett, still in the chair, which was about five feet out from the giant section of cement wall. I pulled a pair of foam earplugs from my shirt pocket and twisted them into my ears.

"What the hell are you doing?" Bartlett yelled across the large space to me. "I did what you asked. Now untie me."

"Hang in there," I said, loudly. "You'll be done in few seconds."

I saw him nod.

I touched the screen of the tablet to restart filming, then turned quickly and ducked into one of the small offices. Earlier, I had set the two little remote detonator switches out in the proper order.

I pressed the button on the first one. A fraction of a

second later, the detonators buried inside the blocks of C4 plastic explosive affixed to each top corner of the wall segment fired, setting off the high-velocity explosive and instantly severing the support cables that held the wall in a vertical position.

The huge wall, now standing free, wavered back and forth slightly, unable to decide which way to fall. Bartlett strained in the chair, trying to twist around to look behind him, as he screamed in terror.

I pressed the red button on the second transmitter. A half-pound shaped charge of C4 exploded against the rear of the wall, two feet down from the top edge. The force of the blast pushed the thing violently forward, as though hinged at the bottom, to fall flat onto the floor, crushing Bartlett like an ant under the heel of a heavy work boot.

While I had braced myself for the shock of the explosions in the enclosed space, I hadn't anticipated the violent blast of air that shot out from under the giant wall segment as it fall flat. Like a huge invisible hand, it swatted me off my feet and into a heavy wooden desk that stood in the middle of the room, and the world around me went black.

I came awake to the smell of burned high explosive. I pulled the earplugs out of my ears and the smell was joined by the wail of a distant siren. Sitting up, and then using the old desk to help myself stand, I realized that I had probably only blacked out for a minute at most. I stretched and shook myself, rubbing the large patch of my left side that had taken the brunt of my meeting with the desk. The distant siren was getting less distant.

As quickly as I could, I detached the tablet from the tripod and then spent twenty seconds to film some close-ups of the edge of the wall, which was flat against the floor, along with a pan of the overall scene. I stowed the tablet into my pack, along with the collapsed tripod. I tossed the keys to Sykes' Explorer onto the floor of the office. I opened the door slowly, looking out across the field towards the airport buildings. There was activity there, numerous lights and shapes running around. A set of headlights had started across the field towards the hangar.

Outside, I hightailed it back to the corner of the building nearest the tree line, where I paused for a few seconds to use a small flashlight to signal Tommy. His answering signal came back right away. I ran across the rear lawn to the spot on the fence that Tommy had signaled from, passing my pack over to him and climbing over the fence. We could hear sirens and shouting arriving at the CBC building as we loaded into the car.

"Whew, that was exciting," I said. I rolled down my window to help clear the scent of burnt explosive from my nostrils.

"I bet it was," Tommy said. "I'm sorry I'm missing out on all the action. How was Bartlett?"

"You know," I said, "he really didn't seem like such a bad guy. As a matter of fact, it turned out he didn't support the wall after all."

37

W ilfred O'Donnell turned off the burner when the teakettle whistled, and filled his cup with hot water. His wife of almost fifty years was away, touring the state with their daughter as part of some tourism promotion program, but his long-time mistress—insomnia—was with him still in the house. The stresses of a lifetime in politics, including decades at the top of the legislative branch as a respected senior senator, had wedded the two together long ago. He considered himself lucky that he was able to function as well as he did on just a few hours of sleep each night. At his age, and with his variety of aches, pains, and afflictions, a long, solid sleep was nothing but a distant fantasy.

Looking out the kitchen window across the dark yard as he stirred his tea, he thought about the grand plan he had put together with his billionaire friends, the Kone brothers. The whole thing had fallen apart over the past week or two, though he didn't yet know who was to blame. Who the hell could it be other than the CIA, he wondered, but how could he not have gotten wind of that? At any rate, it was time to cut losses and look for some other way to stir the pot and get that wall built. He regretted ever letting Sykes get involved with those damn Booth brothers, but at least he and Gavin were untouchable.

He dropped his spoon in the sink and went out of the kitchen towards his private study, where at least he could get some reading done.

It was one-twenty in the morning when the senator pushed open the door to his study and entered. With his tea in his left hand, he flicked a switch up with his right as he turned to walk to the massive oak desk, turning on a trio of brass sconces mounted to the dark wood paneling on three sides of the room. Sitting down behind the desk, he pulled the chain on an old fashioned green-shaded banker's lamp, bathing the desktop in a warm light.

"Good morning, Senator," I said, as I stepped out from the darkness in the far corner of the room. His hand jerked in surprise and the teacup tumbled off the desk. As old and frail as he looked, I was surprised by the quickness with which he reached to the underside of his desk. I could tell by the motion of his arm that he was repeatedly pressing the alarm button mounted there.

I raised my left hand to show him the device I was holding, which was about the size of a deck of cards, flat black, and with several colored LED lights and a small digital display. "You can stop bothering with that. I'm jamming any signal from leaving this room or the immediate vicinity. The police in the car outside won't be bothered. Just stay calm so we can talk for a few minutes. I won't take much of your time." I dropped the jammer unit into a pocket.

"Who are you?" he said. "Do you have any idea how much trouble I can make for you? You're no burglar. CIA, right? Or is it someone else?" He relaxed some, changing his position in the chair. I could tell he was reaching for one of the drawers to his right. Either he had not noticed the big automatic in my hand or was unafraid of it for some reason. I let him play out his move.

With another surprisingly fast motion, he produced a large pistol, pointed it at me, and pulled the trigger. There was a substantial metallic click, followed by several more as he manually cocked the pistol's hammer back and pulled the trigger. He deflated as he realized he was trying to shoot me with an unloaded gun. With a dejected look, he set it down on the leather desk pad.

"Really now, Senator, how many times am I going to have to tell people that if you're going to have a gun in the house, you need to be familiar with the thing? As a good son of Kentucky, you should know better. That's a Colt Single Action Army, weighs about two and a half pounds. It would weigh almost a half-pound more if it was loaded." I held out a hand to show him the six shiny cartridges, before dumping them into another pocket.

The room was a classic example of the private study of an old, rich, powerful man. Oak or mahogany paneling, stained darker than it would naturally be and highly polished. Shelves full of law journals and old classics of literature. The big desk was along one wall, with three armchairs, upholstered in rich leather, facing it in a semi-circle from a few feet away. There were three mounted deer heads on the walls; light from the sconces played with the antlers to paint eerie fingers of shadow on the ceiling.

In a lightning-fast motion, I brought up my right hand and shot the three dead deer in their necks. The pistol's suppressor did its job; the sound could not have been heard even from a few rooms away. The three shots had happened so close together that they hit the ear as one. The three ejected shell cases dropping to the office floor made their own barely perceptible thump as they fell to the thick carpet almost at the same time, rolling no more than a few inches before settling in place.

The senator jumped in his chair, pushing it sharply back to hit the rail behind him with a crack louder than my three shots had generated.

"I just wanted you to see that *my* gun is loaded, and I know how to use it. Got it? Now, sit still and don't try anything else that might irritate me."

"I just realized," he said, "you're here to kill me. There's no way you could break into my house, fire a gun, and expect to just walk away. This must be some kind of coup."

"No, no coup," I said, "and I'm not here to kill you. As a matter of fact, I have specific orders NOT to kill you." I kept one eye on him and the gun pointed in his general direction as I scooped up the three brass shell casings from the carpet and pocketed them.

"Orders from who?" he said, jumping in. "Who do you work for? It can't be anybody I don't know. And if you really aren't going to kill me, surely you realize that I'll have their job and you'll be going to jail."

I stepped closer, leveling the gun at him in the light from the banker's lamp. "I said I didn't come here to kill you, and that I had orders not to, but I also advised you not to irritate me, so don't test me." I checked my watch. "I don't have much time, Senator, so I'll get to the point without making it a long story. Gavin Bartlett, Sykes, West, Booth, a bomb in a U.S. city…"

He dropped his chin and sank into himself. The breath went out of him in a deep sigh and I thought he must have lost ten percent of his mass. He shook his head—not, it seemed to me, in denial—but in despair.

"Yeah, that's right," I said. "You get it. That's why I'm here. You want evidence? We've got it all. Phone records, meetings, payments—you name it. But I told you I'd keep it short, so let me show you something that'll cut right to it."

I walked back to the dark corner to get the tablet from my pack, bringing it to the desk to set in front of the senator. I used the touchscreen to start a video. I moved to just beside him, keeping the gun leveled at him, as he leaned in close to watch the screen.

The camera jiggled back and forth a bit as the focus and exposure was adjusted to settle on the face of Gavin Bartlett. A gasp from the senator told me that he recognized him immediately. The camera panned out to show Bartlett taped to a chair, and then out farther to show the chair against the section of cement wall.

"Were you aware of the CBC building out at the airport?" I said. "The wall showroom?"

"I've been there, yes," he said.

I gestured to him to keep watching, and he turned his attention back to the screen.

The camera panned around the room, showing the scale of the wall in the huge space, with Bartlett in the chair in front of it, before zooming back in to focus on his face. He looked right into the camera and spoke.

"It's me, Will. It's Gavin. These people are some kind of government agents and they have me in custody. They know all about Sykes and the other guys, and they know all about the bomb plot. It's all over, it really is. Listen to me, Will—they've got Louise also. They tell me they'll make sure she goes to jail if you don't help them. I don't care about myself anymore, but please, Will, help Louise. The kids need her. Do what they want, Will."

Bartlett appeared to respond to some off-screen instruction, and the camera panned back out. The picture was interrupted for a second before settling again on a long view of the wall. Suddenly, the screen shook and there was a loud explosion. Bartlett seemed to jump and tried to struggle with the chair as he looked around. The whole wall behind him appeared to sway. A second explosion followed and Bartlett disappeared as the wall fell towards the camera and flat onto the floor.

Senator O'Donnell, watching closely, let out a low moan and shook his head back and forth. "No, no, no. You can't have done that. You can't do that. Is he...?"

"Oh we did it alright," I said. "You better believe we did it. He's probably a half-inch thick at this point. Look."

As he looked back at the screen, the picture adjusted as the camera tried to focus through a cloud of dust and dirt. There was a wide view of the huge space with the wall section, cracked and broken in many places, now lying flat out on the showroom floor.

The senator tore himself away from the screen and buried his face in his hands. "You sick bastards. You can't do that. You're a murderer."

"A murderer, ha—you're too much," I said. "Isn't that exactly what you and Bartlett were planning to do? Murder? What would your wife and the other good people of Kentucky think about that? Senator Wilfred O'Donnell, mass murderer of innocent Americans. Not much of a ring to it..."

He looked down in silence for a few seconds before appearing to suddenly realize something. He looked up and spoke angrily. "My daughter, Louise, she had nothing to do with any of this. You say you have evidence, so you must know that. She didn't even know about it. Gavin said she was in custody—why?"

"We have her, yes," I said. "Let's watch the next video."

I fiddled with the controls on the tablet for a few seconds before setting it back on the desk in front of him. The scene this time was very similar to parts of the Bartlett film, with a figure apparently tied to a chair in front of the same wall. This time though, the figure was smaller, and appeared to have long blond hair. From a distance, the person in the chair was still, but as the camera zoomed in, with several cuts and some bouncing around, a woman's face came into focus.

"That's my daughter!" the senator yelled. He started to rise out of his chair; his right arm came back as though he was going to hit me. A sharp smack across the ear with my gun settled him back down, and he sat still.

"Take a breath and watch. This video is a little choppy because the camera fell when the first wall came down."

The picture froze for a few seconds in a close-up of Louise O'Donnell-Bartlett's face. Her mouth was open like she was in the middle of saying something, but there was no sound. Then there were a few quick cuts as the view panned out again to show her taped to the chair, and then out further to show the whole scene again.

"Who the hell are you?" he said. "I don't even think the CIA would do something like this."

"We are the people who do the dirty work, and you, tonight, are just that—dirty work." I looked at my watch again. "Anyway, the Booth brothers are dead, as well as Sykes, West, and quite a few others that got involved in your sick plot. And now your son-in-law Gavin Bartlett too. Squashed like a bug, in fact. Just a stain on a cement floor. As you see in the video, we are prepared to make the same thing happen to your daughter." I made a show of checking my watch again. "That is scheduled for just about ninety minutes out from right now. It will happen automatically if I don't stop it."

"Leave my daughter out of this. What do you want from me? I suppose you want me to resign."

"You're getting warm," I said. "Look, Senator, I'll spell it out for you. You've had eighty-nine good years and a long career of public service. You've kept it a secret so far, but we know about your cancer. You probably don't have more than a year, a year and a half at most. Why not leave on your own terms, with your illness as cover, and preserve your legacy?" I set a small glass vial on the leather blotter in front of him. "My friends at Langley tell me this won't take more than ten or twenty seconds. Alternatively…" I pushed the empty Colt revolver across the blotter towards him, and set two of the shells down beside it. "Sure would be great if I could make the call to cut your daughter loose. She could go on to a good life of running the company and raising your grandchildren. You could avoid the disgrace of arrest and trial for treason and conspiracy to commit murder."

"What guarantee do I have that you won't just kill her anyway?"

"None, really," I said, "except that I would have no motivation to do that. I know she's innocent, and I don't kill innocent people. No, Senator, you do this...this thing, within fifteen minutes, and your daughter will be free and clear. If you don't, well, you have only just begun to know pain and misery."

He sat silently for a full thirty seconds before he spoke again. He pointed across the room.

"I presume the condemned man is allowed a drink? Over there on that side table is a bottle of bourbon and some glasses. If you would please. Join me if you like."

I picked up the bottle and two of the heavy rocks glasses that sat next to it. I was amazed to see that it was a fifteen-year Pappy Van Winkle; bourbon so rare and hard to acquire that it would never be anything but a myth for most people. *Perks of being a Kentucky senator, I guess*. I filled both glasses halfway and set one in front of him. He pushed the vial of poison towards me.

"I won't be needing that," he said. "Nobody who knows me would believe that anyway. I'm tired, and I've done my bit. I'll do as you ask." He raised his arm and pointed his finger at me. "But hear me, young man—if you have any decency in you—I charge you with making sure my daughter is safe and clear of all this."

"It will be done," I said. "You have my word on it. But remember where she's sitting and remember that the clock is ticking."

We both raised our glasses to sip the ultra-rare whiskey, and the taste of its amber fire was glorious. Though later I would understand the idea to be absurd, I briefly felt that the senator and I were sharing some sort of elegant moment. For me, a professional killer largely numbed to the worst that people could do to one another, the fine liquor was a few seconds of respite. For the senator, it was a glass of liquid solace as he faced his final reckoning, and looked into the uncaring blackness of eternity.

Draining my glass, I set it on the corner of the desk and poured more for the senator, leaving him the bottle. I closed the tablet and took it back over to stow in my pack, coming back with a small device that looked like a kind of pocket camera. I held it up for him to see and then positioned it on one of the bookshelves across the room from his desk. With an inspection of the furry necks of each of the mounted stags, I satisfied myself that the new bullet holes were not noticeable. I came back towards the desk, where the senator was nursing his drink, making a show of checking my watch again and rotating the bezel to start timing.

"I think we have an understanding now, Senator, so I'll go outside and give you your privacy. The camera over there on the shelf will transmit images to me wirelessly, so I'll know what happens in this room. Whether or not you leave a note is up to you, but I suggest that anything that will bolster the story we discussed would be good. You now have ten minutes."

Leaving him to his drink and his thoughts, I took the glass I had used and my backpack out of the room and through the house to the kitchen, where I rinsed the glass and set it on the drying rack. The little camera I'd left on the bookshelf—being just some strange model that I'd picked up at a thrift shop—had no connection to me and probably wouldn't be noticed or questioned.

It was almost exactly nine minutes later, just as Tommy picked me up again at the corner of the Rutherford Estate, when we heard the sound of the shot.

"That was interesting," Tommy said. ".45? Certainly not a Magnum."

"You pegged it," I said. ".45 Long Colt. He had an old Peacemaker. In different circumstances I would have stolen it. Nice piece."

Tommy already had us two streets away as we proceeded calmly and quickly out of the neighborhood. "Want me to turn around so you can go back down the tunnel and get it?"

"I'd slap you if you weren't driving," I said. "He had a bottle of Pappy Van Winkle also."

"Are you fucking kidding me?" Tommy said. "The Holy Grail of bourbon? I know you brought it with you, right?"

"No," I said. "I thought about it, but it didn't seem right at the time."

In the light of a pair of passing headlights I saw him shaking his head in exaggerated disbelief.

"You really need a vacation," he said. "We gotta get you

to a sunny beach for a week or two. And I owe you one anyway. Next time you drive and I'll do all the work."

"Vacation sounds good, T," I said. "Let's coordinate that. You know, this job has really gotten to me in some ways. I don't know how much more I can take."

"I understand, buddy," Tommy said. "I understand. All the violence and, you know, the killing—can really take its toll on you."

"Yeah, you're right," I said, "but it's not that. I'm talking about the lying. I hate lying to people. Not my nature at all." Tommy had found the ramp to the highway and hit the loud pedal to get up to speed on the mostly empty road. The dashboard clock proclaimed that it was almost two in the morning. "Hey, if you're up for it, let's see if we can find a bar that's still open. I'll buy you a drink."

"We'll toast to a successful mission," Tommy said. "We can pretend it's the Pappy Van Winkle that you thoughtlessly left behind."

With over a hundred-billion dollars in annual revenue, and employing a hundred-thousand people in sixty countries, Kone Industries was one of the world's largest privately held corporations. With a focus on all aspects of finding, refining, and distributing fossil fuels, the company also had substantial interests in paper production, international shipping, chemicals, mineral mining, and heavy equipment.

The multi-billionaire brothers who ran the company, Charles and David Kone, consistently made the list of the world's richest people, each with a net worth in the tens of billions. Over most of the past twenty years, while still at the helm of their huge conglomerate, the brothers had become better known to most of the public for their outspoken support of conservative and libertarian political policies and candidates.

Over time, the Kone brothers became synonymous with the exercise of behind-the-scenes political influence, in no small part due to the fact that Kone Industries was not a public corporation, and therefore had no obligation to disclose its financial dealings.

When David Kone, the older of the brothers, surrendered the reins of power and went mostly into seclusion due to numerous mental and physical health issues, his brother Charles decided to focus his own energies on ways to use his money and influence to support his political vision for the country. With a serious heart attack and quadruple bypass surgery less than a year behind him, Kone rarely left the security and comfort of his vast estate outside Wichita, Kansas. Most mornings, he grudgingly followed doctor's orders to spend some time on the treadmill before reading through the daily mail, along with various reports and updates related to his corporate holdings.

It was one sunny morning, a week after he had learned about the surprise suicide of Senator O'Donnell, that he slit open a particular manila envelope and started to look over the few pages within. Being an experienced businessman, he quickly realized the first page was what appeared to be an enlargement of a section of some kind of bank statement. He recognized the name of the organization at the top of the page as that of one of Kone Industry's smaller subsidiaries. Someone had circled parts and used a yellow highlighter on other parts in order to demonstrate that the Kone company had made a series of transfers totaling over three million dollars to some other entity.

The second page also showed part of a bank statement, with further highlighting indicating the owner of the receiving account was a company not familiar to him. Kone's expression changed when he read the short paragraph someone had added, which explained that the receiving company was in fact a shell company controlled by Gavin Bartlett of Consolidated Barrier Corporation.

The upper portion of the third page at first looked to Charles Kone like part of a movie script. He was momentarily confused until he saw that someone had added a note at the bottom of the section.

The above was taken from a cell phone conversation that occurred on 18 July of this year. The speakers have been identified as one Gavin Bartlett, CEO and majority owner of Consolidated Barrier Corporation, and Senator Wilfred O'Donnell, both of Kentucky. Note that Senator O'Donnell is Bartlett's father-in-law.

As Kone read the small segment of conversation, he felt several different bodily reactions. His throat suddenly became very dry, and took on a distinct feeling of tightness. He felt warm moisture on the sides and back of his neck, and realized he had started to sweat. He felt a type of pain in the middle of his chest that had become all too familiar to him in the last year. He feared that particular pain and respected it, but after a few deep and calming breaths, he continued to read.

Bartlett: ...so I got that new company all set up, and I see that the money showed up yesterday.

Senator: Good. My friend in Wichita will be happy that we're finally doing something. Hopefully this gets results. He's also sending two people to you that have helped him out in the past... with... unsavory tasks. I'm told that a man named Sykes will be in touch.

Bartlett: He already contacted me. I'm meeting with him tomorrow. Not sure if the other guy will be with him. Man named West is what he told me. I'll get them both on the payroll right away.

Senator: Well, keep in touch and keep me informed. And hang in there, Gavin, we'll get that damn wall built and the company will be in great shape.

At the bottom of the third page was a hand-written note.

Dear Mr. Kone,

This has not YET been shared with the press or anyone else. Watch for further communications via the same channel.

A Concerned Citizen

When Kone finished reading, he sat back in his chair and closed his eyes, devoting ten minutes to the deep breathing technique that one of his therapists had taught him. It seemed to work, slowing his heart rate and easing the overall tightness in his throat and the rest of his body. He reached across his desk to press the button that would summon his personal assistant. A minute later there was a light knock on the door and a man entered.

"Yes, Mr. Kone?" the man asked. He was immaculately dressed in a light gray Brooks Brothers suit and polished wingtips. His conservative haircut framed a lightly tanned face. He looked to be about thirty-five. "What can I do for you?"

"Dan, where did this come from?" Charles Kone held up the manila envelope.

"That was in your private box, Mr. Kone, at the post office. You've made it clear that you want anything that comes to that box to be left in the private tray on your desk, unopened. Is there a problem sir?"

"No, no, Dan," Kone said. "Everything's fine. I think I just got myself confused for a minute. Keep doing exactly that. That's all for now."

Dammit! Kone thought to himself, as his assistant left the room. *How did those Kentucky idiots fuck this up? If this gets out...*

Four days later, another manila envelope arrived in Charles Kone's private IN bin. Coming into his office and approaching the desk with his morning coffee, he glared at the envelope for a full minute before sitting down and picking up his letter opener.

The first two pages of the contents caused him to look away sharply, disgusted, before turning back to take a long, careful look. The first page, printed on matte presentation paper, was a color picture of a dead man, with a notation identifying the man as Bernard Sykes. The man's face was mostly covered in blood, with a jagged hole—a bullet hole, presumably—where his left eye should have been. The second picture was also of a clearly dead man, shown propped against the side of a car. His arms were crossed over his belly, apparently to show off the fact that both hands had been severed at the wrists. The severed hands were cradled in his lap. The note indicated the man was James West.

The several printed pages that followed were annotated and highlighted. For both of the dead men, there was a page showing a history of banking transactions going back more than a year. In essence, the page for each man demonstrated that they had been on the payroll of a Kone company for at least a year in the past. The next two pages showed similar but more current information proving that both Sykes and West had recently been on the payroll of Consolidated Barrier Corporation.

The seventh and last page looked something like a phone bill, being a long list of calls to a certain number, showing dates and duration of calls. Someone had added a note explaining that the receiving mobile phone number was registered to someone named Bobby Booth, militant co-leader of a racist group called The New Confederates. Other notes pointed out that Bobby Booth's phone had received numerous recent calls from both James West and Bernard Sykes.

Similar to the package from the week before, the sender had indicated that more information would be coming soon.

The third package arrived just three days later. This time, Charles Kone only glared at it for a few seconds before tearing it open. There were several photos—apparently crime scene photos—showing what appeared to be a hotel room filled with bodies. Small stickers with notes and arrows had been added. There was Bobby Booth, there was his brother Darren Booth, there was Darren's girlfriend, there were the four other men, all with multiple gunshot wounds. A page accompanied the photos that was mostly blank, with just three typed lines at the top.

- Thirty to forty shots fired in this room, with none hitting walls or furniture.
- Thirty to forty shots fired in this room and nobody reported hearing anything.
- There is no security footage showing Bobby Booth and his two men entering the hotel at any time, nor are there any witnesses.

Charles Kone sat back in his chair and did his deep breathing exercises until his racing heart slowed and his mind cleared.

Somebody is laying the whole thing out, he thought to himself. *And lording it over me. How much are they going to ask for? I can't take much more mail like this.*

Kone placed the latest package into his special "Shred Box." He had long ago issued standing orders to his personal assistant to immediately destroy anything in that box should he ever become incapacitated or otherwise unable to act for himself for any reason, including his death.

The fourth package took four days to arrive. Kone circled his desk several times before cutting it open to find several more photographs inside. The first picture was a wide shot of what looked to him to be an aircraft hangar. The building looked old, but freshly painted and well maintained. Kone recognized the style of the sign attached to the top of the building, and after looking more closely, realized that the sign read "Consolidated Barrier Corporation."

The next picture must have been taken from somewhere high up inside the building, from a catwalk perhaps, Kone thought. The building contained no aircraft, but appeared to have been repurposed as a kind of test site—or showroom—for CBC's wall building business. In the foreground of the picture he could see a huge section of wall, standing upright. An ordinary chair sitting in front of the wall lent scale to the scene, and he guessed that the wall section must have been at least twenty-five or thirty feet high and almost twice that in length. It appeared to be about a foot thick. He could see heavy supporting cables attached to both upper corners of the wall section, and then anchored to fixtures high up on the wall of the building.

The third picture was a ground-level close up of a man tied up in a chair. Charles Kone did not recognize the man and puzzled over the picture for a minute before realizing that the chair the man was tied to was the one shown in the prior wide picture. Now with a man tied to it, it appeared to be eight or ten feet out from the wall. Someone had added a small sticker with a note identifying the man as Gavin Bartlett.

The next picture was another wide shot, but now the huge section of wall was lying flat across the floor. He could see cracks in several places, with large chunks of cement, or whatever the wall was made of, now broken off and scattered in all directions.

Alone at his desk, Kone shook his head in disbelief as he realized the implications of what he was looking at. He felt the dryness in his mouth and the tightness in his chest that had become all too common over the past few weeks. He turned to the last page, which was nothing but another photograph. He realized almost immediately that the last picture was a close up of one edge of the wall as it had fallen to the floor.

That wall must have weighed ten tons or more, he thought to himself, before pushing away from his desk, grabbing his trash can, and violently throwing up into it.

After much thought, Charles Kone decided that, whenever the next envelope arrived, and regardless of what terrible information it held, he would meet with his personal attorney and tell the whole story. Of course he would leave out anything related to knowledge of any kind of domestic terrorist plot or even the Booth brothers. He would spin the whole thing as a complex scheme, engineered, presumably, to fleece him and his brother out of millions of dollars. After all, it would not be the first time that someone had tried to blackmail them. He felt a distinct sense of relief after having made this decision.

The morning when he went downstairs to his office to find the fifth envelope waiting for him, he pushed himself to smile at it, warily ready to get through it and move forward and into battle.

Slitting the envelope open, he found three pages, and willed himself to look at the first one slowly and carefully.

It was a full size photograph of the front gate of his estate. *They had been right outside!*

The second page was a similarly framed photo, but showed a front gate and driveway that he recognized as the entrance to his brother's house several miles away.

When Kone looked at the third and last page, also a photograph, the other two pages, along with the envelope, fell to the office floor as his muscles went slack.

The third picture was a close-up shot of two severed heads.

The heads were sitting in a shallow tray on a tabletop. Their eyes were closed and they were facing straight on to the camera. Kone felt his heart start to beat faster and a hot pressure spread through his skull. *The faces!*

He struggled to catch his breath. The head on the left was his brother David. *My poor sick brother.* The head on the right was him, Charles Kone. He was looking into a mirror, but a mirror showing his own head in a plastic tray. *What...how can...am I dreaming?* His head started to spin, and then the whole room started to spin around him. He stumbled away from his desk.

The pain exploded inside him as though a dozen bullets had ripped through his sternum. The ornately-carved ceiling of his office flashed by as he fell. He neither heard nor felt himself hitting the floor, and then the ceiling became dark, and then darker. The pain was tremendous, but somehow apart from him. He felt it, but it was no longer *him*. Still more darkness came, and with it, an intense quiet...

39

The vast majority of people who visit the Bahamas only get to see the heavily developed and commercialized areas around Nassau—which is the capital, Paradise Island—connected by bridge to downtown Nassau, or to a lesser extent, the island of Grand Bahama—over a hundred miles across the water to the north. What many visitors don't realize is that the nation is made up of over seven-hundred islands. Many of those are nothing more than rough outcroppings of rock, while many others are larger, but still uninhabited. A number of these "Out Islands," are quite large, mostly rural, and support substantial populations of Bahamians along with hosting a small percentage of the tourist trade.

After Tommy and I had finished up with our lucrative work on the BEQ affair, I bought myself a two-bedroom house on the island of Eleuthera, which was a crooked strip of land about a hundred and twenty miles long by no more than three miles across at the widest point. My house was one of a dozen or so that sat on the tranquil and beautiful Ten Bay Beach, just south of the middle of the island on the west coast, and not far from the small town of Governor's Harbor. There were no casinos or malls, and no big resorts, but there were plenty of cozy little bars and restaurants to choose from if you did a little research and didn't mind the drives up and down The Queen's Highway.

It had been almost three weeks since Tommy and I had left Kentucky. With clearance from The Colonel for some time off, we had managed to make it out here to the picture-postcard little bay of white sand, palm trees, and warm, clear, shallow water.

Jenny had been able to get her sister to handle their growing business back in St. Louis, so she had come with me for some much deserved R & R. The house's guest suite was occupied by Tommy, who had surprised me by bringing his ex-wife Becky with him. He explained that they had been tap-dancing around the idea of getting back together for a few months, and things had been sped up by the shock of his recent injury. Though I was surprised, it was pleasantly so. I had always liked Becky and thought it would be just fine if they hooked up again on whatever level they wanted to. How he planned to deal with telling her or not telling her about the work we did was going to be interesting, but I was sure he'd figure it out.

We rented the small beach cottage next to my own from an island neighbor who was away, and extended invitations to other team members to join us. Both Briggs and Sophia had declined with regrets, while Damien had accepted. Tommy and I, along with the ladies, had already been on the island for four days when Damien arrived with Tammy, his new girlfriend. She was a thirty-ish New

Yorker who he'd met recently at a party in Montauk. She was super-smart and made for good company, and the two of them went together well. We respected her bravery in coming all the way down to the islands with him to spend time with us.

Some days, we piled into the rented Range Rover and drove to a secluded cove for swimming and snorkeling, or ventured out for lunch, dinner, or both. The default, though, was to line up our six beach chairs right there on Ten Bay Beach, with a well-stocked cooler in front of us, enjoying the perfection of the sun, sand, and water. Later, we would gather around the blender for fruity rum-based drinks, followed by grilling dinner on the patio. It was a lazy time, and we felt like we deserved it.

Tommy and I were wading out of the water after snorkeling around the rocky point one afternoon, carrying our flippers and masks as we walked back towards the group, ready for a cold beer.

"Seeing you two together with your shirts off," Jenny said, "you look like you've been hanging out at the wrong end of a shooting gallery."

"Yeah, I guess you're right," Tommy said, "but we've been pretty lucky, all in all. Everything still works. Right, Dean?"

Everyone laughed, if a little uncomfortably. I could see that Damien appeared to be quietly explaining something to Tammy.

"I'm working on Tommy to find a desk job while there's still some of him left," Becky said. She looked over at Jenny. "Maybe you can try that too. Good luck. If it works, let me know how you did it."

"Maybe I'll give that a try," Jenny said. She handed me a cold beer as I sat down next to her. "Oh, I almost forgot, the internet must have come on for a while when you guys were out. I checked when I went up to the house, and my email had updated. You told me to let you know."

I was just finishing my beer when the ladies decided they were going to go in for a swim.

"We're going to reload the cooler," I said, pulling myself out of the low beach chair. "Be right back." I motioned to Damien and Tommy to join me, and we started up the path.

Inside, I woke up my laptop and the three of us gathered around as I opened a message from The Colonel.

Hope you are all having a relaxing time. I wanted to give you the news that Charles Kone, the billionaire industrialist and political activist, died suddenly yesterday morning of an apparent massive heart attack. The Washington Post has reported that, based on some anonymous tips they've received, they are investigating the possibility that Kone had recently been working behind the scenes with the late Senator Wilfred O'Donnell to illegally influence government policy...

We had been on the island for almost two weeks when Jenny decided that she had taken advantage of her sister's goodwill long enough and needed to get back to St. Louis to help run the business. It was that same afternoon that Tommy told me he had gotten an email from The Colonel asking us to meet with him in person in three days.

"I got the same email," Damien said, when it was just

the three of us within earshot. "Seems like something big's brewing and he wants all hands on deck. Briggs got called in too."

With travel arrangements all settled, the six of us concentrated on enjoying our last few days on the beach and in the water. Damien and Tammy, the young kids among us, had gotten closer, and started to act like a comfortable couple. Tommy and Becky were doing better than I would have guessed, and seemed to be really enjoying each other like I knew they had in years gone by. We were out for dinner at a favorite beachside restaurant on our last night together, when I held up my glass in a toast.

"Some of us here are older than others, but I hope all of us have a lot more good living to do. I hope we can do this again. I've had a lot of lessons in my life so far. Some I've learned, and others I guess I won't ever learn."

"I've given up trying to learn a lot of 'em," Tommy said, and everyone laughed along with me.

"Right, T, me too," I said. "Before I get too full of shit, I'll get to the point. However young or old we are, it's easy to get caught up in saying 'Those were the days—oh yeah, remember back then? Those were the days…' But what I wanna say is that, really, these are the days, my friends. A week ago, three days ago, today, tomorrow—THESE are the days. It is happening now. Now I'll sit down and shut up. It's been a great time here with all of you."

"You are flagged," Tommy said. "You're right, as usual, but you're still flagged."

Ah yes, those were the days…

40

Inside a second floor apartment in a quiet Kentucky neighborhood, a man knelt in the corner of the bedroom. With the assistance of a small pry bar, he lifted up a foot-long section of floorboard and set it aside. Reaching down into the opening, he pulled out the long metal box that he knew would be there. The box reminded him of a bank's safe deposit box, which, though not inside a bank vault, is exactly what it was.

Lifting up the long metal lid, the man was only slightly surprised to see a large automatic pistol sitting on top of the other contents. He set it aside and pulled out a handful of other items. There were several thick envelopes in different sizes, along with a ragged pile of folded papers, held together with a rubber band. Reaching to the rear of the box, he pulled out the last bundle, about the size of a small brick, and wrapped up in what looked like an old piece of sack-cloth. He unwrapped the bundle to find that he was holding several smaller bundles of banded currency. Seeing that the money was all United States hundred-dollar bills, he guessed that the pile must have been thirty or forty thousand dollars. He re-wrapped it and set it aside next to the pistol.

He went through the rest of the contents of the box quickly, knowing there would be time later to sort it all out. He paused for several minutes to look through a handful of faded old photographs. The pictures were not unlike millions of others that could have been found inside the dusty albums of any American family. Kids at the pool, kids with the dog, mother in the kitchen, father in plaid shirt at the backyard grill, father smiling next to a station wagon.

One picture caught his attention and he looked at it for a long while. It was a picture of two pre-teen boys, smiling at the camera in matching brightly-colored cowboy outfits. He could tell by the long shadows that it had been taken in the late afternoon of a sunny day on some well-manicured patch of grass.

It was a picture of a pair of identical twins.

That was the day Bernie stubbed his toe, he thought to himself. He turned the picture over to read the note written there in the familiar hand of his late mother.

"Bernie and Jason, July 1977"

Sliding the small pile of photos back into one of the envelopes, he loaded the money and the other contents of the box into a khaki-colored canvas bag that he had brought for the purpose. He added the pistol to the bag after wrapping it in a hand towel from the bathroom. The empty metal box went back into the hole in the floor, and the man fit the board back into place. With a last look around the small apartment, he left through the kitchen, locking the door behind him.

Outside, on the deck that connected the garage apartment to the main house, the sun was beating down onto the stained wood surface. A few steps took him to the upstairs door into the house, and from there he found his way downstairs and walked through the rooms. The blood stains had been cleaned up, but there were still several holes in the walls. The realtor that his brother had used for years was in the kitchen.

"Did you get everything you needed from your brother's apartment, Mr. Sykes?" The realtor asked.

"Yes, thanks Joe, I think I have everything now. How long do you think before you can get the place on the market?"

The realtor looked around for a moment and scratched the back of his neck before answering.

"I just need to get someone in to do the patching and painting, then I'll have the cleaners in as soon as I can. We'll take care of the apartment too. I'm thinking about two weeks should be more than enough to get the listing up."

"That's fine Joe, thanks for all your help. I'll be traveling on and off, but you have my number. Just let me know what you need from me."

They shook hands and the man left the house and walked to his car.

Three hours later, he was nursing a double bourbon at one of the bars in the Northern Kentucky airport. He read through his printed travel itinerary, looked at his watch, and then studied the printout some more. If his first flight was on time, he should make it to Atlanta by about seven.

Then, if his connection with the smaller plane went smoothly, he should be able to get out to Nassau, Bahamas before midnight.

Once there, he would find the friend of a friend who had agreed to take him by boat across the water to Eleuthera.

Acknowledgments

As I publish my second novel and begin work on the third, I have learned a lot about the process. At different times, it is all of exciting, fun, thrilling, grueling, and occasionally even boring. Consistently though, it is hard work. I could not have done it without the generous help of several people.

For their tireless and enthusiastic assistance with the numerous stages of the editing process, I wish to thank my friend, Dr. Judy Ozment; my sister-in-law, Heidi Nelson; and my wife, Bonnie Boumiea. (I hope they will all approve of the way I just used commas and semicolons in that last sentence.) It has not been easy for me to "put myself out there", asking for feedback on my work. I appreciate the way these people have bravely provided the criticism I need, while never failing to be encouraging at the same time. Many thanks!

I'd also like to thank Lee Burton of Ocean's Edge Editing, for the excellent work he did on my first draft. His feedback was very helpful to my story and the overall process.